The Dead Husbands Society

ADELINE AIMES

Author's Note

Dear Reader,

I'm so grateful for you spending time with my story; it's the biggest gift a reader can give an author.

This book was born out of a very real ache—and the wild, beautiful ways we try to stitch life back together after loss.

I hope you fall a little in love with Birdie's love story and the beautiful, messy dares she creates!

Thank you for supporting stories by indie authors.

XOXO,

Adeline

Content Warnings

Off-page death of spouses. On-page depiction of depression and mourning. Explicit sexual content. Explicit language. For mature readers, 18+.

To every woman who's ever cried on the bathroom floor, screamed into a pillow, or eaten cold pizza at 2 AM wondering if life could ever feel normal again.
To the ones who loved hard, lost everything, and still showed up.
You didn't need a roadmap—you built one.
This one's for you.
And if you're still figuring it out?
Same, babe. Same.

Prologue

WASHINGTON STATE UNIVERSITY, 1994

"Seriously?"

I stare in disbelief at the ratty pink sock dangling from the doorknob. Again? This is the third time this week. My pillow sits slumped against the doorframe, purple butterfly pillowcase on display for the entire dorm hallway to admire in all its childish glory. Technically, the sock means I'm supposed to disappear, but would it kill her to give me ten minutes' notice? Or at least use a clean sock that doesn't look like it was dragged through a dryer fire? Or better yet, to keep your "visitors" on a schedule and your laundry in a hamper? I clutch my color-coded planner tighter. Breathe, Birdie. Breathe.

Would it be frowned upon to knock and ask for my toothbrush? I debate it for a second, running my tongue over my teeth. While I apparently don't have the right to sleep in my own bed tonight, surely I deserve to brush my teeth like a civilized human being.

I lift my hand to knock, then freeze at the muffled noises from inside.

Nope.

Not worth it. I sigh, scoop up my pillow, and start the long trudge across campus.

I don't even have to knock before his door swings open.

"Sexiled again?" He's leaning against the doorframe like he's been waiting for me.

"Yep." I hug my pillow tighter.

"You can have the bed."

"I can't keep kicking you out of your bed just because I keep getting kicked out of mine," I protest, but I'm already stepping inside. His room is warm and the posters he has hanging on the wall feel more familiar to me than my own room at this point. He'd even hung up a rendition of "Judith Slaying Holofernes" by Artemisia Gentileschi because he knows it's one of my favorites.

"I don't mind." He flashes that grin, dimples and all, and my breath catches before I can stop it.

"This is going to pose a problem when your roommate finally shows up." I try to sound casual as I drop my pillow on his bed, admiring the visceral, raw, and utterly unapologetic Gentileschi rendition hanging above me—Like vengeance in brushstrokes, like how I wish I had the courage to live.

He shrugs and flops into the desk chair. "I don't know if he's ever showing up at this point."

"Mono, right?"

"Yeah. I'm just hoping they don't send him back too soon."

I laugh, and for a moment we're both quiet, just looking at each other. The air shifts, humming with the same what-if that's been hovering for weeks now. It would be so easy to cross the room and sit in his lap. I wonder what his chest would feel like pressed against my cheek. How his lips would taste... Nope, not going there.

He's the perfect friend, and friends can think about other friend's mouths without acting on it. I shake the thoughts out of my head, kick off my shoes, and collapse backward onto his bed, arms flung wide, pillow tucked under my neck. His pillow smells like him—soap and maybe that intoxicating body spray that reminds me of the ocean, cedar trees, rain.

"You know, one of these days, you're going to regret always rescuing me." I stare up at the ceiling.

"Doubt it." He swivels lazily in his chair, biceps flexing as he pushes off the desk with his bare foot. He's wearing sweatpants and an old t-shirt that clings to his shoulders in a way I try not to think about too hard.

"I'm serious. Someday, you're going to have an actual life, and I'll barge in whining about my roommate and ruin everything."

He snorts. "Pretty sure you whining about your roommate is my actual life, and I kind of like it when you show up in my room without notice."

I lift my head to squint at him. "Well, I kind of like your bed." I cringe, suddenly realizing the many ways that could be interpreted.

"Oh, do you? It's the 200 thread count sheets. They seal the deal every time." He stops spinning, leans forward, elbows on his knees. His eyes are warm and focused, like I'm the only person in the world worth watching.

"Don't get cocky," I mumble, rolling to my side to hide the flush creeping up my neck.

"Too late." He pushes up from the chair and crosses the room in two easy strides, making his way to the bed, and my pulse jumps into my throat.

"You're taking up the whole bed, you know."

"I gave you first dibs," I shoot back, but my voice goes soft because he's close enough now that I can see the tiny scar near his jawline.

He leans down, bracing one hand beside my head. "Scoot over then."

I shift left just as he moves in the same direction. It happens fast, a clumsy, off-beat choreography. Our faces turn the same way at the same time, and his mouth brushes mine. Not fully a kiss, but not *not* a kiss either. It's warm, unexpected, soft in the way surprise can be soft.

We freeze.

I feel his slow exhale against my cheek. His face is still close, too close now to pretend it didn't just happen.

"Um." His voice is rougher than usual, the syllable pulled tight like a bowstring. "Sorry."

Neither of us moves.

His eyes flick down to my lips, just for a second, and that second stretches. Something hot and unfamiliar pulses between us.

Outside, someone slams a door, and I flinch just enough to break the moment. He pulls back first, clearing his throat like he's trying to swallow a thousand words.

"So..." My voice is too bright. "Scooting."

"Yeah," he mutters, shifting to the other end of the bed like it's suddenly on fire.

I force a laugh that doesn't sound right before burying my face in his pillow, desperate to erase any awkwardness over the fact that whatever just happened definitely wasn't in the friend-zone rulebook. "Ugh. I left my toothbrush in my stupid room with my stupid horny roommate. My mouth feels like a swamp."

When I peek up at him, he's grinning again, like he's been waiting for this exact complaint. He reaches over to his desk drawer, rummages for a second, and then holds something out.

A brand new toothbrush, still in the plastic.

"Here." He stretches it out to me, scratching the back of his neck with his free hand. "I, uh... picked it up for you. Since this keeps happening."

My heart trips over itself at his sweet gesture. It's just a toothbrush, Birdie, I remind myself all while I feel a goofy grin stretching across my face. "You bought me a toothbrush?"

He shrugs, trying to look casual and failing miserably. "Figured I'd save us both the drama. Plus, you're less grumpy with clean teeth."

I snatch it from his hand, still trying to fight back that silly giddy smile. "You're my hero, you know that?"

He rolls his eyes but can't hide the pleased look that tugs at the corner of his mouth. "Yeah, yeah. Go brush your swamp mouth before I regret this entire arrangement."

I sit up on my knees, still clutching the toothbrush, and lean in just close enough that, for one reckless second, I think about kissing him intentionally—friendship be damned.

But instead, I bump his shoulder with mine, grin, and hop off the bed.

"Don't fall asleep without me," I tease as I slip out the door toward the dorm bathrooms.

"Wouldn't dream of it," he calls after me, and when I glance back, he's watching me like he's memorizing all the parts I keep pretending he can't see.

Chapter One

"Ma'am? Are you alright?"

My lungs are heaving, and not from the mile I've just run. All I can see is the cracked cement blurring between tears as I hold my head between my knees. The sobs wrack my body in between each shaky inhale. Lifting my head, I use the corner of his t-shirt to swipe at my dripping nose. The worn material falls away, black streaks smeared across the grey fabric. Why did I put on mascara before a run?

Oh. Right.

Because even if I'm just jogging, I need to look runway ready.

I knew I should've bought another tube of the waterproof stuff. *Pull it together, Beatrice.* A few limp strands of my long, dark hair have escaped my ponytail, almost like they're begging to be rescued.

Am I alright?

My husband of twenty-six years is dead.

I still snuggle into the imprint on his side of the bed and wake up dreaming that he's holding me.

This is his t-shirt.

It doesn't smell like him anymore.

My mascara is running.

It never smudges, much less runs, certainly not from tears and certainly not in public.

Am I alright?

Nope.

He's gone.

And two years later, there are days where all it takes is an Anise Swallowtail in the park to make me feel like nothing's going to be alright in my world again.

But you can't tell that to a stranger at the corner of Pines and Second.

"I'm just fine." I slip into a reassuring smile, the one I've perfected over the past two years. Enough teeth to show I'm sincere, not enough to look entirely unhinged.

The woman narrows her eyes, nods twice, and starts pushing the stroller and her smiling toddler back down the sidewalk, casting a few curious glances back over her shoulder.

My feet refuse to move for a few more moments before the muscle memory takes over, and my scuffed tennis shoes are once again smacking the pavement. It's the same route we ran together each morning before breakfast. I keep thinking running it without him will get easier.

It doesn't.

As I turn down our idyllic suburban street, I remind myself to look up and notice the green buds pushing out of the mighty oak trees. A few neighbors are mowing their grass. Their lives are carrying on, and I remind myself women who are processing their grief in healthy ways don't want to spit in their home owner association president's perfect yard because her life is fine and mine isn't.

Just before I reach the driveway, the low hum of the mail truck rounds the corner. Noah slows down as he pulls up beside me, already hanging out the doorless cab.

"B!" He tips his mail hat like we're in a Western movie. "Out running before 9 AM? I feel like this requires a victory celebration. Coconut ice cream still your sweet treat of choice?"

I move the back of my hand over the mascara circles I'm sure I have under my eyes, probably making it worse. Luckily, Noah's seen me uglier. And drunker. And crying into a pizza box at 2 AM back in college. He was my friend first, Owen's roommate second, and still the only one allowed to call me B.

"Don't make it weird." I probably look like a deranged raccoon slinking back after a romp in the dumpster. "I'm just reminding my legs they still work."

He tilts his head to the side, the same easy grin that used to talk me off a hundred ledges, back when we were all too young to know better starts to falter. Then his blue eyes are crinkling at the corners as he leans farther out of the cab, and I hate that they still have that don't BS me effect they've had since college.

"Hey, you alright?"

I shrug, then shake my head because lying to Noah never works. "There was a butterfly in the park."

His mouth hardens, and I see his throat bob in a forced swallow. "Yeah? What kind?"

"Anise Swallowtail. He loved those."

"He was obsessed with them. Did you know the caterpillars mimic bird droppings? My brain is full of Owen butterfly facts that will only be useful in a bizarre trivia category."

I chuckle, but it comes out high and strained. "Yep. Most people get into birdwatching, not Owen. He was out there stalking butterflies like a six-year-old with a net."

Noah huffs a laugh, but his is also laced with sadness. "He dragged me along more than once. I think he thought I'd appreciate the wingspan facts. But I clearly only remembered the bird shit ones." He pauses, gaze flicking over me. "It's a good sign though, B. Means they're coming back this season. He'd like that."

My throat tightens. "He'd want me to like it, too."

He shifts in the seat. "You still have his butterfly book?"

I nod.

"I gave my copy to his mom. Thought she might need it more." Silence stretches for a minute. "You want me to swing by later? Bring coffee? Talk about anything but bugs?"

I swipe under my eyes again and manage a watery grin. "I'll be fine."

He nods before rummaging through the pile of mail on his dash and handing me a few pieces: grocery flyer, bill I'll pretend I didn't see, and one addressed to Owen Lawson or Current Resident.

I blink, but it's too late. The tears well up fast again.

"Some days it feels like it's getting easier. And some days it doesn't." Noah's voice wavers.

He doesn't elaborate. I know he misses Owen too.

"You know... your fennel's staging a coup." Noah nods toward my front yard where the feathery green stalks sway like they own the place. "If the swallowtails are here, we need to spruce up the place for them."

I know what he's doing—offering me a lighthearted off-ramp from the emotional spiral currently attempting a triple axel in my chest. But he's picked the wrong plant. My throat tightens, something curling low in my belly at the idea of anyone messing with the butterfly garden.

I've already made a public scene twice today, and I'm not ready to have a meltdown in my driveway for the neighbor's viewing pleasure. "I'll see if I can talk them down. Maybe negotiate some peace terms." My voice is smooth, steady. I am in control.

He leans in a little, mock-serious. "I could come by Saturday. Help you tame them. I've got hedge clippers strong enough to take on a jungle. Found a whole bicycle beneath the overgrowth in my cousin's yard last spring."

I glance at the wild sprawl of the fennel, then back at him. His dark hair is all clean lines and military precision, of course he could conquer chaos. "I don't think there's a bike in there, but who knows. Could be some treasure." I will make it through this conversation without crying.

"I'm happy to risk it, treasure or not. Friends don't let friends get lost in their own flower jungle."

It's past time to trim the garden. Owen would be distraught over how chaotic I've let the space become. The HOA is distraught over it. That alone should be enough to push me to do something about it.

It's the only space I've let fall apart since he died. Everything else, the house, the meals, the fundraisers, has stayed perfectly intact. But the garden? That's where I let it go. "That's nice of you."

He shrugs, easy and unbothered. "Offer stands. Only don't blame me if I decapitate a zinnia."

"I'll take my chances. Now, go be a civil servant."

He lifts two fingers in a mock salute, puts the vehicle in gear, and drives off down the street. I watch for a moment, comforted by the familiar site.

Turning into the driveway, I pause, inhaling and steadying myself like I do each time a memory surfaces and makes it harder to step into the empty house.

I kick off my shoes at the front door. At the one-month mark, I forced myself to move his shoes into the garage.

I make my way down the hallway. At the three-month mark, I removed the pictures of him from the hallway, because it was too painful to have them greet me instead of his face every time I opened the door.

I grab my coffee mug from the cupboard so I can pour myself another cup. At the six-month mark, I boxed up his favorite coffee mug, the "butterflies are the new birds" one with a chip on the handle that he swore tasted better than any other cup in the cabinet.

I don't bother sitting at the table, just pop a piece of bread in the toaster and eat while I stand in the kitchen. At the nine-month mark, I stopped setting his place at the table by accident.

At the one-year mark, I gave away his old college T-shirts, all except the one I'm wearing—because I realized they didn't smell like him anymore, just like me pretending.

There's no guidebook for how to evict a ghost gently. Grief moves in and takes up every room, and the only way to reclaim the house is one tender eviction at a time.

Some days are getting better. But today isn't one of those days.

Wanting nothing more than to wallow in the wreckage of memories that assaulted me this morning, I force myself to change into something slightly more socially acceptable. A plain black t-shirt and dark leggings. Color just feels like it's asking too much on an Anise Swallowtail sighting day.

I rush to the bookshelf, wishing someone had disrupted my color-coded system. When reorganizing by publishing date doesn't work, I run a cloth over the invisible dust on the already spotless surfaces in the living room. Then I'm straightening the shoes and sweeping nonexistent crumbs.

My phone buzzes on the counter as I'm settling in to scroll through museum assistant or exhibition curator job positions I have no intention of acting on before going to another PTA meeting. I can go through the motions. I am going through the motions.

> Harper: Coffee. 3 PM. No excuses. We're making you a social media profile today. It's tough love time. I love you xoxo

I don't respond right away. Instead, I stare at the message like it's a summons to jury duty. My daughter means well. But there's something about the way she says *we're making you a profile* that makes me feel like I'm being dragged to my own execution.

I can do new baked good recipes, coupons for comfy shoes,

and order the occasional bright-colored cardigan. I don't do social media.

Still, I always show up. That's part of the problem. I don't know how not to show up, even when I feel like my insides have been hollowed out and stuffed with cobwebs. I know she's missing her dad and worried about me, and if this proves to her that I'm doing okay, then I can manage it. That's what you do as a mother: put yourself second, or third, or nowhere at all. You smooth things over. Say you're fine.

She's already seated when I arrive at the café, wearing a navy blue hoodie with her college's logo on the front and sipping something that looks more like dessert than coffee. Probably that half-caf oat milk vanilla bean, lavender thing she seems to love so much. I pause, my chest physically aching over how much she looks like us—like him. She has sandy blonde hair, but it's stick-straight like my dark hair. She has his deep brown eyes but has gold flecks that match my honey-gold ones.

That somehow makes it worse because she's us, and now there is no us.

"Hi, Mom!" She bounces up, life and youth radiating out of each step as she wraps me in a warm hug. "You look... like you left the house."

"High praise." I sit, smoothing the invisible wrinkles from my blouse even though I steamed it twice. My lipstick is intact, my hair is curled, my cardigan is perfectly draped, but inside, I feel like a knocked-over display someone tried to restack in a rush.

I hate that I see the concern etched into her features. That she chose a local college so she could pop in during the occasional week night and weekends, that she's sitting at a cafe worried about her mother, mourning the loss of her father, instead of enjoying her freshman year of college.

"I'm great, honey." I squeeze her hand before trying to take a stab at my old sarcastic humor to lighten the mood. "And for the record, I considered making up a headache that I don't have to stay in bed. I also weighed the pros and cons of running off and joining a cult."

This seems to reassure her that I'm not entirely falling apart, and she grins and opens her laptop. "Too late. Your cult leader is here."

"I'm not sure how I feel about being online. And I at least need a tea before we start on this. Maybe a little update on your life." I raise my eyebrows, attempting to look innocent as I try to push the topic back to her. "How's your second semester going? Are you still loving that art history class? You must've hit the Renaissance by now. What I would do to go back to my college days and listen to a lecture about Artemisia Gentileschi. Her *Judith* makes all the Caravaggios look tame. And don't even get me started on Botticelli—*Primavera* still makes me tear up if I think about it too long."

"Nice try, Mom." Harper rolls her eyes, clearly seeing right through me. "And here's your tea: peppermint, bit of honey, burn-your-intestines-hot. No excuses. Sit."

I take the mug, hoping the warmth will calm my nerves. "Grief is private. It's sacred. Not everything needs to be made into a scene, especially on the internet."

"You're not making a scene. And I know you're tackling your grief. You're healing, and I'm proud of you." Harper already has her laptop open, the screen cluttered with so many tabs that just looking at it makes my head pound. "But you're lonely. We're just making a tiny social media profile. One or two sites, that's all. You don't even have to post anything." Her eyes bore into mine. "It might be freeing to talk to people who don't know your past, who don't know you as Dad's widow."

I open my mouth to protest, but my daughter knows me too well. Her voice softens even more as she reaches across the table, covering my hand with hers. "So, let's find a few friends who have lost someone too. No one has to know but you. There are women out there feeling exactly what you're feeling, maybe a little lost and sad and pretending they're fine. You shouldn't have to pretend with everyone, Mom. You shouldn't have to hold this all alone."

I cross my arms, knowing I'm acting like a child. "I'm sure there are other women out there with similar circumstances as mine, and they should all be left alone in peace and quiet to mourn and process. It was good enough for your grandma, and it's good enough for me."

She exhales, closes her laptop halfway, and pushes her chair back. Before I can protest, she steps around the table and wraps her arms around my shoulders from behind, resting her cheek on top of my head like she did when she was little.

"Mom." Her voice catches just enough to crack something in me wide open. "You don't talk to anyone. You won't try a group. You always text me to make sure I'm okay. You haven't applied for any art related positions despite you working toward that for years."

I open my mouth to protest, but she carries on, "Yes, I've seen the tab open on your laptop. And don't think I forgot all the help I gave you sprucing up your resume before Dad died. You don't do anything for you. You're still a part of my old PTA and pretending like everything's okay. And I'm so scared you're going to disappear. I need you. I want you to have people again. Please. You deserve more than this."

"I still have people." I raise my chin.

"Name one person you talk to outside of the women from my old PTA and the occasional nonprofit fundraising coordinator."

I take a long sip of my tea, pretending to contemplate. "I refuse to dignify that with an answer."

Harper raises an eyebrow, a gesture that is a mirror image of her father's.

"I had him." My voice is a strangled whisper, and in desperation, I gulp another sip of tea, focusing on the way it burns as it slides down my throat. "He was my person. And now he isn't."

Her smile falters as she reaches for my hand. "I miss him too. I'm just trying not to lose myself in the sadness, because if I stop and think about it too much it will swallow me whole, and I won't stand by and let it swallow you too."

"I won't let it swallow you." Every mama bear instinct rises up in me. I'll fight grief like I fought the monsters under her bed.

"Let me help you, Mom." Her brown eyes are so sincere, the worry etched into the corners of her mouth.

"Fine." I throw my hands up in the air. "Show me your... grief internet."

Chapter Two

An hour later, I'm back home with a notebook full of passwords I won't remember and a phone that now buzzes with updates from three grief support groups, one meditation app, and something called Widow Wednesdays.

I open my app, adjust my reading glasses, and try to remember how to get to the first group's feed before giving an exasperated sigh and looking at the instructions I swore to Harper I "didn't need." Press the app icon on the screen, enter your login details, pass the two-step verification. Getting into this thing is like breaking into Fort Knox. Finally, my screen fills with an image of a woman live-streaming herself reading a poem to her late husband's urn.

Nope.

The second group is full of images with *"Heaven gained an angel, but I lost my heart."* plastered in Comic Sans over fields of tulips or heavens with angel wings.

Nope.

The third is a stream of sobbing emojis and guilt-soaked confessions that make me wonder if I should feel worse about the kind of wife I was when he was alive.

"I should've let him get the boat. He wanted a boat. I said no. Now he's dead. No boat."

Next comes *"Sometimes I told him the dishwasher was broken so he'd wash the dishes by hand. It wasn't broken."*

Then, without warning: *"He died thinking I liked his mother. I did NOT."*

I click my way out of the groups, feeling worse than when I started.

Instead, I open the general feed and begin what my daughter warned me is a doom scroll. She told me it would be tempting but to try to fight the urge for as long as possible. If the alternative is to pour my heart out in grief groups, I will gladly take the doom scrolling. If nothing else, I can tell Harper I gave the social media world a try, and we weren't compatible.

And then I see her.

She's sitting cross-legged on the floor of what looks like a man cave that collided, perhaps reluctantly, with a yoga studio. There's a neon "Beer" sign unplugged in the corner, half-covered by a leaning full-length mirror framed in gold. An old dartboard hangs above a Himalayan salt lamp. One wall is still painted a deep hunter green, but a tapestry with an abstract sun-and-moon design is tacked unevenly across it, trying its best to soften the space. A yoga mat is rolled out beside a pair of dumbbells, and what might have once been a minibar now holds candles, succulents, and a stack of self-help books with titles like *Radical Acceptance* and *The Art of Stillness*.

She's wearing a bright orange sweater and glittery eye patches under her eyes, hair piled in a messy bun like she gave up halfway through making it presentable. She's surrounded by paint cans and brushes, trying to DIY a bookshelf, squinting at the instructions, swearing softly when a screw rolls away.

In the corner of the screen, her husband appears in a stitched-in throwback video, laughing uncontrollably in a much older clip as she fumbles with a different piece of furniture. His voice, warm and teasing, fills the room for a second, "I think the instructions might really be useful here, babe," and her shoulders instinctively lift toward the sound.

The caption reads: *Don't worry, I'm still messing up furniture without you.*

It's oddly moving.

I click on her profile, ThisIsUs. Her bio unapologetically proclaims: *Wife. Yoga enthusiast. Documenter of our adventures.*

Instead of a page dedicated to grief and regret, her page seems to do the opposite. It screams of over-the-top life. Like she's trying to tell the world, or maybe herself, that he's not really gone. Not yet.

I scroll back through her content, watching the slow unraveling of a life lived in tandem. In the early videos, she's with her husband. He's tall, bearded, with the kind of playful energy that makes you like him immediately. They go on hikes and road trips, try viral dance trends they're clearly too old for, burn sourdough, and make jokes about kombucha explosions. There's love in every frame, even when they're bickering over GPS directions.

And then he's gone.

Not all at once, but slowly. The footage grows quieter. The camera lingers longer on her face. Sometimes she overlays a current video of herself with an old one of the two of them, like she's trying to keep him in the frame a little longer. Or maybe she's trying to keep herself from slipping out of it entirely.

Before I can second guess myself, I'm liking the video with the furniture and forcing my fingers to tap across the screen:

@ThisIsUs: A few months ago an end table my husband ordered before he died finally showed up. I left it in the corner for weeks while I cried. Pretty sure it's still in the garage. I've made peace with not having a nightstand.

I'm about to end my doom scroll, thumb twitching toward the home button, resolve setting in to delete this whole app and pretend I never tried, when another video catches my eye. It's quieter than the others, no music, no face, just the still shot of a knitted blanket folded neatly on top of a queen bed. The camera holds steady. Then a soft, steady voice says, "Today, I let the sadness stay. And then I vacuumed."

That's it. That's the whole video. No clever transitions. No hashtags. Simple honesty.

And for some reason, it undoes me. My throat tightens. My eyes sting.

I don't know why it makes me cry. Maybe because I vacuumed yesterday. Maybe because the sadness stayed then, too.

Or maybe because it's the first time someone's admitted that grief doesn't always roar. It hums. It lingers in mundane chores, quiet rooms, and in the way we try to put ourselves back together in the middle of it all.

I click on the profile: BooksAndYarn. The videos are few and simple—hands, yarn, a ton of knitting projects, the occasional stack of books by a sunny window. In one, a kettle whistles softly in the background while she completes row after row with her knitting needles.

Her hands move methodically in the frame, looping sunshine yellow yarn through her fingers with a kind of reverence. Like each stitch is its own breath. Like she's mending something I can't see. Maybe something in herself.

I stare at her page until I feel the late afternoon sun fade into evening.

Her presence feels quiet and still. I don't know where she lives or how long ago she lost him or even if it was a him. But somehow she makes me feel less alone.

Without overthinking it, I scroll back to the knitting video and leave a comment:

> @BooksAndYarn: You make grief look…
> doable. I don't know the first thing about yarn,
> but now I want to learn.

I immediately wince. Regret settles fast and hard.

The moment I hit send, I spiral into panic. Both comments are too much. Too vulnerable. I go searching for the delete button like it's a life raft. Why is it so hard to find? Nothing is labeled clearly. I adjust the reading glasses that are slipping down my nose while I mash random icons, accidentally following someone named Grief_GuruMama and liking a reel about fermented oat milk.

"Where is customer service?" I mutter, jabbing at my screen like it's personally offended me. My eyes scan my profile for any little information button, which apparently does not exist. I'm lost in the wilderness of the internet, with no map, no water, and entirely too many hashtags. Someone send help.

Fifteen unsuccessful minutes later, I'm still in a mid-panic spiral when two bright red notification dots light up my screen.

> @Birdie71: Who needs that nightstand anyway. Also: welcome. You're officially part of a club that no one ever wants to be in. 💃
> 🖤

I blink at it.

Read it twice.

There's something so casually kind about it. No forced optimism, no sugarcoated advice—just solidarity. And a dancing lady emoji, which pushes a smile through my panic.

Without allowing myself time to second guess, I tap the message icon and type:

> Hi. I'm Birdie. I don't know what I'm doing.
> Can we be friends?

She replies almost instantly:

> ThisIsUs: Hi Birdie. I'm Vivian. Friends call me
> Viv. Call me Viv. u lost your husband? How?
> (Is that morbid to ask?)

Me: Brain aneurysm. In our butterfly garden. One day he was here and the next he wasn't. It's been two years, three months, eighteen days. I still can't bring myself to weed. But I'm clearly moving forward just fine. You?

ThisIsUs: I told myself I wasn't allowed to keep track of the days after I hit the one year mark… But one year, six months, eleven days, approximately ten hours.

Cancer.

Terminal.

He had three months after the diagnosis.

What's your grief starter pack? Wine? Chocolate? Rage cleaning?

I want to reach through the screen and hug her, to offer some kind of lifeline. But I've been around enough well-intentioned sympathizers to know that grief, real, raw grief, has a way of paralyzing those on the other side. You don't want to say the wrong thing, but silence feels like abandonment. So you do the only thing you can: keep going, pretend your words might help.

Me: Grief starter pack includes: running in his basketball shorts, waterproof mascara, and one bathrobe that's seen too much. Do I qualify for VIP status?

ThisIsUs: Only if you've ever yelled at a pillow for "not being the same without him." Bonus points if you wear his hoodie like armor.

Me: I may or may not be wearing his t-shirt right now. Oversized, faded, smells like laundry detergent instead of him. Total grief couture.

ThisIsUs: Ah yes, the widowed woman uniform. Add in limp hair and raccoon eyes and you're runway ready.

I run my hand over my long, straight, dark locks. The curls fell out hours ago. Check.

Me: Okay but truly, I haven't been able to go buy our Saturday morning frozen waffles for the last two years. I miss waffles. I bribed my daughter to go pick some up for me while telling her I was fine. Then I sobbed while I ate them. Then I fake smiled with teeth. You know the one.

ThisIsUs: Oof. The "see, I'm totally functioning!" smile. I gave that to a barista once. She gave me a free croissant and a business card for her therapist.

Me: You win. Though I once cried so hard I accidentally sobbed into a stranger's dog at Target in the deodorant aisle. She didn't move. The dog, I mean. The owner looked horrified.

ThisIsUs: STOP. That was me. I am the woman from Target. Just kidding. But now I wish I was. I would've let you keep the dog.

Me: Honestly I would've taken her. I'm tired of feeling alone. Some days I feel I'm moving forward and other days I feel like I'm starting all over again.

ThisIsUs: I hugged my throw pillow so hard last week it popped a seam. My grief is literally spilling out. But then I stuff it back inside and remind it that everything feels better after yoga and some heart alignment.

Me: You're funny. I forgot that laughing and crying could live in the same sentence.

ThisIsUs: That's the secret. Laughter is the grief buoy. Grab it whenever you can.

We go back and forth for a while, swapping dark-humored grief stories like war veterans trading battle scars. It's like talking to someone who's been through hell and came back with glitter under her nails. It's the first conversation I've had in months that doesn't feel like small talk wrapped in pity.

The sun dipped behind the skyline hours ago and the rumbling of my stomach reminds me it's past time to get some dinner.

I'm about to close the app and maybe even consider watching something that doesn't involve true crime or weeping British detectives when I see another notification.

BooksAndYarn: Thank you. I was terrible at knitting at first. You just have to start.

Simple.

I stare at the message for a long time before inhaling. I just had a perfectly wonderful conversation with a stranger on the internet.

I can do this.

The tightness in my chest loosens slightly. Something shifts inside me, not a miracle, not healing, but a flicker of warmth. A door opening, just a sliver.

And before I can talk myself out of it, I message her the same question:

Hi. I'm Birdie. I don't know what I'm doing. Can we be friends?

BookAndYarn: Hi, Birdie. I'm Marin. I'd like that.

Chapter Three

"Can you help me start a group chat?" I try to make the question sound casual as I slide the salad onto the kitchen table. It's my third attempt because apparently the first bowl was too rustic and the second one had a chip I couldn't unsee. This one is just right, arranged like something out of a food magazine, with the arugula fluffed and the tomatoes evenly spaced.

Harper has already set up the iPad, and I can see Matt giving me the side eye through the screen.

"I mean, I have managed the PTA newsletter for a decade, and I coordinated the neighborhood Christmas cookie exchange during a snowstorm," I add quickly, as if my long history of clipboard excellence might shield me from digital ridicule. "And no one has ever complained about my spreadsheets. Or my themed centerpieces. Not once." I smooth an invisible wrinkle from the tablecloth. "I'm very organized. Remember that art show at the rec center last spring? For the kids in the after-school program? We hung every piece like it belonged in the Met. One little boy did this wild, blue-and-orange self-portrait that looked like early Picasso, if Picasso had used glue sticks and googly eyes. It was magic." And I'm rambling. It's my dead giveaway when I'm nervous, and both of my kids know it.

Harper raises her eyebrows at her older brother, and they share an obvious look.

I rush to fill the silence once again. "It's not a crazy question. It's a group chat... thingy."

"Mom, you're the most put-together person I know. Even after Dad died, you didn't let the house go or miss a single nonprofit fundraising event." Matt takes a big bite of whatever protein bar is his pick of the week, chewing thoughtfully. "But that is kind of a crazy question for you considering that you haven't wanted to talk to any other human beings about anything grief related in the last two years and now you're wondering about grief group chats."

"Matt! We should be encouraging her. She's only fifty-one! Her whole life is still ahead of her."

"Hey, young lady. Watch it. Forty-nine! Don't age me before my time."

Harper beams, and I'm sure if Matt wasn't all the way across the country in Boston, she'd be elbowing his ribs. "It's all thanks to yours truly. I got Mom hooked up with a few social media accounts, and now she's diving in deep to the grief groups. Which group was it? My math professor swears you'd love the one he suggested for his mom."

"Wait? Your math professor knows about this?"

Harper shrugs, her long blonde braid swinging wild with the movement, before she stuffs a bite of salad into her mouth. "The point is, the grief groups are helping. You're coming out of your shell."

"I hardly think I was in a shell." I point my salad fork in her direction. "I haven't missed hosting a single Sunday family dinner."

Matt chuckles, his brown eyes sparkling. "She has a point, Harper. The woman is a machine."

"So, what group did you join?" Harper narrows her eyes.

"Um..." I try to stab a cherry tomato a little too hard, and it flies off my bowl and rolls onto the table. "It's not exactly a group. Not a formal one. It's more of a conversation."

Harper's eyebrows go up so high I worry they'll disappear into her hairline. Matt leans in closer to the screen, squinting like he's trying to read my soul through the pixels.

"Mom." Harper's voice drops low. "Are you telling us you joined a secret grief cult?"

"What? No!" I sputter. "It's the magic of the internet, I guess. One minute you're sobbing over a butterfly, the next you're sharing trauma with two women you've never met in real life, bonding over furniture and knitting needles."

Matt nearly chokes on his last bite of protein bar, his wavy blonde hair flopping into his eyes. "Please tell me 'The Reclining Stitchers' is the name of the group."

"It's not," I mutter, focusing very hard on my salad. "But now I wish it were."

"So what's this non-group called?" Harper presses, her voice suspiciously sweet. She twirls her fork like she's conducting an orchestra.

"It doesn't really have a name," I lie. Then wince. "Okay. It does. But I didn't mean for it to be a thing. It just happened."

"Mom." Matt has mastered the all-knowing-big-brother tone. "The Dead Husbands Society."

Harper and Matt's jaws both drop open, and I forge ahead. "I didn't set out to create a Dead Husbands Society. Who dreams of something like that? Serial killers, maybe. But not me." I glance between my kids. "I spent twenty-six years dreaming about growing old with one man, only to find myself Googling, 'Is twenty seven months too soon to make widow friends?'" I hold up a hand. "And guess what? There's no rulebook."

Harper's fork freezes mid-air. "Did you say, 'The Dead Husbands Society'?"

"It's not like I printed t-shirts." My voice sounds defensive, even to me. "Although now that I think of it, that could be kind of clever."

Matt bursts out laughing. "You started the group?"

I shrug, trying not to look embarrassed. "Technically. I invited two women I met online. That's it."

"Oh my God," Harper breathes. "You started your own widow gang." She squeals and jumps up, wrapping her arms around my neck from behind. "I love it!"

"It's not a gang," I protest.

"Mom's got internet friends. The plan is working!" Matt shakes his head, grinning. "Next thing we know, she'll be running a grief podcast and asking us to smash that subscribe button."

"Very funny." I pretend there's something fascinating to focus on in my salad bowl. "Look, it's not what I expected. But they're real. And it helps. More than any of those professional groups or casseroles from well-meaning neighbors."

They both go quiet for a beat.

"Well," Harper breaks the silence, beaming. "If you do print t-shirts, I want one. XL. Oversized widow-core."

"Make that fifteen." Matt flexes his bicep. "I could get my whole basketball team in on that. Solidarity. Grief gang for life."

I roll my eyes, but I can't help the smile tugging at the corners of my mouth. Maybe I didn't dream of this, of widowing, or group chats, or finding new friends in strange digital spaces, but I'm healing. One day at a time. I'm healing.

Marin: Today I cried over burnt toast. The irony is not lost on me.

Viv: What irony? Isn't the saying, 'crying over spilled milk.'

Marin: It doesn't matter. The point is sourdough bread made me cry. Does this upgrade me to a new level of sad?

Viv: Depends. Was it an exceptionally beautiful piece of toast?

Marin: Viv. It isn't about the toast. It's about what it represents. The meaning behind the toast.

Viv: That's ur problem right there. Burned toast really can't handle that much pressure. Just let it be burned toast.

Me: I'm going recruiting today.

Marin: For what?

Me: For our group.

Viv: Where are u going? And why are you recruiting? I like our group.

Me: The funeral home. And because there might be other women like us who need support.

Marin: Oh, Birdie.

Viv: That's the big leagues! u should start with nursing homes or water aerobics or literally anywhere less depressing.

Marin: Viv. For the love of all that is holy. Please write out the word "you." I beg you. That poor vowel is sitting there, all alone.

Viv: That's your problem, Birdie. You're always looking for other people to focus on so you don't have to focus on yourself.

Me: 1000% not a thing.

It's definitely a thing.

Me: Wish me luck!

———

I walk into Greenwood Memorial & Funeral Home, dressed in my blue blazer and carrying a stack of freshly printed flyers like I'm selling Girl Scout cookies instead of grief. The guy at the front desk runs a hand through his thinning, brown hair before eyeing my flyers. Judging by the look on his face, you'd think I was about to hand him a dead cat.

"Hi." I give an awkward little wave with one hand while setting down my pile of flyers on the desk. "I was wondering if I could post this flyer for a support group I run?"

He blinks and doesn't return my smile. "What kind of group?"

There's a long pause while I wrack my mind for the mental script I'd prepared on the drive over here, because saying it to the rearview mirror in the car and saying it aloud at a funeral home are two entirely different things. "The Dead Husbands Society."

His face tightens, like I just punched him in the soul.

The silence stretches, and my mind goes blank. In my desperation and panic to fill the awkwardness, I can't remember my script. "I figured people come here after their spouse dies, and maybe they need support... or friends... or matching shirts?"

His voice is flat. "We don't have a bulletin board."

My years of trying to sell baked goods at school fundraising events kick in and I counter, "Well, do you make recommendations?"

"Yes. For florists. For grief counselors. Not... clubs." He pushes a corner of one flyer to the side, and the sun filtering through the large window catches the copious amount of glitter I used to outline the letters. Damn it, Viv. More glitter doesn't equal better.

I pivot. "I've been a stay-at-home mom for twenty-three years. My last big recruitment effort was getting people to volunteer for a bake sale. I'm a little rusty." Then I tack on a forced laugh that falls flat in the silence between us.

He doesn't join me.

Then, I swear, I black out for a second, not a medical blackout, simply a moment when my mouth keeps moving but my brain is on vacation.

Suddenly, I hear myself say, "It's not just a club. It's a safe place for women whose lives fell apart. For people who've stood next to a casket wondering if they should feel relief, or rage, or nothing at all. For those of us who are sick of casseroles and polite small talk!"

He stares at me like I'm unraveling right there in front of him. Which, honestly, I kind of am.

Then I add, "I didn't mean to start it. One day I'm thinking that I'm healing, and then I'm sobbing in the park, and the next thing I know I'm trauma-bonding with two women I've never met on the internet over knitting patterns and furniture and yoga and Target."

And then because I apparently have lost all people and recruiting skills, I add, "Have you ever lost someone?"

A long pause.

"My wife."

Oh.

Panic strikes again, so I blurt, "Well, maybe you need a club."

That's when I realize I have to leave before I spontaneously combust, but not before I lose a few flyers off the top of the pile in my haste, leaving a trail of glitter in my wake.

I relay the entire ordeal to our group chat, ending with:

> So I thanked him, apologized, took my flyers,
> and walked out with the grace of a broken
> Roomba stuck under a couch.

> Viv: it's like a car crash. I can't look
> away.

Me: I accidentally traumatized a man in a suit, implied he needs a support group, and learned that funeral homes don't like fun clubs. So... progress?

Marin: I bet you made him cry. Like toast.

Viv: I'm making us shirts. Matching black ones. With glitter. Lots of glitter.

Marin: More glitter is not better, Viv. I think we established this with the flyers.

And for the first time in a long time, I laugh so hard I cry.
Or maybe I cry so hard, I laugh.
Either way, I don't feel so alone.
There might be others like us out there, but for now, three feels like more than enough.

Chapter Four

I breathe in deep, the scent of rain and zealous spring blooms curling through the air. Seattle isn't for everyone, but I've always loved the vibrant, unapologetic way it screams life into existence in part because of the grey, foggy, rain-filled days. My shoes pound the pavement, and I match my breath to the rhythm.

Viv and Marin now message me faithfully in our group chat every morning, telling me to go put on my shoes and hit the pavement. Viv always adds, "It's not about Owen, it's about caring for your glutes. You're still allowed to do something you love that also makes that booty pop!" Of course the full-time yoga instructor would say that.

I round the bend on my route, enjoying the way my legs don't burn as badly as they did when I started up again a few weeks ago. Progress.

That's when I see him. A hunched-over, gray-muzzled lump of a dog, dead center in the middle of the road. Not sitting. Not lying. Just planted there like a large, unkept, furry yield sign.

I slow my jog to a stop.

"Hey, buddy." I lower my voice to a soothing tone, as if speaking to a cantankerous neighbor instead of a shaggy dog the color of mashed prunes, who clearly hasn't seen a groomer since the Obama administration. His floppy ears twitch, but he doesn't move. Doesn't even blink. He stares at me with big, searching brown eyes. Eyes that somehow look like mine—as if they've seen too much life and are officially over it.

Cars aren't common this time of day on our street, but still, I glance both ways. "You're gonna get yourself flattened, pal. Let's move it."

I inch closer, clapping softly.

Nothing.

"Oh, for the love—" I mutter.

I crouch halfway down and attempt some very bad leashless coaxing before deciding it's best to lift the silly boy out of the road.

"Okay. I'm your friend, and I'm trying to help you." I stretch out my hand, letting him sniff me and reluctantly abiding a few slobbery kisses before I try to position myself under his body. "I feel we should be on a first name basis before I try to lift you."

The dog raises his droopy eyes toward me.

"You look like my old first grade school teacher. He had hair like yours, but you didn't hear it from me. Can I call you Frank? I'm Birdie." I stretch out my hand and run my fingers over his bristly head.

Frank smells like wet laundry and sadness, if sadness had a smell. And as much as I hate the thought of muddy pawprints on my clothes, I can't leave him.

"I get it," I mutter, crouching next to him, preparing to lift. "If I wasn't worried about getting run over, I'd lie down here with you."

As I'm about to heave, I hear a familiar sound approaching.

"Should I call animal control, or is this a rescue mission?" Noah leans out the white mail truck, grinning like this is the best thing he's seen all day.

"Depends." I straighten my back, brushing at the dog hair that's already managed to find its way to my black yoga pants.

"Do they still make Lassie-style Lassos for middle-aged women trying to guilt-trip stubborn dogs?"

He parks, hops out, and walks over, his long legs easily closing the distance between us. His navy uniform is slightly wrinkled and sun-warmed, his sleeves pushed up. And when he kneels beside the dog, who still doesn't move, but gives a theatrical groan, Noah frowns.

"He's hurt. Back right leg." He gently presses the dog's hip, and the old boy yelps.

I wince. "I knew something was wrong. I didn't want to leave him in the middle of the road, but I can't lift him."

Without saying a word, Noah slides one arm under the dog's chest and the other beneath his haunches, and raises him up. His forearms and biceps flex as he adjusts his grip before turning his attention back toward me. I feel a hot flash starting from deep in my center, radiating through my entire being until I feel like I'm on fire. It has to be a hot flash, right? Because there's no way my guilt would ever let me feel anything for another man, especially my long-term friend and dead husband's best friend.

I clear my throat, fanning my flaming cheeks. "Thank you. That's, um. Impressive."

"Perks of hauling Amazon boxes for fifteen years." He grins and starts toward my house like it's the most natural thing in the world, carrying the fifty-pound mutt like a sack of potatoes. "Where are we putting him?"

"We?" I follow, a little breathless, not sure if it's from the impromptu jog or the fact that my perimenopausal, irrational body responses were short-circuited at the sight of veins on a man's arm. "I don't even know if I'm keeping him." Luckily, we're only a few houses down from my modest two story colonial.

"You found him. He sighed at you. That's basically a blood pact."

I snort. "I was trying to save his life. Not adopt him."

"Finders keepers. I'd say you're about to be bonded for life. What's his name? You named him already, right?"

My nose scrunches up in snobbish horror. "Of course I didn't *name* him."

Noah levels me with the "no BS" look, the same one he used to give me in college when he knew I was lying about my study habits from the night before, and like I always did back then, I crack. "Fine. It's Frank."

"Like I said, he's yours now." Noah nods toward the front yard, and I unlock my door and gesture to the worn beige rug.

"Put him there. If he pees on it, you're buying me a new one." The rug might be faded, but it's vacuumed every Sunday like clockwork. There's an exact corner where shoes go and a basket for umbrellas that I rotate seasonally. The idea of muddy paws and dog hair at the threshold makes my eye twitch.

As a second thought, I rummage in the closet for the old pile of towels I keep stacked precisely for emergencies—mostly to mop up the rain when it dares to follow my shoes inside. They're folded by size, because of course they are.

"Fair." He lowers the dog down with surprising gentleness, not waiting for me to finish finding my thickest towel, and gives him a slow head rub. "I'll even throw in a chew toy and one of those ridiculous bandanas."

"You're really pushing for this to be a Hallmark movie, huh?"

His eyes crinkle with a smile. "Always cheering for that happy ending."

"I gave up on those." I try to shrug off the surprisingly dark comment with a sunny smile and a little side-eye, all while knowing my shoulders are slumping, giving me away. "You've always had a thing for Hallmark movies."

Noah's mouth pulls into a flat, unimpressed line. "We swore we would never speak of Christmas 1994."

"If I remember correctly–" I fish around in the cupboard for the drinking glasses before pouring us both a glass of water. "You begged me. And I offered my silence in exchange for the last five gummy bears. I really should've driven a harder bargain."

He groans and covers his face with both hands. "You *definitely* should've. I would've traded my soul for that night to stay buried in the past. I was emotionally compromised."

And just like that, we're back there—December '94, the dorms deserted and echoing with leftover finals-week chaos. Everyone had vanished home for the holidays, but both of our plans had crumbled last-minute. Owen had invited me to come home with him to meet his parents, but it felt too soon, too *serious* for someone who had started casually dating a few months earlier, and my parents were on some midlife crisis cruise in the Bahamas.

Noah had nowhere to go. At least nowhere he wanted to.

We crossed paths in the lounge, both of us clutching cheap microwavable dinners and pretending we didn't care we were alone. By nightfall, we'd both agreed it was silly not to commiserate together, and we drug our mattresses into the common room like middle schoolers at a sleepover, a tiny TV balanced on a plastic crate between us.

He insisted on a Hallmark marathon.

"You don't understand." His eyes were glued to the screen as a predictably rugged widower fell in love with a plucky Christmas tree farm owner. "I *need* this. No yelling. No slammed doors. No one forgetting I exist. No drama. You know it's going to end with a happily ever after." His voice softens. "Sometimes, you need to believe that you can have that."

He didn't look at me when he said it.

When he teared up during the scene with the snow globe proposal, I pretended not to notice. Just shoved the gummy bear bag his way while he mumbled something about allergies.

That night, we both stayed up until sunrise, cocooned in cheap blankets and the soft glow of the television broadcasting holiday magic and second chances at love.

Back in the present, Noah drops his hands and gives me a sideways glance. "I still watch them, you know."

"I figured." I grin. "You always did have a soft spot for unrealistic men and improbable snowstorms."

He smirks. "And you always pretended you didn't cry at the one with the single dad and the wish list."

I roll my eyes. "That was a fluke."

He leans back, smug. "Sure it was."

The dog gives a pitiful moan and Noah tilts his chin toward him. "I think we should take it to the vet. That leg needs a bandage or a cast or something."

"Frank, remember?" The words come out before I can stop myself. I don't know why. Naming something already implies permanence, and I have no intention of keeping him.

"And yes... we should take him to the vet." Another sentence I can't explain. Logic says I should call a rescue or animal control. Someone with a soft spot for dogs and a budget. But something about his disheveled prune-colored fur makes me think no one else is coming.

Noah's eyebrows quirk upwards but, to his credit, he doesn't say anything. He takes the glass of water out of my hand and glances down at his watch. "I've got a few more streets to hit, but I'll see about working a half day. I have so many unused vacation and personal days that my post master will be thrilled I'm taking an afternoon off. Can you manage for a bit?"

"Manage a dog with a limp and my deep, engrained, soul-crushing sense of maternal responsibility?" I give a half shrug. "That's my entire personality."

He smiles, easy and unbothered. "I'll swing back by when I'm done, and I can help you take him in, if you'd like."

Then he lifts Frank off the carpet, moving him onto the plush green towel I've laid next to him like it's nothing.

He sets Frank down gently before turning toward the door. "Back soon!"

I nod. "Go deliver the nation's coupons."

I'd forgotten how easy it is to talk to Noah. How much I used to love it. I'm still grinning like a middle schooler with a crush, and I don't love the way my stomach flips as he walks away. It used to do that for Noah. And then I met Owen. And the rest is history.

I close the door and exhale—maybe a breath I'd been holding, or maybe a sigh. Or maybe it's grief again, doing that thing where it shapeshifts into longing and shows up in places it doesn't belong.

I look down at Frank. He blinks up at me like he knows.

I'm too old for this.

Too worn down.

Too... widowed.

Still, I grab my phone and type out a message.

> Me: Hypothetically, if someone felt a flicker, a flutter, an uncalled-for awareness of someone's biceps. Would that be a symptom of perimenopause, or do we blame that on grief too?

> Marin: ...what kind of biceps?

> Viv: BIRDIE. WHAT DID YOU SEE. WHO DID YOU SEE. WHERE CAN I FIND HIM.

> Me: There was a dog. I named him Frank. He hurt his leg. One of my good friends, who also happens to be my mailman, carried him back to my house. He was best friends with Owen. I shouldn't notice his biceps.

> Marin: Hormones. You'll live. Also, please describe the lift in greater detail.

> Viv: NO. I need to know his name, route, availability, and if he owns a flannel.

> Me: Focus, ladies. Frank. Smile. Lift. Biceps. Guilt.

———

Noah pulls back into the driveway as I'm wrapping Frank in an old beach towel. The poor dog looks like a disheveled burrito.

"Ready?" He nods toward the pickup truck idling in my driveway. He's still in his uniform, though his shirt is a little rumpled now, and there's a speck of dirt on his cheek that, if I were someone else, I might feel something about.

Instead, I gesture toward the green towel where I've already cooked Frank a chicken breast and given him a big bowl of water. "He's not great with small talk, but he appreciates the ride."

"Good." Noah shoots me another one of those annoying smiles. "I can carry the conversation."

He lifts Frank again, easy and sure. I follow behind, heart steady, breath even, nothing stirred—guilt and mourning firmly back in their rightful places.

Frank groans dramatically from the backseat of the truck as Noah pulls out into traffic.

"Vet's probably going to ask how it happened." Noah nods toward the back. "What do we tell them?"

"That he was contemplating the meaning of life in the middle of the road and miscalculated the curb."

"I'll let you handle that. You clearly have a gift with words."

The sun rests low in the sky—golden in a cinematic way that makes people fall in love by accident.

I don't.

But I do notice that Noah adjusts the radio when it's too loud, and that he drives with one hand on the wheel and the other resting near mine. Owen used to drape his hand over the center console and rest it on my leg. It's been a long time since someone's done that.

We drive a few more streets in comfortable silence, save for Frank's occasional groan and the dull tap of turn signals.

"I think this is the most we've talked in years." As soon as I say it, I regret it. We're hardly talking now.

"I wasn't sure where I fit after Owen passed." Noah keeps his eyes on the road, his voice low. "Wasn't sure if I should check on you, or really how, outside from delivering the mail."

"Even before that."

Noah's face flushes, and his eyes bore into the road. "I wanted to respect Owen. Still do."

I wait for further explanation, but when none comes, I add, "You could've called."

"Don't have your number anymore. My phone fell in the lake on that fishing trip Owen and I took a few years back. Lost all the contacts." He lets out a small breath that might've been a laugh but doesn't quite get there. "Felt weird asking for your number after so many years. If I needed to talk to you, I could talk through Owen."

I nod, letting the silence stretch a second too long.

"Still, it's nice. Talking like this."

He glances at me briefly and smiles.

At the vet, he opens my door before I can grab the handle.

My stomach still does a little flip like it always did when he opened the door for me in college. "You don't need to do that."

He shrugs. "Old habits die hard."

The vet clinic smells like antiseptic and anxiety. The tech takes one look at Frank and ushers us into a room.

"You his people?" Her voice is clipped and all business.

I hesitate. "Apparently."

She takes him back for X-rays and leaves us in the main room. Noah leans against the counter while I sit in the vinyl chair, arms crossed tight.

"You're quiet." He nods in my direction.

"I'm usually quiet."

He smiles. "You forget that I've known you for over two decades. You're only quiet when you're uncomfortable. You didn't have to bring him in, you know. Or let me come with you."

"I know." I fix my eyes on the generic art in the waiting room so I can avoid his gaze. A watercolor landscape—meant to soothe, I guess, though the horizon line was crooked and the trees bled into the sky like someone gave up halfway through. Owen and I used to joke that waiting room art was the visual artist's version of a novel that never left someone's hard drive.

I still found myself mentally tracing the brushstrokes, wondering what the artist was trying to get right. Or what they'd given up on.

"But it was either this or leave him to become an allegory in the road. And there's no way I was lifting him into the car without you."

"Still," his voice is gentle, "not everyone would've stopped."

My eyes never leave the abstract beach scene on the wall. "I know what it's like to lose your person and not know where to go."

"I know what that's like too."

The vet comes back a few minutes later, cheerful and brisk.

"Poor boy's leg is sprained. I would guess he's around eight years old. No chip and no tag." Frank hobbles over to me in his bright green bandage and rests his head in my lap.

"Do you need me to call a shelter?"

I don't hesitate. "No. He'll be coming home with me."

The vet's lips twitch up in a smile before she turns back to her other patients. The receptionist sends us on our way with pain meds and a bill.

Back in the truck, Noah carefully settles Frank into the back seat again.

"He'll be fine."

I nod.

"And so will you."

I don't answer. But the part of me that felt something when he lifted that dog, or smiled in that slow, quiet way, stirs a little.

And I blame the hormones.

And the packages.

And grief.

Mostly grief.

Chapter Five

Do you believe you deserve love? Not like
from your kids or your cats, but actual love?

I pose the question to our little grief group's message thread before laughing over the meme that Viv sent in response to yet another pair of socks Marin is knitting.

As I hit send, Frank groans beside me, curling his old-man body into the couch like he's been doing this his entire life. I stroke his wiry fur absently, already used to the way he sighs like an overworked union rep every time I move.

Viv replies first, as she always does, with her full chest:

> Viv: Obviously, yes. Romantic, messy, hot love. I didn't spend my twenties figuring myself out to shrivel into some tragic cautionary tale. We're not corpses, Birdie. We're widows. Huge difference.

> Marin: Not sure. I think I used it all up. Or never even got it in the first place. My cat cuddles with me consistently. That's more than he did.

Viv: Marin, that's not right. Also, don't try to justify owning eight cats.

Marin: Seven. And they're judgmental, which feels familiar.

Viv: You need a vibrator.

Marin: I knit. That's enough repetitive motion for one woman.

I laugh, in that weird bark-sigh way that still surprises me. Then Viv, relentless as always, circles back.

Viv: Speaking of love... how'd things go with your mailman?

Me: There's nothing going on with the mailman. He's Owen's old college roommate and ex-best friend. We were friends in college and remained friends after that.

Viv: Details. Now.

Marin: We need a visual.

Me: Tall. Dark hair, blue eyes. Built like someone who splits firewood for therapy, but still somehow reads books with tiny print. I had the biggest crush on him before I met Owen. But meeting Owen was like finding a missing piece of my soul. I never looked back, never bothered to ask if Noah felt the same. Didn't want to know the answer. We were good as friends. Now Noah's been our mailman for years. Always kind of there. I never really noticed.

Marin: And now you do??

Viv: Oh she notices.

Me: No. I don't. It's not lust or love or anything in between. It's perimenopause. Fluctuating estrogen and the emotional side effects of too many Doritos and running endorphins.

Viv: Maybe. Or maybe it's being human. You can miss someone and still want something. Or is it an urge that needs to be tended to? You know, you can have grief and urges. They're not mutually exclusive.

Marin: Oh my God.

Viv: I'm just saying. You're alive. You're allowed to want someone to admire your new flannel pajamas besides us.

Me: I knew I shouldn't have sent you two that picture!

Viv: You need to read a spicy book. Reignite the flame of love for your own body and its amazing potential. Get reacquainted with yourself.

Marin: Viv, you're going full-on granola-crunching hippie enthusiast on us.

Viv: I'm trying to save all of your yonis. I'm sending you a link. You need to go on Reddit. There's a thread called r/RomanceBooks. Trust me. It's steamy and enlightening.

Before I can object, the link lands in our message thread, and after washing the dishes, reorganizing my spice drawer, and color coordinating my sock drawer, my curiosity wins.

I scroll, skimming past a thread about morally gray vampire boyfriends, alien anatomies, and a post about girth that makes my face heat to a thousand degrees. Then I see something that I wasn't expecting to find there.

Click.

Posted by: GinnyHotFlash1945

Title: Romance Checklists: The Love Reboot for Whenever You've Stopped Waxing

Hi.

This is Ginny. I don't know how this works, and it's only after sharing this message that I realized I accidentally added a picture of my left elbow along with it, but let's press on.

My friends and I finished helping our younger friend, Emma, find love. She works at our assisted living center, and let me tell you, we put her through the wringer. Dancing in the park, sexy baking dates, meeting the parents, costume changes, even a fake heart attack.

It was glorious.

Here's the thing: it all started because we were tired of seeing Emma give up on love, but not only love, on life. Watching her believe that she didn't deserve the real, heart-throbbing, panty-dropping, life to lead with full abandon and passion, the kind of life we read about in spicy books.

She deserved to live it, and this time we could yell at her instead of at the pages when the heroine made a terrible decision (putting your whole life on hold for a man with a motorcycle and no helmet? Ma'am...).

So we made a romantic checklist. A list of all the tropes that she should try. Here's the kicker, it wasn't just about a slow burn, workplace romance, or forced proximity. It was about helping her see she could trust herself to fall in love with someone, with herself.

And you know what? It worked. She got her HEA.

So now we're thinking, maybe it's not only for Emma. Maybe it will help someone else too.

If you're stuck. If you're lonely. If your love story feels like it ended after one too many bad dates, or the person you thought you knew left you with a house, a goldfish, and a tax mess, maybe it's time to write a new chapter.

Start small. Our friend started with spilling tea on a sexy psychiatrist on a bus. Yours might start with arguing over the last rotisserie chicken at Costco.

If you want a copy of our checklist, we've stashed it on Helen's computer (in a fancy kind of file thing that Emma told us about. Don't ask, it's a whole situation).

Know this: love doesn't go out of season like shoulder pads or crinoline.

(Helen and Betsy say I don't need to put this, but this is Ginny. Writing on behalf of all of us, even though Helen swears she doesn't "have any needs" ((liar)), and Betsy keeps asking me to go to the coupon thread ((she's got a problem)). But I still love them both.)

I scroll past it. Then scroll back up.

Read it twice.

The corners of my mouth twitch at the image my mind's forming of the women behind this post. My eyes subconsciously wander to my large bay window and the empty street outside.

Noah's mail truck had driven by hours ago. Frank had followed his urges and barked valiantly at the poor man while he tried to deliver my mail.

What would it be like to complete a romance checklist? I chuckle at the idea. Completely ridiculous for someone my age to even think about such a silly thing.

But my fingers start to move anyway.

Username: BirdieLawson49

Okay. I wasn't going to post. I was simply lurking. But something about this made me laugh, and ache, a little too hard not to say something. I lost my husband a little over two years ago. Suddenly. No warning. Brain aneurysm.

One minute we were arguing about lawn fertilizer, the next I was calling 911 and forgetting how to breathe. I'm not looking for romance. I mean, unless you count my mailman who keeps offering to trim my fennel plants (which is probably not a euphemism, but who even knows anymore?) and is also my dead husband's old college roommate who I previously had a crush on.

Yeah, it's complicated.

But I've realized there's something I miss.

Being seen. Being known. Being happy. Is it okay to be tired of being sad?

I'm not signing up for a romance checklist or a dating app. Not yet. But maybe I'll let the mailman prune the garden.

Thanks for the post, Ginny. And tell Helen she's not fooling anyone.

Reply from: GinnyHotFlash1945

Oh, sweetheart. I read this out loud and now we're all teary over here (except Helen, proper ladies don't cry at things on the internet and all that, but she did blink more than usual, so she was clearly moved).

Listen, grief's a heavy coat. Some days you wear it like a classic trench, buttoned up tight, shoulders squared, looking put together. Other days, it slips off your shoulders like last season's ratty, worn-out cardigan, and you feel the sun on your skin again. No one can tell you when to take it off, but you can always change the fit. Maybe try something that breathes a little. You don't have to toss it aside, just loosen the seams.

(Betsy says grief can't be compared with fashion. Which isn't true. Everything is a metaphor for fashion. She also wants me to add: You're not broken, Birdie. You're still you. And whoever he was, he'd be damn proud you're still putting one foot in front of the other. She also wants you to know she has coupons for Froyo, if you need sweets.)

(Helen says, and I quote): "It is not inappropriate to accept help from a mail carrier if one's hedges pose a hazard."

We're rooting for you. Whether it's a checklist or a chat with the mailman.

Love,

Ginny, Betsy, and Helen (who reminded me it's impossible to love someone on a Reddit message stream. Don't mind her.)

I don't reply again.

And I don't upvote because I'm still not exactly sure what that means.

But my fingers do move to save the post.

———————

I'm still thinking about that ridiculous Reddit thread, the one with the romance checklists and spicy book tropes and the overly confident women, and now I'm spiraling through the idea of grief checklists, too. Is it possible for both to exist? Can there really be room for love and sadness at the same time, like mismatched socks you wear anyway because the laundry didn't get folded? It's all starting to feel far too philosophical for this early in the morning, which is a surefire sign that I need either a run, a nap, or a therapeutic stroll with Frank.

I settle on the stroll option, because it turns out existential crises don't pair well with sports bras.

I've wrangled us out the door, me in one sneaker and one sock, Frank circling like a senile rodeo horse, when I hear the unmistakable sputter and hum of the mail truck turning onto our street.

Of course.

Perfect timing.

If I hustle, I might be able to make it down the porch steps and around the corner before Noah sees me. I'm not sure why I want to avoid him, exactly, just that the thought of bumping into him while I'm knee-deep in feelings about love, death, and dogs makes me feel itchy in my own skin.

I call Frank, who is now moving with the glacial urgency of a retired sloth. I swear, the dog can hear the mail truck too, and he's in no rush to leave his morning routine of stretching, barking, and offering Noah his best guard dog impression.

"Frank. Let's go."

He blinks at me like I've ruined his day, and because I'm feeling too restless to deal with passive-aggressive dog stares, I give his bottom a gentle shove to get him moving. He lumbers down the porch like an arthritic goat, and I tumble forward after him, still hopping on one foot, trying to jam my other sneaker on without untying. Frank's leash ends up clenched between my teeth, one shoe skids down the front steps, and I'm pretty sure the neighbors are watching me lurch around like a feral Muppet.

All I can think is: Please let me avoid Noah and my feelings and whatever potential mail is addressed to Owen today.

But the truck's already parked in its spot a few houses down from mine, and Noah and his impressively long legs are moving with confidence toward my front door.

I'm not going to make it.

"So..." Noah stretches out the syllables as he eyes my half-shoed state before popping the mail in my mailbox and looking at Frank, who's casually stretched out on my porch. "Looks like you're keeping the dog? And going for a walk?"

"I haven't decided yet, on the dog, I mean." I finish lacing up my tennis shoes.

"Looks like you were on the fence there with the walk too."

I figure it's better not to mention the fact that I've already memorized the sound of Frank's peculiar snoring and know exactly how he likes his ears rubbed. "We're coexisting."

Noah raises an eyebrow, leveling me with a stare that speaks volumes. "I dare you to keep him."

I feel it rise, automatic and hot. The ridiculous pull of a dare. He knows what he's doing. In college, he and Owen would make up the most absurd dares just to see how far they could push me. They learned fast: I could never resist one. Not since third grade, when Emily Bishop double-dog dared me to eat an entire packet of Pop Rocks without closing my mouth. I did it. Then hiccupped purple foam and got to go home early.

Worth it.

"You're evil." I glare at him before snapping the leash on Frank and giving it a gentle tug.

Noah shrugs, that same infuriating, irresistible grin spreading across his face. "Maybe. But it doesn't change the fact that the dare's been extended." He backs down my porch slowly. "So I guess I'll be seeing you... and Frank... around." And then he's whistling a catchy tune while striding down the street.

I want to tell him that he can shove his dare and his cocky grin where I like to shove coupons for 10% off oil changes and commemorative stamps featuring endangered birds, but instead I just try not to enjoy the way his pants hug his ass.

Something flickers in my chest, something restless and real, the kind of feeling that makes you want to text someone something brave and then throw your phone into a lake. And then it's squashed by the bottomless guilt.

I stare at the empty driveway for a few minutes before Frank presses his wet nose into my palm, clearly wondering why we were in such a hurry to get out the door only to sit and stare at the concrete. But all I can think about is the word *dare*.

Maybe that's the whole thing.

Maybe I don't need a romance checklist or a grief checklist. Maybe I don't need structured steps, self-help books, cathartic journaling prompts, or fifteen stages of healing, none of which ever actually feel like progress.

Maybe what I need is a list of good dares.

Not reckless ones. Not eat-an-entire-bag-of-cotton-candy-in-ten-minutes dares (though, let's be honest, I'd still do it). But brave ones. Silly ones. Hopeful ones.

Like walk into a hardware store and purchase the screws to fix the fan, because Owen isn't coming back to do it for me.

Or buy something with stripes, polka dots, and patterns because you can still wear color.

Kiss someone when you're not entirely sure how it will end.

Keep the damn dog, even if he did pee on your favorite rug.

Want something just for you. Not because it's sensible. Not because it's expected. Simply because you want it.

Tell someone the truth, even if your voice shakes, especially if it does.

Tell yourself the truth. Not because it'll fix anything. But because it might remind me I'm still capable of wanting, of choosing, of being me.

Grief doesn't evaporate. But I can win against it in a stare-off and dare it back into its sad corner now and then.

Maybe healing doesn't always look like softness.

Sometimes, it looks like saying yes to keeping a dog with a coat that resembles mashed prunes because someone raised his eyebrows and dared you to.

Damn it. I guess that's it. I have a dog.

Chapter Six

"The eighth... is it the eighth?" I scrunch my eyebrows trying to work the math, but the weeks all blur together. "No matter. This meeting of The Dead Husbands Society is officially starting. I have several things on the docket to discuss today."

I adjust my headphones as Frank tugs the leash forward. The sidewalk is damp and smelling sweet from a fresh drizzle, and the pink sky reflects in the puddles like cotton candy soup. We never did make it on our early morning walk, so he's overly excited about our evening one. My boots squish satisfyingly as I walk, one hand holding my phone up so I can see the screen. It always helps to walk when I'm processing, brainstorming, or discussing ideas.

Viv rolls her sapphire eyes so hard that it's a wonder they stay in her head; then her camera shakes as she flops backward onto what looks like a velvet floor pillow. "Good *God*, Birdie. Who died and made you Parliament?"

"Technically?" I glance down at Frank, who has stopped suddenly in his tracks and is now hyper-focused on sniffing a dandelion. "All of our husbands."

Marin's square lights up in a small smile as she pushes a few strands of brown hair away from her pale grey eyes. She's in her usual oversized sweatshirt, yarn in her lap, cat curled behind her on the couch. "I actually really like the structure. I need structure. It's the one thing Theo gave me that I still appreciate, a love of structure."

"I'm walking Frank right now, so breaking structure a little." I angle my phone slightly to show the pink sunset trying to break through the overcast sky and the puddle-filled sidewalk. "But I do my best thinking when I walk, so if I cut out, it's probably because he saw a squirrel and tried to end us both."

"You're the only person I know who holds a grief meeting during cardio." Viv tucks a strand of bleached strawberry pink hair behind her ear, lounging like a grief-stricken Greek goddess. "You know I'm all for movement to cleanse the thoughts, but today I'm opting for yoga pants without the exercise. They make me feel emotionally limber."

Frank veers to the right, yanking me slightly off-camera. "Okay. First item: *someone* forgot to mark themselves safe from another round of dating app disasters."

"Why do you say *someone*?" Marin leans way too close into the camera, giving us a deep and personal encounter with her nose hair. "We all know Viv is the only one brave enough to still date, much less join an app. Although, to be honest, I always thought it looked kind of fun. Like something a spy would do."

"Marin! You should join! I have a list of viable options."

Marin shakes her head vigorously at Viv's request. "Nope. Not ready."

Viv lifts a hand, her hot pink nails flashing with the movement. "Fine. I'll confess then. Guilty. And I thought this one had promise. He teaches breathwork and sound bathing."

"That does sound promising." Marin sets down her knitting needles, fully supportive even though I'm pretty sure she knows about as much about sound bathing as I do.

Viv sighs. "He brought his singing bowls *on the date*. Set them up right there on the table at the vegan café, told me he couldn't connect with me properly until he aligned my root chakra."

I wince. "Please tell me that's not code for something else."

"Oh, it was." Viv's voice is Sahara-Desert-dry. "But not in a fun way. He said my 'energy body had walls.' Then he asked if I wanted to do acro-yoga in the Whole Foods parking lot."

Marin starts to chuckle, but a look from Viv causes her to stifle it down into a snort. How Viv can convey that much contempt through a web camera is a gift in and of itself. "You always find something wrong with them. Could it be because none of them is your husband?"

Viv doesn't miss a beat. "No, it's because none of them are sane. Also, I draw the line at doing downward dog over a cart corral." Then her eyes soften. "And after each date, all I want to do is call him and laugh about it because he would understand..."

I let the moment settle, the image of Viv's social profile splashing across my memory: ThisIsUs. No past tense. Viv's silence lasts a second too long to be breezy, but she snaps back into her usual sparkle before anyone can call her on it. "Anyway, he refused to eat chocolate. Who doesn't eat chocolate?"

"Speaking of chocolate..." I barrel ahead even though the segue makes zero sense. "I went down a Reddit rabbit hole the other night."

"Oh, tell me it was the lumberjack one!" Viv sits up, suddenly alert, her chest practically spilling out of her off-the-shoulder top. "The guy who builds her a bookshelf and then slow-burns her into oblivion?"

"No, I didn't finish it."

Viv gasps. "You *bailed* on social media's hottest fictional contractor? The discussions happening on Reddit are enough to get your engine primed."

My face reddens, and I look around the deserted street, despite the fact that no one can hear inside my headphones but me. "I took a detour. I found a post by a woman named Ginny. She was writing about a young friend of hers and some romance checklist the women at her assisted living home gave her. It was ridiculous. And kind of sweet. And weirdly inspiring."

"I like weirdly inspiring." Marin hasn't picked up her knitting needles again, so I'm counting this meeting as a win. "What did they do?"

"Well, the checklist was full of tropes. Like forced proximity, slow burns with emotional baggage, and forbidden workplace relationships. But the point wasn't the romance. It was that these women wanted the girl to actually *live*, to stop hiding behind sarcasm and safety nets and take a chance on her one messy, beautiful, unpredictable life. And it made me think about us."

Viv groans. "Here comes the homework."

"Viv. It's a grief group. Not homework. We should do things to process what's happening." I stop walking, the phone steady now as Frank lies down in a patch of clover.

"Fine. A romance checklist sounds fun," Viv concedes.

I put down the camera to fiddle with the backpack I slung over my shoulder for this occasion. The hot pink, glitter-covered notebook stares back at me, and I wonder for the millionth time since grabbing it at the office supply store if I should've gone with the plain, black spiral one.

"We're doing a list of double-dog-grief dares!" I yell it into the screen because right now, they're both looking at the slightly overcast, pink sky.

I hear Viv's voice echo out. "Dares? Like we did in middle school? Now sexy dares I can get behind. Tell me, Birdie. What romantic tropes do I get to play out, because there's a hot young thing who started at my yoga class, and I can think of a few things I'd like to do with him and to him."

I pick up my phone in time to see Marin's knitting needles click together as her mouth forms a perfect, shocked O.

Before Marin can pretend her internet connection is unstable and end the call, I plow ahead. "Not like that. Not a sexy lumberjack dare. *Grief* dares. For each of us."

Marin tilts her head, suspicion radiating from her face. "What kind of grief dares?"

"The kind that nudges you out of your stuck places. Things that scare you. Or stretch you. And here's the kicker, we write them for each other. I am putting each of your notebooks in this mailbox now." I set the phone down again and let the loud creak of the mailbox speak for me before holding up the one I kept for myself. "We're going full *Sisterhood of the Traveling Pants* and writing one in each other's notebooks before sending it on to the next person until it finds its way back to the original person. Then we complete the dare and pass them around again."

Viv blinks. "Wait. So *you* get to write *mine*? And Marin writes yours? Wouldn't it be easier to tell each other the dare?"

"That's true," Marin adds. "And save on postage."

I sigh, saying goodbye to my traveling pants idea, and nod. "Fine. We can do it that way, but yes, we are still writing the dares for each other, and we are doing it in physical notebooks. The act of writing is therapeutic and all that." I wave my hand and make the statement with authority of someone who doesn't still avoid frozen waffles and knows how to process grief.

Viv narrows her eyes. "Now Marin writing one, I can handle. It will probably be something related to knitting needles. You, on the other hand, you're probably going to make me go on a date with no makeup and talk about my feelings, aren't you?"

"No. But maybe I'd dare you to take yourself out on a date next week. And show up for yourself without the persona. Tell yourself the truth. Not the funny story. Not the curated version. Just honesty."

Viv blinks, her long lashes accentuating the motion. "Okay, but that's far more terrifying."

Marin clears her throat gently. "What would mine be?"

I glance down at the screen, meeting her eyes as best as I can through the camera. "Write a letter to your husband that says everything you didn't get to say."

Marin flinches like I've reached through the screen and touched a bruise. She opens her mouth. Closes it. "There were plenty of things that were said. Too many things. It's why the divorce papers are still in a shoebox, in the closet. I haven't even —" She stops again, eyes blinking fast. "I don't need to say more things. I need to take things back. I mean, he went for a drive to cool off after we fought over the logistics of the separation. Nothing was final. Until everything was final."

Silence stretches, thick, but not uncomfortable.

Viv speaks first, softer than usual. "That still counts as grief."

"Maybe you have more to say than you think?" I whisper.

Marin nods.

Frank barks at a squirrel off-camera, giving us a beat to breathe.

Viv recovers first. "Okay. So we're doing this now? Grief Olympics? Do I get to assign you one?"

"Go for it."

Viv tilts her head dramatically. "I double dog dare you to flirt with the mailman."

Marin gasps. "Vivian!"

Viv shrugs. "You said this was about pushing each other. And that man has been bringing her mail with looks that make me think he should be auditioning for a leading role in a rom-com movie."

I laugh, trying to cover up the pounding in my chest, the ringing in my ears at the mere thought of flirting with another man. "What does this have to do with my grief?"

Viv ignores me and plows ahead. "I think he wears fitted Henleys and smiles like he knows your favorite coffee order."

Marin giggles. "That's very specific."

Viv points at the screen. "I want eye contact. Full smile. And if you really feel bold, maybe ask him if he likes rain."

"If he likes rain?" I can hear the skepticism in my voice.

Viv squints at me. "You've got a tall, broody mailman delivering packages to your porch, and you haven't rain-troped him yet. You know, accidentally bump into him while it's pouring, drop your umbrella, stare into his deep blue eyes like it's a Nicholas Sparks trailer. Come on, Birdie."

"You want me to rain-trope the mailman?"

Viv leans back into her velvet purple cushion, her eyes serious.

"I want you to stop pretending your needs don't matter. That all you were was a good wife and all you are is a proper mother. That you aren't someone outside of those roles. That's what this has to do with your grief."

Marin's pale eyes widen. "Viv, that's actually really good."

Viv throws her hands in the air, bangles jangling like warning bells. "Of course it is! I contain multitudes."

"Alright." I take out the pink flamingo pen that was the obvious choice to go with the sparkly pink notebook. "We each have one week to complete our grief dares. And yes, there will be check-ins."

Viv's perfectly plucked eyebrows launch toward her hairline. "Check-ins? Deadlines? What is this, emotional algebra? I didn't do homework in high school, and I'm certainly not starting now."

Marin gives a tiny, ladylike snort. "It's not like we don't talk every day, regardless, Viv."

"Yes!" I jump in. "Exactly. We already show up. Accountability is what we need."

"Not talking about it and getting into bed with potential new candidates is what I need," Viv mutters, folding her arms dramatically. "Preferably ones with strong forearms and no emotional baggage."

Marin smirks. "So, fictional men then."

Before Viv can launch into her ideal, emotionally-disconnected but physically fully-connected ideal fling, Frank suddenly veers off the path, nose to the ground like he's on a mission from God.

"Oh no," I mutter, tugging at the leash. "Not here, Frank. Not now."

But it's too late. He circles once, twice, the universal sign that my next five minutes are about to get undignified.

I glance at the screen. "Well, I won't subject you all to watching me help Frank handle his digestive journey."

Viv lets out a cackle. "Before you go, I need to say, the notebook and pen is perfection. When will mine be here?"

"I splurged and didn't want to chicken out, so I overnighted it. Viv, can you write down Marin's? I'll write down yours, and Marin can write down mine. Don't forget to add it's a double-dog dare. No take-backsies. I didn't chicken out on the playground, and I'm not starting here."

"Still sounds like homework, but I guess the flamingo does make it better. My next challenge had better not have anything to do with catching feelings on dates. Or I'm quitting." Viv levels me with a fierce stare.

"You can't quit! It's in the bylaws." I reach for the little green plastic bag with a sigh. "The eighth meeting of the Dead Husbands Society is officially adjourned."

The screen fills with waves and eye rolls, and on that note, I click "end meeting" and get to work addressing Frank's needs.

Chapter Seven

I swipe on mascara like I'm getting ready for a red carpet, not my front porch. It's the first time I've worn makeup in weeks, and no, it has nothing to do with the mailman. It's about the dare. I don't half-ass a dare. Even if my hands are shaking, my heart is pounding, and I'm 100% sure that flirting with Noah will win me the Worst Widow of the Year trophy.

"Stop spiraling, Birdie." I give myself a stern glare in my entryway mirror. "It's just a normal Wednesday."

A normal Wednesday where I happen to be wearing my favorite jeans, the ones that make my butt look like I still do daily Pilates, and a snug, floral blouse that has no visible dog hair.

Frank watches me from the rug by the front door, his head tilted like he's trying to figure out who I'm trying to impress. I smooth my dark strands and avoid eye contact with his judgmental brown eyes.

"I'm allowed to be curious about a person," I mutter, checking the time. "It's not a crime to be aware of another human being. And this is about moving past grief and developing my sense of self. And proving to the girls that things are moving along nicely in the emotional baggage department."

He blinks.

I raise my eyebrows, which I may or may not have plucked this morning. Just because they needed plucking, mind you. "I'm not flirting. I'm being neighborly." Why am I trying to justify this to a dog? And why does my dog seem so judgmental?

The truth is, I've timed the mail delivery. It usually arrives between 9:36 and 9:46, depending on how bogged down Noah is with packages for the day. I glance out the window for the third time in five minutes, then force myself to sit on the couch and pretend to read a book. It's some romance Viv recommended and it's not doing anything for my nerves. I keep glancing toward the driveway like a teenager waiting for their prom date.

When the mailbox clangs shut, my heart hiccups.

Frank lets out a single bark.

"Nope." I bolt up. "We're not running to the door. We are not chasing the mailman." I give Frank a pointed look. "We are calm. We are composed."

We are peeking through the curtains like it's a neighborhood stakeout.

Noah is halfway down the driveway, the sun catching the dark waves of his hair. He's wearing his usual navy USPS polo, and somehow, it fits him as if it were tailored. He looks like he belongs on one of those fake calendars Viv would ironically order—Hot Mailmen of the Pacific Northwest.

Before I can talk myself out of it, I open the door and attempt to look casual, as though I were passing by and not peeking out of my curtains every twenty seconds.

"Noah!" My voice is entirely too loud, and I'm pretty sure I hear a few birds stop midsong in panic.

He turns, surprised. "Hey, Birdie." He walks back toward me, casual, his gait loose and confident. "Did I forget a package? You look nice. Going somewhere?"

"Oh! No." I run a hand through my long, dark hair, which I'm sure makes my stick-straight bangs stand on end. "I wanted to say hi."

He raises an eyebrow, amused. "Hi."

"So, how's the weather?"

He glances up at the sky and squints. "Sunny. Few clouds."

"Oh. Yes. Um, I knew that."

We stand there for a beat, quiet, except for the distant sound of Frank licking his own paw.

Noah runs a hand over the scruff on his jaw, and I watch it a little too long. It's a very attractive jaw. And a very attractive hand. Why is that suddenly a thing I notice? My stomach flips with nerves and guilt. Always guilt.

Before I can stop myself, I blurt out, "Have you ever auditioned for one of those, uh, hot USPS mail delivery calendars? I don't know if they have one, but if they do, you could definitely make a little extra cash. Not that you need money. I don't know your finances. I meant—it would be a favor. To the calendar industry. And housewives everywhere."

There's a silence so thick it could be cut with the edge of my embarrassment.

Noah chuckles and then laughs, an actual laugh, deep and low, that sends heat rushing to my cheeks.

"I'm not flirting," I blurt.

Why did I say that? How did those actual words come out of my actual mouth?

I wince and scramble. "I mean—I am, I guess. But not on purpose. It's part of this, uh, grief dare. You know how I am with dares. A thing my widow support group is doing. Like exposure therapy, but for sadness. And romance. And personal growth."

Noah raises an eyebrow, clearly trying not to laugh. "Romance?"

"Not romance..." I continue helplessly. "I'm not saying we love each other."

Did I just say love? Backtrack. Backtrack now.

"I mean, I'm not objectifying you. You're not a piece of meat. Or a calendar. Never mind. This isn't about that. I'm trying to show up for myself. Not looking for something extra on the side. That sounds like I meant something, uh, inappropriate. I didn't mean that. Of course, nothing inappropriate. Calendars are not inappropriate." Oh my God, I need to stop talking.

Noah chuckles again, the sound warm and deeply amused. "I think the last time I saw you this flustered was when we got separated from the group during that five-day class trip to Washington, D.C."

"I was right to panic!" I point a finger at him, grasping in desperation onto the topic change. "We were supposed to be studying Public Policy and Institutions, and I was not about to get a bad grade because I couldn't read the bus schedule. I hated that class."

Noah pulls his lips into a dramatic pout. "Wow. That was the only class we ever had together, and I'm not going to pretend I'm not a little crushed that you hated it."

I smirk. "Okay, the best part of that class was you. Happy now?"

"Marginally." He leans back, shuffling a few pieces of mail between his hands. "If I remember correctly, you were the one who confidently led us in the wrong direction for three metro stops before realizing we were headed toward Maryland."

I groan. "In my defense, I'm pretty sure there's some bus schedule gremlin who enjoys seeing people get on and off at the wrong place."

Noah just beams, continuing on, "And then we tried to call the chaperone, but your phone was dead and mine was... Damn, I don't remember where it was."

"That was the same problem we had back then. You never could keep track of your phone. I'm pretty sure we found it in your checked luggage." I roll my eyes. "Who does that?"

"An optimist!" His hand is on his heart. "I believed in the structure of the itinerary."

"And yet there we were." I start laughing as the full memory floods my mind. "Stranded, hungry, and terrified we were about to end up on some missing students flyers."

But even then, under the city lights, shivering on a park

bench, I was only half-panicked because Noah was there. I always felt safe with him.

"Speak for yourself. I was more scared of you stabbing me with a pencil because I asked to be partnered with you when you wanted to be partnered with Lucy Fennec."

I shrug. "You weren't wrong. She got the best grades in the class, and you wore a corduroy suit jacket, ironically."

"It wasn't ironic." He purses his lips, clearly pretending to be offended. "It was practical. And you weren't complaining when it stopped your shivering on that park bench, remember?"

I smile despite myself. "Yeah. I drowned in that thing. It smelled like Calvin Klein and spearmint gum." I don't tell Noah that I still love corduroy because of that stupid jacket.

He chuckles again, the kind that crinkles the corners of his eyes. "Still, not a terrible night. We walked ten miles and discovered an all-night diner with cinnamon pancakes the size of your face."

"Yep. Paid for it with that horrible duet you had us sing in those hats we found. Never before and never again."

"I think we could've made a career out of busking!" Noah argues.

I level him with a stare. "The years are eroding your memory, my friend. If it hadn't been for that drunk old man who dropped us a $100 dollar bill, which I'm pretty sure he thought was a $1, we would still be there trying to turn 'Barbie Girl' into a duet and arguing over who had to be Ken."

"Is that why you drug Owen and me to so many nights of karaoke after that? You always were a perfectionist. Was it about redemption at that point?" Noah stares like all the missing pieces of a puzzle are falling into place before his eyes.

I scoff. "No."

"It totally was! Owen and I know way too many vocals to way too many songs because of you." Noah's eyes are wide in horror.

Know. Present tense.

I guess Noah forgets sometimes that he's gone too.

Maybe Noah senses the shift, sees the way my eyes start to water, because he's adding, "Don't forget the hour we spent rating historical monuments on hotness during that trip. You gave Alexander Hamilton a nine, which still feels generous."

"He had confidence." I sniff, pulling back the unexpected tears, grateful for the topic change. "That's sexy in a man. Looks are 50% genetics and 50% confidence. And I did get 82% on the final for that class."

We're quiet for a beat, just long enough for memory to settle in.

"You know—" I give a tentative smile "—as awful as that night started, it ended up being one of my favorite parts of the trip." I twist my finger through the air like I can still feel corduroy brushing my shoulders.

Noah glances at me, and something in his expression shifts. Softer. Sadder. "Mine too."

I groan and cover my face with the stack of mail. "Maybe it's just easier to focus on the past. Back then, everything fit—him, me, the life we made. You and my ridiculous side quests. Now I feel like I've wandered into someone else's story."

He doesn't answer right away, just looks down at the ground between us like it holds some kind of map.

"Yeah." When he does speak, his voice is tight and strained. "It was simpler then. You were his. I was... me. And we all knew our parts."

The breeze shifts, brushing past us like it's trying to move something along. It brings that scent of cedar and rain and Noah —something so familiar it hurts. One of the envelopes slips from my pile. As I bend to pick it up, so does he, and his fingers brush the inside of my wrist.

The jolt is immediate.

Electric.

Uninvited.

Unfair.

Too much like how Owen used to touch me.

My chest tightens like I've been punched. Like Owen's ghost has curled a fist around my ribs.

He steps back, mirroring my own retreat.

Frank barks from the porch, startling us both.

"Thanks for the mail." The words come out too fast, and I'm already backing away, blinking against the tears pressing behind my eyes.

Noah straightens, his own face riddled with guilt. His voice shifts into something professional and distant. "I should get back. I've got... a ton to do."

"Right. Yeah. Of course." I nod like a bobblehead in a windstorm. "Deadlines. Mail. The world keeps turning."

He gives a faint smile that doesn't reach his eyes. "Take care, B."

I watch him walk back to his truck, the distance between us growing with every step, and try not to wonder why my grief suddenly feels lonelier now than it did before he showed up.

Frank lifts his head and follows me back inside, like he's seen enough.

I close the door, heart racing, and lean my forehead against it. "Frank, that was not neighborly."

Chapter Eight

The email pops up like a ghost, uninvited, inconvenient, impossible to ignore. I don't even remember signing up for notifications from the Seattle Art Museum's HR department. Probably one of those late-night impulse subscriptions, back when hope felt like a luxury I could afford.

Subject line: Now Hiring–Exhibition Curator Internship.

I stare at it. My stomach does a flip. I click it open before I can think better of it.

A paid internship opportunity with the Seattle Art Museum's Exhibitions Department. Ideal for emerging professionals in the field of curation and art history.

Emerging professionals. That's a polite way of saying twenty-two-year-olds who can speak fluent Excel and wear wide-legged trousers with confidence.

Still, my heart gives one pathetic little flutter.

Once upon a time, before diapers, lunchbox notes, and mortgage payments, I wanted to work there. I used to imagine myself walking through those halls in kitten heels, naming exhibitions and hanging art labels like they were tiny poems. I got my degree in art history for that girl. The one who envisioned her life would be surrounded by beauty and stories before the narrative changed.

Could I apply?

Nope. Not a chance. I haven't written a cover letter in decades.

I slam my laptop shut. And then, two seconds later, I open it again. Not because I'm applying. The Dead Husbands Society meeting starts in two minutes, and if I'm late again, Viv will send a search party, and Marin will send a strongly worded text. Neither of which is ideal.

I hover over the email. I should delete it. Just be realistic, save myself the embarrassment of even imagining.

But instead, I flag it. Not because I'm going to apply. Simply so I don't forget it's there. Just in case.

Viv appears first, her camera slightly angled from above. Her background is lit by Himalayan salt lamps. "Well, I failed the challenge." The words lag slightly behind the frame as my internet catches up, and the sound is garbled as she flops back on a cushion.

"At least you're not trying to cover it up. Did you fail or bail?" I nestle further back into my muted blue sofa.

She scoffs. "I *attempted* a solo date. I really did. Took myself to this chakra alignment thing at a healing café."

Marin joins with a quiet "Hi," and Viv gives her a signature smile, all sunshine and perfect teeth, before continuing. "Marin. Date challenge fail at a chakra alignment healing cafe. Now you're caught up."

Viv barely stops to suck down a quick sip of air before plowing forward. "And there was this man with this *incredible* aura. Looked like Jason Momoa if he worked at a co-op. Long braid. Sandals. We ended up splitting a turmeric latte and doing partner yoga. The universe clearly wanted me to realign in his arms."

Marin blinks. "You mean your solo date turned into a *real* date?"

"My chakras insisted." Viv gives an unapologetic wave of her hand. "I'm respecting the flow of energy."

"You're allergic to being alone." I make the statement with the full authority of someone who's now watched several trending mental health videos.

"I'm allergic to ignoring divine signs. I'm basically following orders from the universe."

"Viv." Marin's voice is so gentle that it almost doesn't make it through the speaker. "Do you think maybe it's less about energy flow and more about not wanting to sit in your own stuff?"

Viv's smile falters for a second. "I do sit in it. Briefly. Like a cold plunge. In and out. Rejuvenating. Then I move on."

Marin doesn't flinch. "And why do you think that is?"

Viv looks off-screen, like she's debating whether to bolt. "Because if I marinate in it, I might stay stuck. Or worse. What if it's bottomless? What if I don't come back up? What if it swallows me?"

I shift in my seat, heart tugging. "Viv..."

She waves a perfectly manicured hand. "Nope. You're one question away from pulling out a pen and saying, 'How does that make you feel?' and I am not about to be the subject of tonight's emotional excavation."

"But we care about you," Marin adds.

Viv sighs, a long, dramatic exhale like she's deflating. "I know. That's the most annoying part."

I smile. "So maybe next time take the plunge. Just for a little longer. Let yourself know it's okay to be you without him."

Viv gives us a look, half exasperation, half gratitude, and grabs the fizzy concoction in the glass next to her to take a sip. "Fine. But if I drown in my own emotions, it's on you two. I expect tasteful memorials."

I raise my hand as though I'm pledging allegiance. "On my honor."

There's a beat, then Marin exhales slowly. "I did mine."

Viv's eyebrows lift. "The letter?"

Marin nods, holding up a folded piece of notebook paper. "Actually, I did write it to him."

Viv's brows lift, and I straighten in my seat.

"I wasn't going to," Marin continues, voice trembling slightly. "But once I started, it all poured out. And it got ugly."

She glances toward the opposite wall, like she's ashamed to even look at the letter or us. When she speaks, her voice is low but steady. "It wasn't soft or sad. It was messy. Brutal, even. I told him I hated that he left me with all of it, telling the kids, sorting through a house filled with things we didn't even like anymore, rewriting a version of our story I hadn't agreed to."

Her eyes glisten, but she doesn't blink them away. "I said he died like he lived, ducking out when things got hard. I called him a coward and then circled it and underlined it a hundred times. I wrote that he abandoned me one last time, and somehow, still gets to be remembered as this great man. This devoted husband. This amazing dad." She lets out a bitter little laugh. "But no one knew the truth. Not really."

We're all quiet, waiting. Marin takes a breath like she's steadying herself and continues.

"I kept our struggles to myself for years. Because I didn't want to be the wife who complained. I didn't want people looking at me like I'd failed. So I smiled, and made everyone's lunches, and went to the accounting office, and crunched the numbers in perfect little boxes, and told myself we needed to push through a rough patch. Except the patch never ended. It only shifted. We were barely speaking by the end. We were in the process of separating. Divorce, even. But we hadn't told the kids yet. We hadn't told anyone."

She finally looks up at us, eyes filled with a quiet kind of grief. "So when he died, it was like I lost him and didn't lose him all at once. I was grieving someone who was already half-gone. And now I'm expected to mourn like we were still something sacred. Like I should only feel devastated. But what I feel is so much more complicated than that."

Her lip trembles. "I asked him, in the letter, if he was planning to leave me first, if he gave up before I did. And I'll never know the answer."

Viv doesn't say anything at first. And neither do I.

Finally, Viv reaches for her glass and whispers, "Jesus."

I feel my chest tighten.

Marin lets out a shaky breath. "And then I cried. Because part of me meant it, and part of me didn't. But that's all I've been holding. Everyone talks to me like I should only be sad, like I lost the love of my life. But I also lost someone I was furious with. I'm grieving a thousand things at once, and none of them make sense."

There's a long pause. Then Viv presses a fingertip to her camera screen, as though she's trying to absorb some of the hurt from across the internet. "Marin, thank you for saying that out loud."

I nod, unable to speak right away. My throat tightens. "You don't have to carry that alone. Or tuck it away because it doesn't look like how grief is supposed to look." I do air quotes around "supposed to" and think Harper would be proud.

Marin swipes at her eye and manages a shaky smile. "It felt like I let something out that's been rotting inside me. And now I'm scared everyone will think I'm awful."

"You're not awful." Viv's voice is firm. "You're honest. And that letter is the most real thing any of us has said tonight."

Frank barks once in the background. "See!" Viv points at the camera. "Even Frank agrees."

We all laugh, the release necessary after everything Marin shared. Viv seizes the moment and clears her throat dramatically. "Okay, that was emotional and beautiful. But can we all agree that my chakras are not the enemy here?"

I grin, grateful for her comic timing. "We agree."

Marin's smile is hesitant. "But maybe next time, try eating dinner alone first? It could be therapeutic. That letter was."

Viv groans, tossing her head back. "You people are relentless.

You know I have an adverse reaction to red meat and emotional vulnerability."

"Both things you insisted were good for us." I can't resist pointing out the irony.

"I said I was open to them. There's a difference."

There's a beat of silence, the kind that feels warm instead of heavy. And then Viv tilts her head, a glint returning to her eye. "Speaking of emotional beef, Birdie. How did your flirting dare go? Did you throw yourself at the mailman's feet?"

"Oh God," I groan, covering my face with both hands. "It was a disaster."

Viv perks up immediately, the coral pink streaks in her hair reflecting the warm glow of the Himalayan salt lamp. "Delicious. Do tell."

I peek through my fingers. "I wore mascara and my good jeans. Frank stared at me like I was a total stranger without my signature t-shirt and bathrobe. So that was a nice confidence boost. I kept peeking out the window like a deranged teenager. And then, when Noah actually showed up, I panicked and asked him about the weather like it was 1952. And then, then, I asked him if he'd ever auditioned for a sexy mailman calendar."

Viv makes an audible choking sound. Marin's eyes widen. "You did not."

"I did. And then I blurted out that I wasn't flirting. Which was, of course, also a lie. He told me I was terrible at it, and honestly? He wasn't wrong."

Viv fans herself. "But did he say it in a mean way or a hot way?"

I hesitate, guilt washing over me in waves. There's no way it's appropriate to call him hot. But then again, I did compare him to a male calendar model, and I do tell the girls everything. Finally, I mumble, "A hot way. He kind of brushed my hair out of my face, and it was too much. Too intimate. I short-circuited and basically ran back inside."

Marin lifts a brow. "That sounds kind of sweet."

"Not sweet," I mutter. "Vulnerable. Awkward. Gave me way too clear a look into my issues, which is why I hated it."

Marin's voice stays warm, like she's used to holding messy things without trying to clean them. "And what issues are those?"

Her knitting needles click gently in the background while I lean down to rub Frank's head, hoping it'll calm the pounding in my chest.

"That I built my whole life around Owen." My voice is a whisper. "And now the loss is swallowing me whole, because I don't know who I am if I'm not someone's wife. Or someone's mother."

The silence that follows isn't empty. It's full of breath I don't want to take.

Viv's voice, usually flippant and wild, comes soft this time. "So who are you without those things?"

I dig my thumbnail into a spot on my jeans until it hurts. "I don't know. I wish I did. I keep reaching for pieces of myself but all I come up with are his things. His stories. His friends."

I glance at the screen. "Do you think I shouldn't have flirted with Noah?"

Neither of them answers; they both just hold the silence for me.

"I mean, he and Owen were close," I go on. "We all were. In college. It feels... wrong. Like I touched something I wasn't supposed to. And weird."

Still quiet.

"They played poker together every Thursday night for years. He came to Owen's funeral. He brought us macaroni."

Viv lets out a slow breath. "Macaroni is quite the hill to die on, Birdie."

I laugh, but my throat's too tight for it to last. "It just feels close. Too close to the past. Like I'm... disrespecting it."

Frank nudges my leg with his nose and I reach down again, grateful for something solid to touch. "I don't want to feel like

I'm stealing something. Like if I let someone see me, even just flirt with me, I'm erasing Owen. Like I'm rewriting our story."

Marin's cat climbs over her keyboard, blocking her face with a blur of calico fur. "Maybe you're not rewriting anything." Her voice carries through the fuzz. "Maybe this is just... chapter two."

That feels too generous. Too hopeful. My voice wobbles. "But what if people think I moved on too fast?"

Viv snorts. "Anyone judging a grieving woman's timeline can come talk to me and my chakras."

Marin's quiet. "Grief makes everything weird."

"Yeah," I whisper. "It does."

I look at them both. "I just want to find myself again without feeling like I have to bulldoze over the woman I was. The life I had. I want to move forward, but I don't want to lose her. Or him. Or us."

Viv's smile is full of sparkle, her blue eyes passionate. "Maybe you don't have to step over her. Maybe you have to bring her with you."

Something in my chest crumples and rearranges itself.

I blink fast, my voice hoarse. "Okay. That's enough emotional beef stew for one night. Someone please say something wildly inappropriate."

Viv grins. "Do you want me to ask Noah if he's open to a holiday-themed shirtless mailman calendar? For research purposes only."

I laugh. "God, no. But also, maybe."

Marin smiles. "I'll design the cover. I'm a wizard with Canva."

"So we all got vulnerable today." Marin looks at Viv, and the message is clear.

Viv clears her throat, stares past the camera, picks at her cuticle, and then, seeing we aren't letting this go, throws her hands up in the air. "Fine. I know I make jokes about the chakra guy, but the truth is I miss my husband. I miss having someone to talk to at night. I miss being picked. And when I'm alone, the silence is so loud it feels like it's echoing off the walls. So I keep trying to fill it.

With people. With videos. With noise. With turmeric lattes and imitation Jason Momoas."

Marin gives her a look that's more love than judgment.

Viv shrugs. "Grief is lonely."

"It is," Marin agrees. "Even when it's shared."

We sit with that for a second.

Then I take a breath. "Okay. So. What if we each build on what we started this week? But make it specific."

Viv raises an eyebrow. "You mean more homework."

"Dares," I correct.

"Dares do make it sound more dangerous. Can we add the word 'danger'?"

"Fine. Grief danger dares," I concede. "I'll go on an actual date. Not a failed flirtation in front of my house, but me showing up as a woman who still exists outside of what she's lost."

Viv starts slow clapping. "That is one impressive dare."

Marin nods. "I'll keep writing letters. The ugly ones. The ones that say all the things I didn't get to. Maybe it'll help me start to forgive myself for not being more honest while he was alive."

We both look at Viv.

She groans. "Ugh. Fine. I'll take myself to dinner. Alone. No co-op cuties, no alignments. Just me, some quiet, and maybe a journal. But if I get emotional, I'm allowed to order dessert."

"New rule." I grab my flamingo pen and start to write. "We are all allowed and encouraged to add chocolate to each grief dare."

"Deal," Marin echoes.

Viv lifts her tea like a glass of wine. "To grief dares."

We all raise invisible glasses in solidarity.

"To grief dares," Marin and I chant.

And in the background, Frank lets out an approving snore.

Chapter Nine

Me: There's some major plot holes in this grief dare.

Marin: For example?

Me: How am I supposed to actually go on a date if no one has asked me out?

Viv: 🤣🤣 ... Wait... are you serious? 😳

Me: Yes, I'm serious. Last I checked, asking someone out was the guy's job. I read a book in college that said men need the thrill of the chase. I can't do the chasing.

Viv: That book was written in 1954 by a woman who probably hated orgasms or a man who hated women.

Me: I don't want to emasculate him by being too forward.

Marin: You're not proposing marriage. You're talking about coffee.

Viv: Or fennel. Didn't he say something about trimming your fennel plants?

Me: That's not code, Viv.

Viv: Make it code. "Yes, Noah, I would love it if you came over and handled my delicate blossoms."

Me: Absolutely not.

Viv: Suit yourself. But he offered. The least you could do is hand him a pair of shears and a flirtatious smile (not the one where you don't blink. Or show too much teeth. Maybe skip the smile for now.)

Me: This still feels inappropriate. I'm flirting with my dead husband's best friend.

Marin: Well, when you put it like that... It does have the makings of a reality tv show. But maybe remember that Noah is more than that. He's someone who knew you before Owen.

The video call comes through and I drop the little wrench I'm fiddling with to slide the answer button over. Viv's face fills the screen, followed quickly by Marin's.

"This was too important for the group message thread. An intervention is needed. I have some though—wait, what are you doing over there?" Viv squints at me through the screen.

I grunt as I wedge a bolt into the underside of the table I've been building for the past hour. The instruction manual is taunting me with cartoon diagrams that make no anatomical sense. One leg keeps leaning inward like it's contemplating early retirement.

"Putting together this side table from IKEA. Or, you know, attempting it without adult supervision." I flick a rogue wooden dowel off my lap into the growing pile of leftover hardware.

There's no way all these pieces are necessary. I think they just throw in extras to test your self-esteem.

I sit back and exhale. "Owen ordered it, said it was time to replace mine after the leg finally gave out. But it was on backorder and when it came, I didn't have the heart to deal with it. It's been sitting in the garage ever since."

I run my hand over the half-built tabletop, steadying it even though it's still a little crooked. "He was supposed to put it together. But I finally dragged it out and figured, why not me?"

I shrug, like it's no big deal, even though it kind of is. "It doesn't have to be perfect. It just has to stand."

Viv blinks. "Is this the same table that started our whole conversation? The same piece of infamous furniture?"

Marin blinks. "And you're building it? By yourself?"

"Why does everyone sound so shocked? I can follow a diagram. I once diffused a fistfight between two dads over gluten-free muffins. This is nothing."

I jiggle the table. It wobbles. Not ideal. Hopefully, neither of them noticed. But the point is it stands.

Viv lets out a low whistle. "Well damn, Birdie. Look at you doing things imperfectly. On purpose."

"Honestly?" Marin adds. "I think that's kind of badass."

I try not to smile, but I might. A little. I tuck the last screw into the drawer I'll never use and pretend I meant to do it all exactly this way, even while my brain itches to go find the level.

"This leads to my point. Things don't always have to be done perfectly. Sometimes the best things start out a little messy." Viv nods before taking a sip from one of her many pottery mug projects.

Marin nods from her kitchen table, where I can see a half-eaten brownie and a knitting project competing for elbow room. "Yeah, like that table."

"You started this grief dare book," Viv goes on, pointing at the screen with a painted pink nail. "You're my fearless leader. Don't chicken out now that we're heading into battle."

Marin nods solemnly, then spoils it by grinning. "Now text him."

I pause, wiping my hands on my jeans, which are now smudged with whatever mystery grease came from the bag of bolts. "I don't have his number. That wouldn't be appropriate."

Viv leans in, raising a single, judgmental eyebrow. "Step one: Get his phone number. Step two: fennel. Go."

———

Frank gives his trademark warning bark before the mail truck even pulls up, and I glance at the clock like it's suddenly responsible for my fate. 9:39 AM. Too early to look like I tried. Too late to pretend I didn't.

I open the door as Noah steps out of the truck, his baseball cap slightly askew, box in hand, mail tucked under one arm. He's wearing a fleece jacket this time, thank God, though the sleeves are still rolled up to his elbows. Of course.

"Morning, Birdie!" His voice is cheerful in a way that makes me suspicious of anyone who delivers bills with a smile.

"Hey. Mail day!" I point at the package in his hand, and then wish I could take the words back.

"Technically, Monday through Saturday is mail day." He gives me a crooked smile.

"Yes, yes. Anything good, or am I the proud recipient of more home gardening magazines?" I tilt my head toward the box in his hand.

He hands it over. "Just this. And it appears you've been chosen to receive what appears to be a magazine featuring a very important set of seasonal throw pillows."

I look down at the magazine cover. "I hate how accurate that probably is."

A brief silence settles, and I flip through the few pieces of mail, hoping for a conversational lifeline. "Well, this one's from a seed company, so I might get some real plants to accompany the fake ones on my impending throw pillows."

Noah nods. "You do have a beautiful garden. Besides the rogue butterfly garden."

He set it up perfectly. "Oh! Speaking of that…" I pause, mentally slapping myself for being so obvious. "You mentioned helping with trimming them."

His eyebrows shoot up, and he shifts on his feet. "Offer still stands."

"Well." I blink. "They're very fennel-like. Still wild. Still weedy."

"I grew up helping my grandmother prune her garden every spring. It's oddly satisfying work."

I nod, the idea sounding oddly intimate now that he's repeating it out loud. "I might take you up on that."

There's a pause. I hold the box a little tighter.

"I don't want to cross any weird lines." My voice comes out fast and breathy. "I know you and Owen were close and then not so close. You knew both of us, together. And it's probably strange that I'm even talking to you like this. About fennel."

Noah tilts his head slightly, his expression unreadable. "Owen and I will always be close. But that doesn't make it weird. Unless you think it does."

I open my mouth. Then close it. "I don't know what I think. Most of the time, I still expect him to walk through the door with a grocery bag and ask where we keep the cumin."

He doesn't flinch. Just nods and stares at the plants, as though he's trying to figure something out that I'm not aware of.

"I'm not trying to be inappropriate," I add, my voice smaller now. "It's hard to know what's allowed. After."

His voice is gentle. "Grief doesn't come with rulebooks. Only a lot of people pretending it does."

I glance down at the box in my arms again. "I didn't mean to keep you."

"You didn't. Always a pleasure to talk to you." His face breaks into a charming half-smile.

I hesitate. "Could I text you, you know, if I decide the garden needs a trim?"

"Sure." He tips his baseball hat and turns toward the road.

"Noah!" I call after him.

"Yeah?"

"I don't have your number."

"Oh." Then with a slight smile, "So is this you awkwardly trying to ask for it?"

I blush. "I—maybe. I mean, yes. But in a very professional, plant-care-related context."

"Got it." He pulls out his phone. "Strictly botanical."

I grin, finally. "Exactly."

He rattles off his number, and I punch it into my phone, labeling him *Noah—Mail/Fennel*. That feels safe. Distant. Appropriate.

He gives a small wave as he walks back to his truck. "See you around, Birdie."

And I'm left on the porch, holding a box of something I don't remember ordering and the phone number of a man who's not my husband.

It didn't take me long to text him. I can't back out of the dare, which was a date. Not just getting a number, and I already know that making this to count as a date will be a far stretch.

The clippers make that satisfying snip each time Noah lops off another dead bloom, his forearms flexing with every motion. I'm pretending to be helpful by carrying the bucket of trimmings, but let's be honest. He's doing all the work.

What is it about a man doing yard work? The primal sweat? The dirt smudges on his forearm? The quiet grunt when he shifts his weight to reach a stubborn branch? The way his fingers, strong and sure, navigate the thorns without flinching? It's like my subconscious is trying to send my confused perimenopausal hormones over the edge with every glance.

And then, just as predictably, the wave crashes in: Owen, standing in this very spot, nurturing the plants, singing some offline version of Johnny Cash, excited over what butterflies will stop here. Guilt spreads in my chest like the plant's roots, deep and stubborn.

"You okay?" Noah turns in time to catch me staring.

"Yep. Appreciating your technique." I gesture vaguely in the direction of the bush, mortified.

Noah smirks, and I feel another wave of heat wash over my cheeks. I guess I could've skipped applying blush to my pre-non-date make-up regime.

Noah wipes the sweat from his brow with the back of his forearm, fingers still wrapped around the pruning shears. "You've been neglecting these guys."

I cross my arms and squint at the thorns. "I've been a little busy trying to patch my life back together after my husband died of a brain aneurysm in this garden."

Great. Now I'm oversharing.

Noah doesn't answer. And like I always seem to do around him, I barrel ahead. "They were always Owen's responsibility, and they remind me too much of him."

I can see the fluffy white clouds reflected in the crystal clear sea blue of his eyes. "Fair enough."

I glance down, straightening the delicate gold watch on my wrist, trying to appear casual. "It's getting a little late. Would you like to come in for a bite to eat?"

Noah stands, dusting the dirt off his fitted blue jeans. "I never turn down an offer for free food." It's clear most of the mud isn't going to come off. "But maybe we could eat it on the porch?"

The image of my cozy screened-in back patio fills my mind. Owen and I had hung the lights together, and I had potted and cared for fresh herbs in the raised beds he made for me. How would it feel to share dinner with someone else on *our* patio? Realizing that the silence has stretched too long, I quickly paste on a smile. "I hope you like lasagna." I move toward the front door.

"Only if it's burnt around the edges." I can feel Noah's presence behind me, firm and sure.

I lead the way through the front door, kicking off my shoes instinctively before remembering Noah might not follow suit. But when I glance back, he's already toeing off his boots by the mat.

"Bathroom's second door down the hall on the left. Take your time. I'll serve the food!" I call, already moving toward the kitchen.

"Back patio okay?" I tilt my head toward the back door, already balancing two plates in one hand, when Noah walks through the door.

"Perfect." He takes one of the plates before I can drop it. "Smells incredible, by the way."

I almost tell him I used three cheeses, made the sauce from scratch, and assembled it like a bricklayer with something to prove, but I don't. No one needs to know I measured the noodle placement like it was an architectural draft. "It was no big deal."

He stares at the perfectly even dish. "Looks like a big deal. You're setting a high bar."

My mouth twitches. High bars are my love language. I once remade an entire casserole because the cheese bubbled unevenly on one side.

We nestle into my worn wicker chairs, plates balancing on knees, Frank curled between us. There's something about the early evening light, shy of golden hour, that softens everything. Even me.

"Thanks again for the garden rescue." A light breeze rustles the herbs in their planters, and the porch lights blink on, timed like a memory.

Noah nods, and for a while, we eat in comfortable silence. The lasagna *is* slightly burnt around the edges. Victory.

Then Noah breaks the quiet. "You know what's funny? When Owen told me he'd scored your number, I didn't believe him. I thought you were completely out of his league."

I raise an eyebrow. "Yeah, right."

"No, I mean it." A gentle smile skates across his face, warm in the sunlight. "You'd shown up at my dorm room because your roommate was getting it on, and Owen finally showed up like six weeks into the term after his mono. I was out at the library and next thing I knew, I was walking in on you talking about Suzanne Valadon with him like she was your soul sister."

I laugh. "God, I was insufferable."

"Maybe." He grins. "But captivating. With that wild perm and deep brown eyes, I thought you were going to conquer the world."

A brittle laugh leaves my lips, and its bitterness surprises me. "Yep. That's me. Taking over the world, one dirty diaper, PTA meeting, and perfectly curated dinner at a time."

Noah leans close, our arms almost brushing as he stretches across his wicker chair toward mine. "That's not an easy world to conquer. I haven't found a single person I'd like to enter that world with and now I think it's a little late."

The words hang between us like something delicate and dangerous. I reach for my lemonade, trying to swallow the lump in my throat with the ice.

The intimacy scares me, and I retreat. "I forgot that's when we met." I set my empty plate down and start twisting a dark strand of hair around my finger, the wedding band I haven't taken off glimmering in the fading sunlight. "I remember Owen trying to impress me with bad metaphors and talking over everyone."

"He was good at making an entrance."

I nod. "And I was good at pretending I didn't like it."

Noah leans back against the wicker seat, the wood creaking slightly beneath his weight. "You two were something, though.

Volatile and golden. Like you'd either take over the world or burn it down together."

My smile is soft now, touched with something else, the wedding band pressing into my finger. "We almost did both."

"Remember the first night we met?"

My breath catches, heat pooling at the back of my neck.

"How could I forget?" I laugh, but the undertone is nostalgic now, pulled from a place that aches a little. "I was so sure I had this whole college thing figured out. I knew exactly where I was going with my little map, first week on campus, ready to conquer the world, and I walked straight into the wrong dorm room, not even the right building."

Noah chuckles, leaning back, his elbows braced on the creaking wicker armrests. "I'd just finished unpacking and was laying down to rest and there you come, sauntering into my room like you own the place, staring at my Pearl Jam poster like it had personally offended you."

I close my eyes, letting the memory rush back in: the stale hallway air, the too-big map of campus stuffed in my pocket, the unlocked door that I thought was mine, until a sleepy boy with dark tangled hair and a crooked grin sat up in bed and asked, *"You planning to rob me, or...?"*

"I had made a terrible life choice, choosing West instead of East," I tease, nudging his ankle with my toe from across the porch. "But you didn't even yell at me. Just sat up wearing nothing but those basketball shorts and asked if I was there to steal your ramen."

"Hey. Moving was hard work and I was sweaty and gross and not at all ready to face the communal showers." He tips his head back, eyes closing, grinning like he's twenty again. "And what was I gonna do, kick out the prettiest girl I'd ever seen? Besides, my roommate wasn't showing up till the next day, so technically, I had the whole room to myself."

"Right." My voice catches again. "Owen. He is always late. Was always late."

Noah's smile flickers, but he doesn't look away. "Yeah. But in his defense, he did have mono and missed the first few months. It wasn't poor planning. Well, unless you count sharing a straw with Sarah Finney poor planning. Left me to guard lost freshmen and make sure they didn't wander into the wrong bed."

"Oh, please." I roll my eyes, but the flush rising in my cheeks betrays me. "You practically begged to walk me back. Barefoot. Half-asleep. Quizzing me about my major like I wasn't two seconds away from dying of embarrassment."

He shrugs, casual, but his eyes never leave mine. "Couldn't let you get lost twice. You didn't even have a cell phone then. Something about it being a tool of the system. Only that brick you called a pager."

I snort. "God, we're old. And I was so rage against the machine." My fingers twist a lock of hair around and around, my wedding band catching the last bit of sunset light.

And for the first time, I wonder, really wonder, what my life might have been if I'd lingered with the barefoot boy and his bad posters and kind blue eyes a little longer, before the golden one swept in with promises big enough to drown in.

I drop my gaze, my throat tightening. "Bet you wish you hadn't found me that night." My voice comes out too quickly, too lightly.

Noah's smile is gentle, edged with something too deep for either of us to touch. "Nah. I liked finding you."

The warmth between us spikes, bright and terrifying. It scares me enough that I stand up so fast my chair scrapes the patio. "I should, um, top off my glass. You want more?"

He lifts his half-empty beer, eyes still on me. "That'd be great, B." He must sense the tension because when I return, he asks, "What do you think is next for you? I have yet to meet someone as passionate about art history as you are. I still know way too many facts about Artemisia Gentileschi's Baroque raw depictions of women."

My cheeks redden, and the flagged email from the Seattle Art

Museum flashes in my mind. "Oh. I don't know. I haven't thought about what I would like to do since Owen and I got engaged, and I got pregnant with Matt in a matter of seconds."

"Might be something to think about now."

We sit with that for a moment, watching as the sun dips lower, throwing gold across the floorboards.

"You ever miss being married?" The boldness of my question surprises me. We've never talked about his failed marriage. I know I miss being married, but my partner was taken from me. His left.

Noah rakes a hand through his short, dark hair, his gaze drifting toward the yard like he might find the answer buried beneath the hydrangeas.

"Yes and no," he says finally. "I don't miss being married to the wrong person. That was... hell." He gives a small, tired shrug. "But I do miss what I thought marriage could be—with the right person. That version gutted me."

His eyes darken, and I immediately wish I hadn't asked.

"I ended up declaring bankruptcy," he adds, voice low. "That's actually how I got into the mail service. Freelancing with a lit degree wasn't cutting it, and Owen—he's the one who helped me land this route. He found out your last mailman was close to retiring and pulled a few strings. The guy could charm anyone."

I blink. "I had no idea."

Noah nods, then pauses. "Yeah. He was one of the good ones. I don't think I ever repaid him for helping me put the pieces back together. I meant to. But he was gone."

"You ever think about that?" My voice is a whisper in the early twilight. "What it means to still be here when someone else isn't?"

His smile fades into something that mirrors my own broken, battered heart. "Yeah. More than I wish I did."

Something shifts. I can feel it. A tug between familiarity and something else. Something new. Something full of longing. Something wistful. My brain short-circuits trying to label it.

"Well." I clear my throat, trying to lighten the air. "If the lasagna's any good, I do accept praise in the form of home repairs and light gardening."

He chuckles. "I'll keep that in mind."

Frank stirs and stretches, groaning like an old man. Noah looks down at him and grins. "Frank, you didn't even contribute."

"I, uh, I should probably..." I gesture toward the house, or maybe the kitchen. I don't even know what I'm doing anymore.

He leans back slightly, watching me with a bemused expression. "You okay?"

"I don't know." The darkness that has seeped into the evening makes it easier to be honest. "You were his friend. You knew us together. And now you're here trimming my fennel and eating my overcooked lasagna and being nice. It's weird, right?"

I sense him studying me in the dim light for a long second. "Is it?"

I hesitate. "I mean, I didn't plan to flirt with you," I blurt. "Not that this is flirting. It's yard work and prolonged eye contact."

Noah laughs. A low, real laugh, warm and deep, and the sound surprises me and also fills me.

Then he quiets. "Do you want to do this again?"

I blink. "What?"

"If you ever need help with the yardwork, or want a friend to have dinner with, you can text me. Now that you've got my number and all." His grin is a lazy Sunday morning, slow and sweet.

"Which I won't freely use."

Noah cocks his head to the side. "Why not?"

I open my mouth, then close it again, then manage to sputter, "I am trying to be appropriate."

"Birdie. I would never expect anything else but that from you." His voice is gentle. "But know you can text me about plants. Or lasagna. I won't read into it unless you want me to."

And just like that, he stands, stacking our plates without

another word, leaving me in the kind of silence that has a heart-beat. I hear his voice traveling from the kitchen out onto the patio. "I'll pop these in the dishwasher, grab my boots, and let myself out."

"Oh. You don't have to do that. I'll take care of it."

His face appears through the screen door, lips set and serious. "Let me help you."

I'm thankful for the darkness and the fact that he can't see my obvious blush. "Thanks for helping with the garden."

He gives me a look that Viv would best describe as a smolder. "Anytime, Birdie."

Chapter Ten

"You finally tackled those weeds in the butterfly garden!" Harper bursts through the door and grabs me in a back-realigning hug. "I'm so proud of you! I was getting ready to call one of those landscapers who keep leaving their obvious flyers on the doorstep myself. It was really getting out of control, you know."

I open my mouth to let her know who took care of that task, but before I can say anything, she's already releasing me to race back to the front door where she's deposited a grocery bag. Frank is barking and attempting to prance around her feet, begging for attention. "Thank goodness I brought drinks to celebrate!" Harper pulls two probiotic sodas out of the bag. "Two grams of sugar per can and enough fiber to keep you regular all week. It's a celebration for both ends!"

I again try to interject that there is no reason to celebrate, and I'm a weak woman who can't bear to cut the plants that most remind her of her dead husband. Worse than weak, I'm a woman who had another man come cut said bushes and then invited him for dinner, where he sat in the same spot as her dead husband.

"I drank one of these on the way over here, and I really need to pee!" Harper is already halfway down the hall, waving a half-empty lemon soda can in the air.

I haven't said a single word yet. I'll tell her later, I decide. No sense ambushing the girl mid-bathroom emergency.

I grab the bowl of popcorn and call out, "Harper! Honey, it's starting!" I manage the bowl, her weird fizzy drink, and her favorite white cheddar seasoning with the balance of a seasoned circus act as I shuffle toward the living room.

Harper flops onto the couch beside me just as the camera pans to Matt on the bench, bouncing his knee. "Do you think he eats protein bars during the game too, or just before?"

I smirk. "I guarantee he's had four already. So, discussing his snack preferences while watching him on TV—that's what we call family dinner now?"

"If it includes popcorn, then yes." She grabs a handful, then her voice shifts slightly. "It's kinda weird, though. Watching him play without him texting us afterward."

I nod. "He's busy. Growing up."

"Do you miss him?"

There's no point sugarcoating it. "Everyday. But you know how it is. You're both growing up, becoming your own person. It means I've done my job right." I shift, trying to sound casual. "You guys are always going to be the biggest priority in my book, though."

We fall into a comfortable rhythm, cheering at good plays, criticizing the refs. But it doesn't last long.

"So…" Harper starts, without looking at me. "How's The Dead Husband Society going?"

"We talk every day." I keep my eyes fixed to the screen as Matt makes an impressive pass up the court. "It's been nice. Unexpectedly nice."

She nods slowly. "I think it's good you have that. Even though I never would want you to have that. But now that everything's happened, it's good that you do. Sometimes, it feels like life's changing so fast, you know?"

I glance at her, trying to read her tone, but she's staring at the screen again. So I reach my hand across, placing it on hers. "I know." Sometimes that's all there is to say.

"Like you joining the internet world and then courageously facing Dad's garden. I haven't even stepped foot in here yet."

It's now or never. I feel every muscle in my body tighten, bracing myself. "I didn't take care of the flower beds this week."

Harper snorts. "Well, ignore my previous comment. What company did you hire?"

"Noah did."

Her head snaps toward me. "Wait—Dad's friend Noah?"

I nod. "He offered. I didn't ask him to, but I said yes."

Harper's expression shifts—eyebrows pinched, lips pressed into a thin line. "That's... a little weird, Mom."

I swallow. "It wasn't like that. He just helped out."

She doesn't respond right away, and my pulse starts to flutter in the silence that's stretching much too long. Harper's eyes don't leave the screen, even though it's halftime and we're currently watching some horrible commercial for soap.

"Are you... seeing him?"

"No." The word comes out too quickly. "No. I'm not seeing anyone. But I guess I've started wondering what that would even look like. If it would ever feel okay. Maybe I don't want to be alone forever, because he's not coming back." My voice sounds strained, despite my efforts to keep it calm, sure, in parent mode.

Harper pulls her knees up to her chest, hugging them. "It just feels fast. Or maybe not fast. I don't know. I thought I was okay with everything, but then I imagine someone else in Dad's garden, and it makes my skin crawl a little."

Guilt floods me, washing over me in waves that make my chest ache and my heart pound. "Harper, I'm sorry. I didn't mean to upset you. Of course you'd feel something about it. I do too."

She shakes her head, eyes shiny now. "No, I'm sorry. You didn't do anything wrong. I just... I haven't figured out how to let go of him yet. And every time something changes, it feels like I'm supposed to be ready for it. But I'm not. Not all the way."

I nod, throat tight. "I get it. I really do. You don't have to let go of him, honey. He'll always be some of the best parts of you."

She leans her head back against the couch cushion. "You deserve to have a life. I know that. I want that for you. I'm just not totally there yet. I might need a little more time."

I might need a little more time too.

"Take all the time you need, sweetheart."

Harper wipes at her cheek, then reaches for another handful of popcorn. "Okay. New topic. Root beer or ginger ale? You're allowed one probiotic soda and one emotional landmine per night."

I laugh, relief and love bubbling up all at once. "Root beer."

She holds up the can solemnly. "To the root of our problems."

I clink it with mine. "And to not making any gardening metaphors for the rest of the night."

"Thank God." She pops the tab and settles back in. "Now, what are the odds Matt does his hair flip after his next free throw?"

"Well, he's a show-off, so... That goes without saying."

Viv appears on-screen first, her face covered in a green and goopy substance, and there's something that looks like smoke drifting in the background. "Okay, don't freak out, but I'm detoxing my aura."

I squint at my screen. "Is that sage? Or is your kitchen actually on fire?"

"Nope, just sage. And a little eucalyptus. And maybe an essential oil I bought from a woman named Moonlight at the farmer's market." Viv's face vanishes briefly as she waves smoke toward the camera with a giant feather. Then she's back and picking up what appears to be a chunk of rose quartz, swinging over her heart like it's a defibrillator for her soul. "I'm aligning my heart chakra," she announces dramatically, "because apparently, some people think I'm emotionally constipated."

Definitely skipping pleasantries.

"That wasn't this week's dare," Marin deadpans as she logs on, and I search her thumbnail for signs of self-care, only seeing a simple cup of tea as her contribution to our weekly girls' pampering evening. "For the record, I'm also pampering myself." She holds up a spoon, apparently reading my mind. "Chocolate mousse. Straight from the fridge. No regrets. I'm also preparing to put on my red light mask."

I lift a foot and carefully swipe a brush of coral polish across my left toes before realizing I really need my reading glasses to get any kind of clue if I'm actually hitting the nail or not. "You two do not know how to do a girl's night."

Viv snorts. "You're painting your toes with a glass of wine in a sippy cup next to you. Don't throw stones, Birdie."

"It has a lid." I hold up the spill-proof wine cup as if it were evidence in court before slipping on my glasses and returning my attention to my toes. "I'm being practical."

They all laugh, and for a moment, the screen feels like a real living room. Not three women in different zip codes doing their own unique versions of pampering.

Viv spins her feather. "Marin, you first. How's the letter writing going?"

Marin sighs and pushes her spoon around the mousse cup. "Surprisingly hard. I started writing what I was mad at Theo for, and I ended up filling four pages. Then I felt guilty and made his favorite meal. I think I'm a little emotionally unhinged."

Viv shrugs. "That means you're doing it right."

I look up from the smudge of coral I'm trying to remove from the side of my foot. "It's real, though. You're allowed to be angry at someone who hurt you, even if they're not here anymore to deal with it."

Marin offers a small, grateful smile. "Thanks. I think I needed to hear that."

"I did it." Viv swings her hand over her forehead, and I wonder if she's preparing to faint at the memory alone. "I took myself out to dinner. Sat alone at a tiny table for one. Ordered wine. Made eye contact with no one. And felt very pathetic."

Marin snorts, almost spitting out the huge bite of chocolate mousse she just took a bite of. "You were supposed to sit with your grief. Not throw it a pity party at Olive Garden."

"It was a very chic little bistro, thank you." Viv points her nose in the air. "But fine, yes. I was deeply uncomfortable the entire time. The server asked if I was waiting for someone, and I nearly said, 'Just my dead husband,' to make it awkward for both of us. No reason for me to suffer alone."

I glance up from the clear polish I'm applying to my toes. "Honestly, you'd be giving that poor server a go-to icebreaker for every awkward first date when he's looking for an interesting conversation topic. In a roundabout way, a part of you would be going on dozens of first dates vicariously."

Viv leans in toward the camera. "Birdie. I'm proud of you! That was a very me thing to say. But the alone-date did something weird. Sitting there, by myself, I realized how much I fill every inch of silence. With my phone, with noise, with jokes. Being alone with my brain is not relaxing."

Marin nods. "It never is at first."

Viv points at the camera. "Okay, therapy club leader. Your turn."

I prop my phone up on the coffee table and snuggle my knees up to my chest, trying not to smudge my wet nails. "Mine involves lasagna and mild emotional panic."

Viv leans in. "You cooked for a man?"

"You went on a date?" Marin waves her spoon.

"I reheated," I correct. "For Noah. He helped with the garden and then we sat on the porch. Talked. Ate."

Marin lifts her eyebrows. "Talked?"

"Only talked. About Owen. About college. About life. It was

weird. And not weird. He remembered things I forgot. Things about when we all first met. It was sweet, but also…"

"Loaded?" Marin offers.

"Exactly." I pause, taking a swig out of my sippy cup. "There was a moment where I almost forgot I was supposed to feel guilty. And then I remembered. It's like my brain keeps flashing Owen's face anytime I let myself enjoy something."

Viv softens, rubbing the goo from her chin. "Birdie. You fed a man. That's not betrayal. That's lasagna."

I smile despite myself. "It was burnt around the edges. Just how Owen liked it. But still," I add, "it was the first time in a long time I didn't feel completely alone."

Viv sighs and flops dramatically back into her chair. "Okay, I'm officially the least emotionally evolved of the group. You're out here reheating heart-healing lasagna, and I'm trying not to cry into crème brûlée for one."

Marin lifts an eyebrow. "You ordered crème brûlée?"

Viv sits up and points at the screen, as if she's been waiting to be asked. "Yes. I sat through dinner and even went for the final round—dessert. At a bistro. With a candle. And a server who definitely thought I'd been stood up."

Marin nods. "That is brave."

Viv beams. "Thank you. I mean, I was sweating through my Spanx and couldn't make eye contact with the couple next to me, but still. Progress."

"You're doing great." Marin waves her spoon at the camera. "Even if your chakras are still hostile."

Viv points a jade roller at the screen. "Watch it. What are our grief dares for this week?"

It's now or never. I clear my throat. "Okay, I have a request. It's a little out there. But I want to make a suggestion for my dare this week, otherwise I know I won't do it." I feel heat rush up my neck. "Do you remember my neighbor, Sharon?"

"The one who makes Bundt cakes for people she openly dislikes?" Marin narrows her eyes in solidarity and suspicion.

"The one who flirted with Owen two days before he died and then dropped off a dozen cakes after the funeral out of guilt and possibly confusion? The one we all don't know, but all dislike?"

I need to stop sharing so much in our text thread.

"That's the one," I sigh. "Well, she's running the neighborhood block party again this year, and she invited me. And the way she said it, like she assumed I'd still be too sad and broken to leave my house, it just, ugh. Then the thought of showing up sad and broken and alone, double ugh."

Viv leans closer. "So you're going to go, and you need us to crash it with you in coordinated outfits?"

I let out a small laugh. "Not exactly. I want to wait to cash in my you-two-coming-to-my-rescue card. But I want to go, to prove to her and myself that my life hasn't completely stopped after Owen's passed. But I don't want to go alone. And, before you say it, I *know* last week's challenge was a date, but I thought maybe that could be my grief dare this week. To ask someone to go with me. To see if I even remember how to ask."

Marin's expression softens. "Birdie, setting your own grief dare? I think that's a new level of awesome!"

Viv claps her hands. "I love this for you. Can I pick your outfit? I have a top that would make your eyes and chest pop. It has your name all over it."

I roll my eyes, but I'm already smiling. "No to the shirt. Maybe to some outfit advice."

Marin narrows her eyes. "Wait, *ask someone*? You already have someone in mind, don't you?"

"Of course she does!" Viv gasps. "It's Butterfly Garden Guy. I *knew* it. You've got ongoing tension following the trimming session!"

"Viv," I groan, covering my face. "Maybe."

She winks. "It's a real phenomenon. The man handles weeds and shears. He's a poetic lumberjack. Don't act like we didn't notice your swoon when you talked about it earlier."

"Okay, *maybe* I've considered asking him."

A look from Viv pulls the rest out of me. "Fine. He's the only person that I would ask. Besides Frank. And going with Frank won't send the right kind of message."

Hearing his name, Frank lifts his head. "But I haven't done it yet. And I'm not even sure it's appropriate."

"You have shared history. Why is this a problem?" Viv never sugarcoats anything.

Marin tilts her head, thoughtful. "What Viv *means to say* is, he knew Owen, but he *knows* you. And you're not asking him to be your plus-one for life. It's one night. At a neighborhood potluck."

Viv grins. "Exactly. Not 'till death do us part.' More like, 'til Sharon serves her aggressively moist lemon cake.' Low stakes."

I laugh despite myself, feeling lighter. "Good point."

Viv lifts her roller triumphantly. "Operation Weed is a go. The grief dare train is chugging right ahead."

"It's a potluck. What should I bring? I always used to bring creamy white enchiladas, but they're Owen's favorite, and I haven't been able to bring myself to make them since."

My screen fills with a visual of Marin tipping her container upside down, scraping the last remains out with her spoon, as she clears her throat. "May I suggest a chocolate mousse?"

Chapter Eleven

Me: Noah. Salutations. I hope this message finds you well.

Noah: Birdie. Greetings. Why are we talking like we're in a 1950s job interview?

Me: You told me to text you. About plants. Or lasagna.

Noah: Or grief... What's the topic tonight?

Me: The fennel plants look good.

Noah: I'm glad. They've got good soil over there.

Me: Also, I burned the leftover lasagna when I was reheating it. (But I ate it anyway.)

Noah: Says a lot about your character. Can't waste food. I admire that in a person.

Me: I keep picturing my grandmother shaking her hand at me, telling me about starving children in Africa. It was crispy in a very intentional way.

Noah: Crispy is the new al dente. It's rustic. Any grief updates?

Me: Nope. I'm thriving.

Noah: Didn't I see you rush inside in your bathrobe the other day on my route?

Me: A midday bathrobe is not a mark of sadness. I'm living my best widow life. I'm even thinking of going to this block party next weekend. Sharon invited me. Although in the name of honesty, it was a very sad-sounding invitation. Like she was worried I'd forgotten how to leave my house.

Noah: Are you asking me to go with you?

Me: I'm thinking of thinking about maybe asking you.

Noah: That's very decisive of you.

Me: I didn't want to sound weird. Or make it weird.

Noah: You opened with "salutations."

Me: Touché.

Noah: I'd go. Just say the word.

Me: Okay. Maybe. Maybe you'll see me (not in my bathrobe) on your route tomorrow.

Noah: It's a date... Well, not a date. Simply one mailman talking about pasta and plants with a widowed bathrobe wearer. (Very normal.)

Me: Extremely normal.

GROUP CHAT: The Dead Husband's Society 💀 🩶

Me: Hey! Quick check-in. How are we feeling about our grief dares this week?

Viv: Wow. Straight to business. No "hey queens" or "what's up"? Cold, Birdie.

Marin: She's deflecting. Did you chicken out?

Me: Absolutely not. I'm a woman of courage. I texted him.

Viv: Did you ask him?

Me: I technically sent some words into the void. Not sure what category that falls into.

Viv: Category: cowardly.

Me: I said something about lasagna and flowers and chaos. Which, in some cultures, is the same as asking someone out.

Marin: What cultures have you been studying? Clearly not this one.

Me: Okay, FINE. I panicked. But enough about me. Viv, how's that singles group you were thinking about joining?

Viv: I see you. I see you're deflecting. I will address that later. The singles group is sad. Not anything like our group. Motion to change my grief dare for this week?

Marin: You picked a dud. I'm the only one who looks like I'm nailing this week's dare. Is judging other obviously sad people considered progress?

Me: Maybe the group's not a dud. It's showing you that people can be happy by themselves with their own thoughts.

Marin: I say it counts as progress, but stop judging me.

Viv: Your plan backfired. That group proved the opposite.

Marin: Fine. How about we change your dare to a solo yoga session in nature? No class, no teacher, just you in the grass (no smoking it) and some time to process.

Viv: That one speaks to my soul. And my glutes. I shall commune with the Earth and pretend not to notice the ants crawling on me. Very healing. Very primal.

Me: Nailed it, Marin. How's your grief dare coming?

Marin: I wrote Theo a letter and then immediately shredded it. My feelings varied from great to violent to something like healing? Maybe?

Me: Your challenge was to decide if you were going to tell the kids about what you and Theo were going through.

Marin: I know. I wrote it out in a letter to Theo. Like we were trying to decide together. I don't know if it will do more harm than good now. He's gone.

Me: Want advice or a sounding board?

Marin: Right now, sounding board.

Viv: Whew, okay. That's a relief. Because I've got zero advice for this one, and you know the universe and I are usually on a first-name basis. Always here for you, Marin.

But Birdie, your grace period has officially expired.

Me: 😬 Oh my. Look at the time. I got to go, um, take Frank out.

Viv: TOMORROW. We're not dragging this out. You don't want to let Sharon and her bundt cakes win, Birdie.

Marin: We believe in you. But also, tick tock.

I stand on my porch, gripping the banister, as if it's going to help me find the courage I clearly left inside next to Frank and my Spanx. Noah is a few houses down, walking his route with the same easy rhythm he always has.

Today's the day. I'm going to ask him.

I smooth my hair, adjust the waistline of my floor-length, floral skirt, like I'm preparing to walk down the runway, instead of stepping off my porch.

"Noah—"

But before I can say another word, a sugar-coated dagger slices through the air in the form of Sharon.

"Noah! Noah!"

I watch his jaw tense from here. The grimace flashes across his face so fast he probably thinks I didn't catch it. But I did. I bite the inside of my cheek to keep from laughing.

Sharon approaches with a bounce in her step, her perfectly permed blonde hair bobbing with each overly rehearsed movement. She's dressed in workout clothes that have probably never seen a squat and is carrying what looks like a flyer and a mission.

"I thought you couldn't hear me." Her voice is breathy and amused, and she titters as she runs a manicured hand over his arm, apparently checking it for durability. "I know you aren't an official neighbor, but we're having a neighborhood block party, and I would love for you to attend. You've been doing this route for years, and I made a motion to make you an honorary neighbor."

She shoves the flyer into his hand and what looks like a little "official Maple street neighbor certificate." Her hand lingers longer than I feel is necessary for a flyer handoff. "My Bundt cakes are famous around south Seattle for a reason, you know. And if you can't find a dish to bring, I'll let you share mine."

My mouth falls open a little in quiet horror. Her flirtation is so bold it should come with a legal disclaimer. I'm tempted to ask whether her short, balding, beige-sweater-wearing husband, the one who quotes traffic laws at dinner parties, would be thrilled to hear she's offering to share her Bundt cake with the mailman.

But I bite my tongue. Proper women don't tear down other women. At least that's what the bumper stickers say. What kind of message would that send about sisterhood and the feminist cause?

Sharon turns, finally acknowledging me. "Birdie knows how incredible my Bundt cakes are. She's been trying to duplicate one for years."

I haven't. I baked a chocolate cake for the first block party years ago, not knowing that cakes were Sharon's domain. And it came out a little over-baked. Sharon has never let me forget it.

She winks like we're in on a little secret, but in suburban housewife code, that's a full-on culinary smackdown. "Tell him, Birdie."

I paste on my practiced grin, the one I use to look good, keep the peace, stay prim and proper, and pay the price for my honesty —and apparently my cake. "It is delicious."

"See?" Sharon beams. "What do you say?"

Noah glances at me for half a second. Then, casually, too casually, he grins. That annoying grin that makes my perimenopause hot flashes act up. "Actually, Birdie already asked me to go with her."

My eyebrows shoot up. I did not. I very much did not.

He nudges my elbow, as though this is a team sport we agreed to play, but there was no secret meeting about block parties and subtext and Bundt cake defense strategies.

Sharon's smile falters enough to be satisfying, then she recovers. "Oh! Well, that's, um, how lovely," she chirps, though her voice goes up half an octave. "I guess I'll see you both there. Jim and I will be thrilled to see you out of the house, Birdie."

She walks away, hips swaying with enough force to get her an audition for a high-heel commercial. I wait until she's a safe distance down the street before I turn to Noah.

"Did you say I invited you to a block party?"

"You're welcome." He doesn't even bother to hide the grin.

"I was about to do it myself! You robbed me of a chance to be brave. To push the feminist movement forward."

He quirks an eyebrow. "With a potluck?"

"Yes!" I huff. "With a potluck. There was going to be courage and intentionality and possibly a sweaty armpit situation. But no, you had to swoop in like some Bundt-cake-blocking hero."

He shrugs, holding out a few letters to me. "You hesitated."

I scowl, even as my cheeks betray me with a blush. "Next time, I'm inviting someone else. Maybe the UPS guy. He brings exciting boxes, and you just bring bills." I snatch my mail. "Bills and obnoxious flyers and catalogues that suck my time and my money!"

Noah stands there, that annoying, lazy smile firmly in place. "Does the UPS guy ask about plants, lasagna, and grief?"

"Nope. But he can deliver roses and lasagna, and that medicates the grief. I'm all covered." I storm up the porch steps, before turning on my heel. "You don't even live here and Sharon accepted you into the fold—with lamination!"

He leans against the side of his mail truck. "In my defense, I earned this with years of loyal Bundt cake acceptance. I've delivered to Maple Street since 2017. At some point, they started acting like I belonged. That counts for something."

I tilt my head. "What made you choose the mail route? I know Owen helped you get it, but do you actually like it?"

He shrugs, folding the flyer again, slower this time. "I've grown to like it. After the divorce, I needed the stability. As you know, my literature degree was everything I wanted, but—" he gives a small, sad smile—"turns out reading *The Brothers Karamazov* doesn't pay divorce lawyers."

I give a sad smile back. "No regrets?"

He shakes his head. "None. I'd choose it again. It gave me something worth carrying. Even if now I mostly carry catalogues and real estate mailers."

There's something unexpectedly tender about that. A man who loves words but delivers credit card offers instead. I swallow against the ache that rises in my chest.

He lifts the laminated certificate and salutes me with it. "Honorary neighbor, delivering the mail. It's what dreams are made of."

"We need to work on your dreams."

He grins, unapologetic. "What time should I pick you up?"

"Seven." I'm not sure why I still sound so hostile. Probably because I'm still upset he robbed me of the chance to properly ask him.

"I look forward to it."

"Me too!" And then I slam the door.

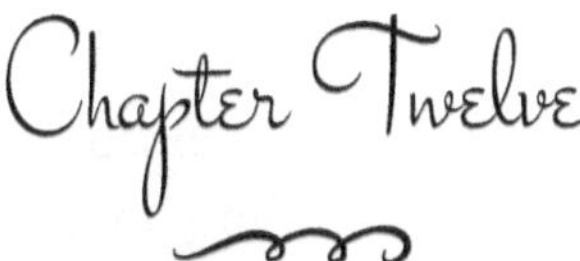

I adjust the webcam, then immediately regret it. What is it about this angle that makes my chin look monstrous? I lean back, tilting the screen down.

Better.

"Will you stop moving the camera!" Viv's voice fills my bedroom.

Harper is sprawled beside me on the bed, holding two hangers like a judge on Project Runway. On-screen, Viv and Marin wait, respective beverages in hand, judging the lighting and my posture. Apparently I've stepped into a high-stakes fashion consult without knowing it.

"Okay." Viv waves her fingers, twirling her kombucha in her wine glass. "Spin around. Full twirl, Birdie."

"I'm not twirling." I shuffle, pulling at the taut material of Harper's "flowy" blouse, which is anything but flowing on me. My chest is bulging out. "This isn't prom. It's a block party with questionable lukewarm potato salad and HOA drama."

"Exactly why you need to look incredible." Marin takes a sip of her herbal tea. "Distract them with a blouse so bold they forget to ask invasive grief questions."

"Can't I wear this?" I move toward my signature black conservative knit sweater. It's the one I've worn for most outings since Owen passed.

"Mom." Harper lets out an exasperated exhale. "I'd never seen you wear that a day in your life before Dad died. It can't be all you wear now. Time to go back to some color. Give your wardrobe life again."

She holds up my silky blue, cropped-sleeve top. "This one's good. Less 'recent widow,' more 'cool mom who might flirt with the mailman.'"

"Yes." Viv nods in approval. "That one's so much better than that sad little black thing. We should burn that top."

I shoot my daughter and Viv a glare but take the blue top anyway. Ducking out of frame, I shimmy into the shirt and a pair of just-tight-enough jeans. They were Owen's favorite, and he said they gave me "an ass that just won't quit."

"I feel ridiculous." I waltz through my closet door. "This is supposed to be a casual event. Not something that requires three women and wine in order to properly prepare."

Viv leans toward her screen. "It's not about the clothes. It's about showing up. That's the dare. But I am a firm believer that clothes help you show up with more confidence."

"We're proud of you!" Marin cheers.

Harper tosses me a pair of silver earrings. "Besides, if you're reentering society, you might as well look good doing it."

I laugh despite myself and fasten the earrings, the silver catching the glow of the lamp. I glance back at the screen, where Viv is doing a slow clap and Marin has lifted her pottery mug in an apparent toast to my beauty.

"Alright, ladies." I smooth the invisible wrinkles out of the shirt. "What do you think?"

Viv grins. "Grief's got nothing on you, girl!"

Marin leans in, squinting for one final assessment. "You're ready for *Thriving and Thirty* magazine."

I snort. "Is that a thing?"

Harper, now curled sideways with a throw pillow under her

arm, doesn't miss a beat. "And will they mind that you're well past your thirties?"

I toss a pillow at her, which she deflects without blinking, already scrolling through her phone. On screen, Viv and Marin dissolve into laughter.

"You're lucky you're cute," I mutter to Harper.

She grins. "What can I say? You gave me good genetics."

———————

The sun dips behind the trees when I step outside. A warm breeze tugs playfully at my messy bun as Noah's truck rumbles into my driveway. He climbs out slowly, his blue jeans hugging his ass in a way that causes me to briefly forget all my manners and openly stare. I might drool. Just a little. Then he leans one elbow on the passenger door.

"You, uh..." He scratches the back of his neck. "You clean up alright, B."

His voice is quieter than usual, and I wonder if he feels it too: that thinking it, much less saying it, borders on betrayal.

"Is that flattery?" If the drool didn't give me away, is it inappropriate to mention how well he cleans up? His white button-up shirt accentuates his tan skin, and he's put some kind of gel in his short hair, causing the dark strands to stand up in delicious disarray. "Or are you buttering me up so I'll carry your mystery dish?"

He lifts a foil-covered casserole with a flourish, and I hate that I notice how his forearm flexes as he does it. "Nope. I take full credit for this beauty."

I fall into step beside Noah, my own foil-covered dish warm in my hands as we head up the street. The evening is golden, twilight setting in while porch lights begin to flicker on in a quiet applause for summer.

"You cooked?" I go to nudge him with my elbow but pull back at the last minute, worried about unwanted hormonal surges that apparently accompany any kind of physical touch.

He smirks. "I'm a single bachelor who likes to eat. Of course I cooked."

I raise a brow. "And what did you bring into existence?"

"Jalapeño mac and cheese." He raises the dish in mock reverence. "With bacon. Possibly too much bacon."

"There's no such thing. Bacon is both flavor and philosophy."

He glances down at the dish I'm carrying. "And what about you? What's under that expertly folded foil?"

"Nachos." I fight the urge to let my bangs fall over my face. "I could've gone fancier. Honestly, I usually do. I've been known to hand-stencil labels for artisanal dips and cut fruit bouquets. Owen used to joke that I had a pathological need to win the potluck."

Noah snorts. "That tracks."

I laugh, but it's tight in my throat. "After he died, I couldn't bring myself to care, so I stopped going. Managing the sadness took too much energy. So tonight, I told myself that I was going to throw something together and be done with it."

He tilts his head, curious. "And what's on these so-called 'thrown together' nachos?"

I sigh before gritting out the words, knowing how not casual they sound. "Black beans, ground steak, roasted corn, green onions. Three kinds of cheese. A homemade guac on the side. I dusted the chips with lime zest and sea salt before baking."

Noah stops walking and turns to look at me fully. "Birdie, that's not phoning it in. That's you still giving it your best."

I shrug. "That's still dialed back Birdie. I didn't want to feel like I was trying too hard to impress everyone, because that's not the point. I want to show up and not perform for once." Why was I telling him this? He had only asked a simple question about nachos.

"It's okay to show up with your best." His voice is gentle, as warm as the sunlight caressing my back. "But it should be because you want to. Because you love feeding people. Not because you think you have to earn their affection with perfectly melted cheese."

I blink, caught off guard by how accurate he is.

He nudges my arm, less teasing now, more grounded. "You don't have to hustle for anyone's love, Birdie. Prove that you were the perfect wife and now the have-it-all-together widow. You get to show up. However you are."

I look down at the dish in my hands. They're just nachos, but they also aren't. They're the halfway point between who I was and who I'm trying to be.

I meet his eyes, grateful. "You're still kind of annoyingly insightful, you know that?"

He grins. "I've been told."

The block party is already in full swing. Lights zigzag across the cul-de-sac, folding tables groaning under the weight of communal carbs, and children darting between lawn chairs like over-caffeinated squirrels. I clutch my nachos, trying not to feel like I'm walking through a minefield instead of a simple neighborhood event.

"Birdie!"

The voice cuts through the murmur of the block party. I turn to see Mildred marching toward me, her sensible flats slapping against the pavement with a purpose that says she's got questions and zero concern for boundaries.

Still spry at seventy-something, she's dressed in her signature twinset and pearls, looking like a church lady with a gaze that could slice deli meat.

"Oh, sweet girl." She reaches out to pat my arm with a hand weighed down by a ring the size of a gumball. "I wasn't expecting to see you here."

Before I can answer, Janet, who lives across the street and always smells vaguely of eucalyptus and Cheerios, appears with her toddler on one hip. She shifts the child and gives me a soft, tilted-head smile that somehow manages to feel both sympathetic and performative. Her short, brown bob accentuates the movement. "We've all been wondering, how are you doing? Truly? It's such a tragic thing. We loved Owen. He always cut my grass when John was out of town for work."

I force a small smile, the one I've been practicing in the mirror. Not too bright, not too bleak, not too much teeth. Somewhere between "I'm fine" and "please stop talking."

"Taking it day by day," I offer, my voice as even as I can manage.

Mildred nods like she's tasted something bittersweet and intends to chew on it all night. "Of course. Of course. And have you given any thought to selling the house?" She leans in slightly. "It must feel so big now. All alone like that."

The words hang in the air. I open my mouth, either to laugh or scream, I haven't quite decided, but before I can do either, I catch a flash of copper hair and dread coils in my stomach.

Missy.

She's weaving her way through folding chairs and collapsible coolers, a heat-seeking missile... And I'm the target. Her auburn braid swings behind her, a smug little metronome, keeping time with her unsolicited opinions.

"Birdie!" Her voice drips faux-surprise. "Is this the first time at a neighborhood event since, um, Owen's unfortunate passing? I totally understand why you've needed time, but it's so good to see you around the block. Running into you at the occasional PTA meeting isn't cutting it." She places a hand on her heart, eyes misting in a way that screams rehearsed. "And this is the perfect opportunity to talk about prom this year. I know Harper graduated, but you're still such a vibrant presence."

I barely get a chance to mumble something noncommittal before Karen swoops in from the snack table: a vulture wearing Tory Burch.

"Birdie!" She wraps me in a warm embrace, and I feel the

tension I'm holding in my spine relax a little. "Don't pay them any mind. I'm so happy you're here!" Her eyes flick toward Noah, who's still planted loyally at my side, and I debate the ethics of using him as a human shield. "And how lovely that you brought a friend. I want to hear all about how you're doing and if you need anyth—Oh, will you excuse me a moment? It looks like Ted needs me." I follow Karen's line of sight across the yard where her husband is standing holding their two newborn twins while their toddler throws marshmallows at Missy's cat.

Before I can beg her to stay and then feel guilty for needing her, she's off across the yard yelling, "Come find me! I have a huge piece of chocolate cake with your name on it!"

Karen's warmth bolsters my confidence, and I stride toward the tables, setting down my nachos just as Sharon sets down her infamous Bundt cake. She's wearing a floral apron and pumps that are so high they have no business being worn to a block party.

"Noah!"

Sharon's voice rises over the hum of the party, all sugary notes and sharp edges. She practically glides toward him, wielding a paper plate with a piece of Bundt cake.

I don't miss the fact she doesn't address me.

"I have to get your opinion," she trills, thrusting the floral plate into his hands. "Tried a brand-new recipe. It's lemon poppy seed, with a hint of almond and the faintest whisper of lavender. All organic, of course. I milled the flour myself."

I blink. Of course she did.

Noah, ever the gentleman, raised on politeness and probably traumatized by church potlucks, takes a forkful like it's his civic duty. He chews, then gives a polite nod, the kind you reserve for when someone's newborn baby isn't cute but you've committed to the lie.

"Wow." He pauses to swallow. "That's amazing."

Sharon beams, clearly basking in his approval. Then, with practiced sweetness, she swivels toward me. Her smile stays in place, but her eyes gleam with the kind of challenge you only see in a small-town bake-off or a Real Housewives reunion.

"Birdie," her voice is all faux warmth and condescension frosted in charm, "you have to try it too. You know, just to practice." Her voice lilts. "That poor chocolate cake is forever in my memory. Oh, what was it…" She taps a manicured finger to her chin. "A little dry? But bless your heart for trying."

I stand frozen for a beat. My eyes drop to the platter of nachos still cradled in my arms, my half-hearted attempt at rebellion. My attempt at saying I'm showing up as I am. But the truth is, I'm not quite there yet. Not really. I still care what these women think. Maybe not as much as before, but enough that her words still land.

Noah leans in, his voice low, only for me. "You don't have to prove anything to anyone."

I glance back at Sharon, who's holding out a plastic fork. Her smile is tight and toothy, eyes glittering with expectation. Around us, the neighborhood women hover, clearly invested in the outcome of this bundt-showdown.

And then, like muscle memory, I reach out and take the fork. Because that's what I've always done: smile, be agreeable, keep the peace. Don't make waves, Birdie. Keep your voice sweet and your posture poised.

I scoop a bite from Noah's plate and chew slowly. For a second, I try to do it the old way. Try to find something neutral to say, something safe. But the weight of it, the fake smiles, the pretending, the ever-present urge to earn a gold star for existing, it all feels so heavy.

Too heavy.

It feels like I should've bought cheap tortilla chips and decorated them in a pre-shredded cheese blend.

I square my shoulders.

"Actually—" My tone is calm but firm. "This cake tastes a little like despair."

The air around us tightens.

"And dish soap," I add.

A stunned silence follows, thick and delicious. Sharon blinks once. Twice.

Noah makes a sound that might be a cough or a laugh being strangled to death.

"Well," Sharon sniffs, her voice clipped, "it's been a hit with everyone else."

Color drains from my face as the words catch up with me. "I—sorry. That slipped out."

Noah leans in again, his breath warm against my ear. "Bold review. Don't apologize now."

Across the lawn, the other women stand in a half-circle of shock, their mouths forming synchronized Os.

Noah gives them a casual nod. "Ladies."

Then he gently guides me away with a hand at the small of my back.

"What came out of my mouth?" I whisper, stunned at myself.

He smiles. "Apparently? Honesty. And it looks good on you."

The evening was off to a bit of a rough, or possibly glorious, start. After my confrontation with Sharon, the rest of the neighbors stand a few feet back. I figure I should make a polite exit after twenty minutes with a half-hearted excuse about "needing to check on the cat."

Wait. I don't have a cat.

Needing to check on Frank. Yes, that's much better. Frank sounds like a dog with gout. Very believable. And there's no reason to fake Frank because Frank is real. Maybe I'll take him for a walk around the cul-de-sac tomorrow to prove his existence.

But then Noah appears at my side, with a confident smirk and blue-eyed mischief.

"So." He holds out a paper plate, a warrior with a paper

shield. "I dare you to try every single dish on this table. No exceptions."

He nods toward the chaotic spread of questionable casseroles and ambiguous Jell-O molds, the kind of offerings that could only come from a family reunion or the seventh circle of culinary hell.

I narrow my eyes, crossing my arms over my chest. "Are you sure about that?"

"Positive." He steps closer, so close I catch the warm scent of cedar and laundry detergent, something too domestic for how feral he looks with that cocky grin.

"Well, I dare you right back." I grab a second plate and slap it against his chest, throwing down the paper plate gauntlet.

He puffs out his chest, in some kind of middle-aged dare showdown, and I can't help but notice how his shirt strains across his shoulders with the motion. Rude.

"I'm not worried about me." His voice is low, teasing. "I'm worried about what's lurking inside that crockpot over there."

I follow his gaze to a bubbling mass of beige something, possibly potatoes.

"Don't look directly at it," I whisper. "It knows."

We stand shoulder to shoulder, surveying the buffet table like we are entering battle, which, in a way, we are. There are no name tags on the dishes. No allergy warnings. No ingredients list. Just total chaos. The PTA would have a fit, and as an honorary member of the PTA, I should have volunteered to make hand-written signs in my perfect calligraphy.

I grab a scoop of something mushy and violently green, plopping it into a red Solo cup for dramatic effect. Turning towards Noah, I lift it in both hands.

"I present to you," I intone with the kind of solemnity reserved for ceremonial toasts or nuclear codes, "the infamous Mystery Dip. I overheard Janet say it's 'family famous,' which either means delicious or potentially hazardous."

Noah leans in, squinting at the sludge. "This feels like a prank from someone's great-aunt who lived through the Depression."

I dip a chip in, hesitate, and take the tiniest bite.

It hits me with a sucker punch of sweet, tangy, and, was that tuna? No. Pineapple. Wait. Both? "Oh no. Oh no. That is, well, that's aggressive."

Noah scoops a bite for himself and recoils. "How is it simultaneously gelatinous and crunchy?"

"Is this how I die?" I cough. "Taken out by pineapple-fish paste at a neighborhood potluck? I always knew I'd go out dramatically, but I hoped for something with better seasoning."

He leans in, eyes crinkling. "At least you'll die fancy. Your earrings are working overtime."

I roll my eyes and move over toward an empty spot on the curb, plopping down into the grass. "You know, I used to spend two hours prepping for events like this?"

"No."

"Yes. Hair curled. Lip gloss layered. Way too much time on my slack and blouse pairing. And heels. Always heels."

"How're the flats feeling?"

Flexing my toes, I give a little sigh. "My toes are eternally grateful, and also wondering why I didn't do this sooner."

And then, because this feels much too intimate, I raise my fork toward his in a conversational pivot. "To courage. And gastrointestinal bravery."

He clinks it against mine. "To surviving until dessert."

Right as we are about to take our final bites, a voice calls across the street. "Hey! Birdie! We need two more for cornhole!" and before I can say I'd rather take my chances with the Cool Whip chaser, Noah raises both his hands and rushes forward.

He looks over his shoulder at me, still planted firmly against the cool cement curb. "Come on! Live dangerously. Again."

"Do I look like someone who plays cornhole?" I hiss.

He waggles his eyebrows. "Not touching that one."

"Ugh, you know what I mean."

But then I find myself holding a beanbag, standing barefoot on lumpy grass, wondering when I became the kind of woman who played yard games in flats and fitted jeans. My old self, the one desperate for neighborhood approval, always-smiling, well-manicured version, would be horrified. She would've stood politely to the side, cheering him on, pretending to scroll on her phone and looking for reasons to go "check the oven."

Now? I launch my beanbag with a dramatic arm swing and whoop when it lands squarely on the board. "Take that, Jim!"

Jim, across the lawn in a monogrammed windbreaker, looks personally offended.

Noah whoops behind me. "You're a menace!"

"Am I trash-talking? Is this who I am now?" I turn to him, eyes wide with faux horror.

"I'm so proud of you." He raises his cup in mock salute. "Birdie 2.0: now with sports-based aggression."

We lose the game, barely, and I stick my tongue out at Jim as we pass each other before giving him a gentle side hug and thanking him for the invitation to play.

A little while later, I spot a kid wobbling through the yard, maybe five years old, his face blotchy with tears and his paper plate sliding dangerously sideways.

"Hold this." I hand Noah my lemonade and move on instinct.

I crouch beside the kid, gently righting the mound of food that includes both spaghetti and marshmallows. "Hey, little man. Let's fix this up, huh?"

He nods solemnly, sniffling.

"Alright. Operation Plate Rescue. You steer. I stabilize."

Together, we make our way across the lawn toward a flustered woman waving from a picnic table while trying to wrangle three other kids under five. I pat him on the head and stand up, brushing grass off my knees.

Noah hands me back my cup. "You're good at that."

"What, kid herding?"

"No. That thing where you step in. Without making it weird or performative. Where you want to help people."

I shrug, suddenly shy. "Old habits. I used to think if I were helpful enough, no one would notice I didn't have it all together."

He tilts his head. "And now?"

"Now I'm just helpful and falling apart openly, I guess."

We both laugh, and for a second, it feels easy and simple. The ache in my chest releases, and I forget that Owen is gone and that I'll be going home to an empty bed.

And then the music changes.

Just a few gentle chords, strumming slow and familiar, but it makes me stop cold.

Owen's song. The one he used to play while flipping pancakes in boxers and singing off-key like a drunk lumberjack.

My stomach twists. My hand grips the Solo cup tight, hoping its flimsy plastic will somehow save me from drowning in my feelings. Around me, people laugh and chat and clink plastic forks, but I can't hear anything over those damn chords.

I don't move.

Don't cry.

Just stand there, paralyzed by the ghost of a life that used to be mine.

The guilt snakes around my heart, chastising me for forgetting to be sad the last few hours—for forgetting Owen.

Then, without a word, Noah bumps my shoulder with his.

Just a nudge. No big gesture. No intrusive questions or pity parade. Just demonstrating his presence.

And that, somehow, unravels me more than if he'd said a word.

I glance at him, blinking fast. That song still hangs in the air, a heavy smoke that I can't wave away.

He looks ahead, arms crossed, voice even. "I never knew why Owen loved this song. It's terrible."

I blink again, John Legend's voice swirling around my memories. "What?"

"Cheesy as hell." His voice is casual, like we're discussing who won last night's baseball game and not his dead best friend and my dead husband's favorite song. "Sounds like it was written by a guy who's only ever loved his cat and a deep-dish pizza."

Despite myself, I huff out something between a laugh and a gasp. "Wow. Harsh."

Noah shrugs. "Sorry, Birdie. I respect the dead, but I don't have to respect their playlists."

A beat passes. "Okay, music snob. What's your favorite song?"

He doesn't even hesitate.

"'Return of the Mack.'"

I whip my head toward him. "Are you joking?"

"Nope." He says it with the same calm conviction someone might use to announce they're running for Senate.

"'Return of the Mack'? That's your song?"

He nods solemnly. "It's got everything. Resilience. Groove. A betrayal arc. Love. And that beat drop? Come on. That's how you know love's real, when it survives betrayal and a key change."

I'm laughing now, a real one, loud and sudden and unlady-like. "You're unbelievable."

"But think about it," he continues, totally straight-faced. "You get your heart broken. You go down. You get back up. And then boom—'Return of the Mack.' You're back, baby. That's romance. That's life. That's healing."

I shake my head, still smiling. "You might be insane."

He finally turns, his eyes darting over my face. "Maybe. But it makes you smile. So maybe I'm really winning?"

"Thank you."

"For what?"

"For not making it worse."

His blue eyes reflect the faded sunlight. "You already made steak topped nachos, Birdie. You've got nothing left to prove."

And for once, I almost believe it. "So tell me about your heart-breaks? What inspired this 'Return of the Mack'?"

Noah's smile drops. "There weren't a lot of notable heart-breaks. Just one. And the rest of the women I dated didn't hold a candle to that heartbreak. I ended it before it even had a chance to begin."

I cock my head to the side. "Only one heartbreak?"

He shrugs, eyes studying the sky, avoiding mine. "It's true what they say, you never really get over your first love."

———

We walk slowly, and I wonder if he's also not in a hurry for the night to end. A soft breeze brushes past, lifting the edge of the foil over the container I'm balancing in both hands, half-eaten plate of nachos and all. Noah carries a plastic tub of what might have been someone's attempt at chili, or possibly dessert. Hard to tell.

"Remind me again why you didn't grab your own dish?"

"I'm telling you, Mildred stole my container. It was the bacon. I put too much bacon in it, and people do crazy things for bacon. She took my mac and cheese in the good container and left me with this. She and I will be having words later."

Above us, the stars have come out in full force, scattered like glitter across navy velvet. Crickets sing from every bush and tree, a gentle lilt. The perfect background music for a movie scene I didn't realize I was walking through.

"I didn't expect tonight to feel..." I trail off, trying to wrap words around the squirmy thing in my chest. "Good. But also weird. I've never had that much fun at a neighborhood block party before. Should I feel guilty about that?"

Noah glances over at me. "Do you think you should?"

I snort. "Maybe. But I don't want to."

"It's okay to enjoy life again."

I smile at the sidewalk. "Thank you. For tonight. Even if I did insult a neighborhood matriarch and question the integrity of her Bundt cake."

Noah slows his steps until we stop at the edge of my driveway. He shifts his container under one arm. "Anytime."

A breeze kicks up again, carrying the scent of someone's barbecue and the distant hum of laughter still drifting from a few houses down.

"You were perfect," he adds, so casually that I almost miss it.

I turn toward him. "Don't lie to me, Noah. I was a hot mess and probably committed the equivalent of social HOA arson."

"Maybe. But like... the charming kind. The kind that warms up the whole place."

My mouth opens, a retort halfway out of my lips, but I stop. He's looking at me like he sees right through all the layers I usually keep zipped up tight. I'm not sure if it makes me want to run or stay still forever.

We reach the porch, and I fumble with the key before realizing it's in the wrong pocket. Of course it is. Because being with Noah always causes me to happily toss aside all structure, order, and routine. Apparently the decades have passed but the habits have not.

He waits patiently, not saying anything, shifting from foot to foot and looking up at the sky like he's cataloging stars.

I finally get the key in the lock but don't turn it. Not yet. I lean in closer, my breath catching in my throat. When was the last time I had a first kiss? Am I ready for this?

Noah mirrors my movement, his breath shallow, his lips just inches from mine. His head tilts, like he's ready—but his hands stay at his sides, clenched now. He looks at me, really looks, and something shifts in his expression.

Regret?

Not for wanting this.

For wanting it with me.

His eyes flick away for the briefest second—toward the ground, toward the past, I don't know—and then we both pull back, the brief connection a live wire.

"See you Monday, Mailman?" My voice is lighter than I feel.

"You got it." He turns to go, stepping off the porch with the easy stride of someone who's not trying too hard.

I watch him walk down the driveway before he throws open his truck door and backs out. He doesn't look back.

But I kind of wish he would.

Chapter Thirteen

Zoom meetings with Viv and Marin always start like a group project from hell. Someone's muted. Someone's frozen. Someone (usually Viv) is too close to the camera, like she's trying to have an intimate chat with my pores.

"Can you hear me?"

"Yes."

"Birdie, unmute!" Viv barks. "You're muted again!"

"I'm not... wait, okay. There."

Marin's face fills the screen, half-shadowed by the glow of her fridge light and a comically large bowl of what appears to be fruity cereal. "I'd like to open this meeting by congratulating all of us! Our grief dares this week were smashing successes."

"I didn't realize we were giving ourselves awards now." I settle back on the couch with a glass of wine.

"Surviving the week is the award," Viv mutters. "Barely."

"Oh, come on." Marin points her spoon at the camera. "Viv, you did a full yoga flow alone in the park. No class. No distraction. Only you and the geese."

"Don't remind me about the geese." I can see Viv visibly shuddering. "Do you know what it's like to be in a deep squat while a flock of waterfowl stares at you like you owe them money?"

Marin snorts. "You did it anyway. That was your dare. Connect with your body in nature. And you didn't even post about it."

"I did take a photo of my mat. And the geese. As evidence, if something were to happen to me. But I didn't share it. That's restraint."

"Progress." I raise my glass.

Viv nods toward Marin. "And you finally made a decision. Are you going to talk to the kids?"

Marin's expression shifts. Not sad exactly. More like tired in that bone-deep way only other widows can spot. "Yeah. I think I'm ready. I kept telling myself I was protecting them. But really, I was protecting myself."

Viv and I go quiet.

"Gonna start with Miles." Marin stares into her cereal bowl, as though it holds the confirmation she needs. "He's the oldest. And the most likely to not immediately condemn me about it all."

"You're brave."

"I'm terrified." Marin's voice is matter-of-fact. "But I keep hearing you two in my head. That whole thing about not letting grief shrink your life."

I swirl the wine in my glass, happy to let the moment breathe.

Then Viv leans forward so close her eyebrows fill the screen. "So... Birdie. You went to the block party."

I nod.

"Yep."

"And...?"

I sit back, take a deep inhale, and forge ahead. "And it might've changed my life a bit."

Marin nearly chokes on her huge bite of cereal. "Do tell!"

I let out the breath. "I don't know where to start."

Viv crosses her arms and squints at me through the screen.

"Okay, so this must've been one hell of a block party to shatter your inner Pinterest board."

"I find that the beginning is always a good place." Marin's voice is warm and the push I need to open my mouth.

I groan. "It was supposed to be twenty minutes, max. Just enough time to show the neighborhood I was still functioning, clean pants, polite smile, head held high. Perfectly perfect."

Marin raises an eyebrow. "And?"

"And... the neighbors started talking. You know, well-meaning but relentless. 'How are you holding up? You look amazing. Is that your new boyfriend?'" I make air quotes and gag slightly. "Then Sharon brought over her infamous Bundt cake, which Noah tried, and something in me snapped."

Viv leans in. "Define snapped."

"I insulted the cake. Loudly. Then I accepted a challenge from Noah to a potluck tasting showdown. Then I talked a lot of smack at cornhole but didn't have the game to back it up, but I didn't care. And then..." I pause, wince. "I maybe wanted to kiss him at the end of the night."

Both eyebrows raise on both screens.

"It was probably the stars. Or the lack of human touch for God knows how long."

Viv and Marin continue to stare, eyebrows raised, bemused expressions on their faces.

"And now I feel like an insane person," I add, voice pitching slightly higher. "Maybe it's grief. Maybe it's hormones. Maybe I've finally cracked like one of Sharon's dry-ass Bundts. Regardless, if either of you has a shred of compassion, please say something so I'll stop talking."

They both pause. Marin takes another big bite of cereal, and Viv tilts her head to the side, like Frank does when he knows there's more treats behind my back and I'm refusing to share them yet. Well, that's not going to work on me... Until it does.

"And you know what?" The words are falling out of my mouth, one after the other. "It was the first time in a long time that I laughed until my ribs hurt. I wasn't hosting. I wasn't performing. I wasn't curating anything. I was in the moment. And it was glorious."

The hush echoes over our tiny grid of digital squares.

"It wasn't like some thunderclap moment," I continue. "Not a movie montage or some big rom-com voiceover. Just this quiet click. I realized I've spent my whole life trying to control the way things look. I wanted it to look perfect on the outside, so no one could see I was far from it on the inside."

Viv's eyes soften, and she tucks a loose strand of hair behind her ear. "So what changed?"

"The realization that I've lived my whole life trying to look the way I thought I should, show up the way everyone wanted me to... except the people who loved me most. I've thrown parties for Owen before. Big numbers deserve big parties. I did his thirtieth at a quaint little rooftop place with string lights, signature cocktails, and a jazz trio. His fortieth was a backyard tent situation with caterers and napkins that I spent two weeks learning how to fold like peonies."

Viv whistles. "Of course you did."

"They were beautiful." I hear the defensiveness in my voice before I pause. "And unnecessary. And not what he wanted."

I glance at the hallway, toward the room where Owen's things still sit, as if they're waiting for him to come back from a weekend trip. "I made those parties about aesthetics. About me. I wanted them to be perfect. Parties that people would talk about. And Owen went along with it. Smiled for the photos. Ate the fig crostini even though he hated figs."

"You didn't know he hated figs?" Marin's eyes widen.

"Oh, I knew." I give a wry chuckle. "I figured he'd love an elevated version. Like I thought he'd love the elevated version of me. And he did. But looking back? I don't remember either of us actually enjoying the party. My biggest memories around that party were worrying about the playlist volume and whether the cake was too dry and losing the last five pounds."

Viv whistles. "You went full Martha."

"Oh, Martha wished," I mutter.

"Did he like it?"

"He smiled. He was grateful. But he looked... tired. Overwhelmed. Afterward, he told me he'd wanted a backyard barbecue. Burgers, karaoke, and an inflatable palm tree cooler. Piña coladas in plastic coconuts." The memory twists around my heart.

"I flipped out at the idea and told him I wouldn't be caught dead throwing a party that tacky. He laughed and said, 'Babe, if there's no inflatable palm tree cooler, is it even a party?' And now I'd give anything to go back and give him that stupid palm tree cooler, give him the party he would've thrown if I hadn't hijacked it with floral arrangements and tapas."

They're quiet. Not because they don't know what to say, but because they do. Because this is the kind of thing we all understand now. The things we didn't do. The times we didn't listen.

"So," I shift my laptop slightly, willing myself not to cry, "for his would-have-been fiftieth, I want to do it differently. I want tacky. Loud. I want plastic cheese melted on burgers, bad karaoke, and someone falling into an inflatable pool after one too many piña coladas, served in coconut cups with little umbrellas. I owe him the party he would've loved."

Viv leans back in her chair, arms crossed, one eyebrow already halfway to the ceiling. "You want it to feel like him."

"Exactly."

"And also like you," Marin adds, tilting her head. "The you now. The you that doesn't give a damn what the PTA thinks."

I grin. "Yes. That me."

Viv narrows her eyes. "So what are you saying? You want help planning a tiki-themed griefapalooza?"

"Think more grief luau." Am I doing this? "Less black dresses, more plastic coconuts and frozen drink blenders that will absolutely explode mid-party. Owen's old colleagues, our college friends, a few of the neighbors. All of Owen's favorite people."

Marin gasps, dramatically clutching her cereal bowl like it's a microphone. "Can I emcee the karaoke portion? I do a killer Alanis Morissette."

"Only if I get to sing 'Islands in the Stream' with a cardboard cutout of Owen," Viv adds, already pulling out a notepad.

"You're joking." I don't know whether to laugh, be shocked, or be horrified.

Viv's expression turns uncharacteristically soft. "I'm not, actually. I think it's perfect. The whole point of grief, at least what we've decided in our very official weekly Zoom grief dare therapy club, is to stop letting it shrink us. You're not shrinking. You're throwing a backyard blowout in honor of someone you love. That's sacred."

"And deeply therapeutic," Marin adds.

"I want to remember him laughing." I'm not crying anymore. No, I'm feeling ready. "I want my kids to see joy. I want to stop living as though being composed is the same thing as being okay."

Viv straightens in her chair, eyes bright. "We're coming out."

I blink. "What?"

"We'll come help. With the party. With everything. I've got unused vacation days, zero plans, and a growing need to escape my neighbor who's started naked sunbathing on his back porch."

"I'm in too." Marin brushes cereal dust off her sweatshirt. "What's the point of working from home if you don't change up your office once in a while? And I've got a glitter glue gun and absolutely no shame when it comes to Dollar Tree décor."

My mouth hangs open, and I snap it shut. "I can't believe you're serious."

"Of course we are. We'll help you plan." Marin's already tapping away on her keyboard, presumably activating accountant mode and crunching the numbers. "Keep you from spiral-purchasing a twelve-foot inflatable parrot."

"Speak for yourself." Viv is pulling out what appears to be an old Hawaiian print shirt from a dresser drawer. "I fully support the parrot."

Tears fill my eyes as I listen to the two of them go back and forth about dates and details and plane tickets.

They both pause. "Birdie." Viv's voice is soft. "If we can't show up for a tiki-themed milestone grief bash/dead husband's birthday party, what are we even doing?"

"She's right." It looks like Marin is already rummaging in her closet for a suitcase. "This is what the grief pact was for."

"What pact?"

"The unspoken one we're now speaking aloud," Marin replies. "Support, no judgment, and showing up. Preferably with snacks."

"And backup vocals," Viv adds. "And me doing yoga on your front lawn at sunrise every morning. Clothes optional."

"Oh God," I groan. "My neighbors already think I'm unstable after that block party."

"Perfect." Marin grins. "Let's give them something to talk about."

And just like that, the idea of my dead husband's would-be-birthday doesn't feel terrifying anymore. It doesn't feel like trying too hard or not doing enough. It feels like maybe the best way forward is through the palm tree cooler—the kind of party where Owen would've laughed the loudest.

Chapter Fourteen

I stare at the front door, hoping it might open and swallow me whole.

"I don't know why I'm nervous," I mumble, wiping invisible lint off my ironed jeans for the third time. Harper had mocked me for a full five minutes while I pressed them earlier, complete with air quotes and commentary.

"Ooh, nothing says 'casual-chic' like heat-pressed denim!" she'd teased, draped dramatically across the couch, my own personal fashion editor. "You trying to impress your grief girl-friends or the mailman?"

"It's not like they're royalty," I add now, mostly to myself. "Or strangers I'm picking up for a blind date."

Harper appears in the hallway, wearing a loose sundress, her favorite Bohemian crocheted purse slung across her shoulder, hair pulled up into a messy bun that looks accidental but is absolutely curated. She's the kind of effortlessly cool I used to pretend to be.

"They kind of are royalty." She nudges me aside to grab a granola bar from the counter. "At least in the little world of your grief group. You're basically meeting the Real Housewives of Widowhood. Or like... the Sisterhood of the Traveling Trauma."

"Thanks." I roll my eyes at her, feeling like our parent-daughter roles were just reversed. "That helps."

She grins, unwrapping the bar. "I mean it in a good way. Viv seems terrifying in a fun, aunt-who-drinks-margaritas-before-noon kind of way. Except maybe with her, it's not margaritas. Maybe it's like... pine soda she fermented herself in the woods while aligning her heart chakra with a family of squirrels."

I snort despite myself.

"And Marin's totally the sweet one who pretends she doesn't need anyone except her cats, but the second she meets Frank, she'll fall in love with dogs and realize that maybe her life needs more than zooms and felines and then, bam!, instant family."

I give her a look. "You've constructed full backstories for both of them, haven't you?"

"Absolutely. I've seen your text thread. I had to build lore around them. Plus, someone has to balance out the drama now that Matt's not around to hog the oxygen with his Division II basketball glory."

She says it quickly, but she has the same look on her face that she did fifteen years ago and suddenly I'm transported to our backyard. A memory of the two of them playing in the backyard together flashes across my mind, Harper in tears when Matt wanted to shoot hoops with his friends and didn't want her to tag along. "You miss him."

Harper shrugs. "I do. But also, college Matt is a whole new species. He sends me gym selfies and reels of motivational quotes like he's trying to become someone's favorite podcast guest."

"You're not wrong." I laugh. "He texted me last week asking for protein powder recommendations. I told him, 'Do I look like someone who would have a ready-to-go list of protein powder or more like someone who still eats Pop-Tarts when I'm sad?'"

"I feel like this is a trick question, so I'm going to go with the protein powder list. Where have you been hiding it, Mom? And have I mentioned how nice those gains are looking."

I don't even bother asking what "gains" means. Instead, I take a deep breath and grab my keys and sunglasses, more for something to do with my hands than because I need them. "Okay. Let's do this."

Looking over my shoulder, I fling open the door, glancing behind me to see if I grabbed my phone off the table before careening straight into a wall of hard muscle. My body might have enjoyed it if not for the shock and surprise of running into a sculpted male chest when opening my front door.

Noah.

He's standing on my porch with a Tupperware container in one hand, the other raised to the door frame as though debating if he should knock. I fight back a smile, picturing him waffling on my front step without the confidence of his mail.

"Oh." I try to tamp down the blush I know is turning my cheeks cherry red from the aforementioned physical contact. "Hi?"

"I need you."

I raise an eyebrow at him. "You need me?"

"For a mission. This is Mildred's container. I'm pretty sure she has mine. And I want it back." Noah's voice is low, as though we're already conspiring.

I mimic his tone, leaning my head closer. "What's so important about this container?"

"It's one of those nice ones." His eyes stare into mine, mock serious. "The glass one with the special suction lid. It's my favorite."

That's it. I take three steps back, throwing my hands in the air. "Who has a favorite container?"

"People who like leftovers."

"So why're you knocking on my door with your container peace treaty?" I jerk my thumb in the direction of the street. "Mildred is three houses down."

"I need backup."

"You need me to go with you to retrieve your container?"

"Well, um, yeah. And maybe help me avoid that awkward

conversation with Mildred about how I took three months to return her Tupperware after a holiday party." Noah shoves a hand in his pocket, scuffing a tennis shoe along the worn boards of my front porch. "Plus, I figured since you fearlessly faced Sharon and her Bundt cake at that block party, you might be a good wing-woman to fend off any, you know, hostile container negotiators."

"Scared?"

"Terrified."

Harper appears in the doorway, a bemused smile tugging at the corners of her mouth. "I'm sure Mom would love to go with you, but we're actually running a little late for the airport."

"Airport?" I blink a few times. "Oh, uh, yes." I try to tamp down the sudden onslaught of butterflies staging a full rebellion in my stomach. "Company."

"Company?" Noah repeats. "Family?"

"Just Mom's grief gals," Harper tosses over her shoulder as she strides over to my sensible Subaru.

"Grief gals? How do I have more questions every time you answer one?"

I shrug, looking down at my open-toed sandals. I don't know why I hadn't told Noah about my grief group before. It technically falls into one of our three approved texting categories—"lasagna," "plants," and "grief"—but it never came up.

Harper leans out the passenger door, calling, "They're like a secret society, but instead of secret handshakes, they do group therapy with their favorite respective drinks and grief dares."

Noah smiles in that lazy, lopsided way that makes me momentarily forget I'm a grieving widow and not the lead in a rom-com with a very confusing rating.

"Sounds intense." His voice is warm and a little teasing. "I hope I get the chance to meet them?"

I force a small laugh and try to keep my expression neutral, but my cheeks are heating up again, traitors that they are. This whole thing, Noah on my porch, his Tupperware diplomacy, the way he keeps looking at me like he sees past all the careful armor I've put on, is starting to make me feel uncomfortably alive.

He leans in slightly, not enough to cross a line, but enough that I feel the heat radiating off his skin. "I want to hear more about these grief dares. And if I've been used for any of them."

My mouth opens. Closes. I want to assure him he hasn't, but really, he's been a leading player in most of mine so far.

"I plead the fifth," I mumble, then try to pivot toward the car like I'm not mildly combusting.

He glances down at the container in his hand, apparently remembering why he's here. "Well," he steps back, "I'll leave you to your grief society, then."

"Thanks." I nod too fast, like a bobblehead on a caffeine bender. "Airport run awaits. Have fun with the Tupperware hostage situation."

I'm already halfway to the car before I realize I didn't even ask how he's doing. I didn't offer coffee or small talk or anything resembling the person I used to be. The new version of me, the one standing with shaky hands and a heart doing the Macarena, is just trying not to drown.

Harper waves enthusiastically from the car, shooting Noah a wink. "See you later, Noah."

Noah waves awkwardly. "Later, ladies."

Harper snaps her seat belt into place with a barely contained smirk. "He totally wanted to be invited inside."

"Harper," I warn, gripping the steering wheel. Maybe, if I grip tight enough, it will magically launch me into space.

"What? I'm just saying. You've still got it, Tupperware temptress."

The arrivals area is a circus. Luggage carts zipping. Children screaming. A man in a full unicorn onesie holding a "Welcome

Back, Carl!" sign. Harper's got her phone out, narrating the entire thing like she's a travel influencer with a very niche audience.

"We are live at Terminal 2." Harper's doing her best impression of a mock-documentary voice, angling her phone toward me as I double-check the arrivals screen for the third time. "Mom's having what can only be described as an emotional stroke. Will the grief ladies be normal humans or hyper-organized mourning club cult leaders? Stay tuned."

"Can you not?" I swipe at her phone, which she dodges with ease; years of practice in her teenage years have paid off.

"I'm trying to help you go viral. This is wholesome content."

"I'm already spiraling. Please don't livestream it."

Before she can respond, we hear it: Viv's voice, unmistakable, slicing through the baggage claim din.

"BIRDIE!"

I spin in time to see Viv barreling toward us with a leopard-print duffle bag slung over one shoulder and a yoga mat strapped to the other. She's wearing neon leggings, a tank top that reads "Sage Against the Machine," and big sunglasses, despite being indoors. Marin trails behind her, wearing a beige pantsuit, a stark contrast to Viv. She tries to keep her rolling suitcase from toppling over, looking like someone who has survived the emotional equivalent of turbulence and a crying baby in 15A.

"Oh my god," Harper whispers. "You didn't say they were walking personality quizzes."

Viv hugs me, and it feels like we've somehow known each other for decades, and she's missed me every day. It's slightly suffocating and wildly comforting.

"Birdie, you look even more vibrant in person. Grief looks good on you. Is that weird to say?"

"Yep. But I would expect nothing else." I'm laughing and hugging her.

Viv pulls back, assessing Harper with a keen eye. "You must be the daughter. The one with the astrology tattoo and the suspiciously incredible hair. Do you bleach or is that natural?" Viv reaches out a hand toward her hair. "Natural. You lucky girl!"

Harper blinks. "Are you a psychic?"

"No, I internet stalk. You should consider bangs."

Marin finally catches up, slightly out of breath.

"Hi." She gives a small, shy wave before lowering her voice and looking around. "I brought wine in my checked luggage. Don't tell TSA."

"I love her," Harper proclaims.

We stand there for a moment, in the chaotic swirl of the airport, four women staring at each other, unsure of what comes next.

"Okay." I clap my hands. "Let's go get your bags and get out of here before Viv starts offering to cleanse people's auras."

"Too late." Viv's already eyeing a stressed-out businessman rubbing his temples.

Marin nods toward the exit. "I packed snacks. I feel like gold fish crackers should be part of this reunion."

"Snacks are a cornerstone of healing," Viv adds.

Harper's already walking ahead. "Well we've got pretzels and way too much nacho cheese. Buckle up."

As we herd ourselves toward the parking garage, Marin's suitcase tips again, her knitted handbag fringe getting caught in the wheels. Viv offers to help an elderly woman who's hobbling along by showing her a few yoga poses to loosen her hips. Harper keeps muttering observations into her phone, and I wonder if she's workshopping a grief feature special.

And me? I take a deep breath. Somehow, for the first time in a while, the chaos feels good.

Like home.

Chapter Fifteen

Frank is stretched luxuriously across Marin's lap, tongue rolling out of his mouth, dark brown eyes turned up in pure adoration, clearly a dog who has claimed his person. Marin sits cross-legged on the floor, one hand resting on his belly, staring back at him with the kind of devotion usually reserved for celebrity crushes and espresso martinis.

"I think I'm a dog person," she whispers. "No one tell my cats."

I stare at her and my traitorous dog from across the room, then take a sip of my lukewarm tea. "You own like a million cats and once told me dogs were 'slobbery codependents with unresolved boundary issues.'"

Marin nods solemnly, not breaking eye contact with Frank. "Frank is different. Frank gets me."

Frank snorts, stretches his back legs without opening his eyes, and lets out a tiny old-man fart.

I raise an eyebrow. "He snores and farts in his sleep."

"I love him." Marin's grey eyes don't leave Frank's adoring brown ones.

"Alright." Viv sips kombucha out of a wine glass. "We are not spending our first night together like some sad, post-menopausal knitting circle." She gives a pointed look to Marin's half-finished knitted tea cozy that's already taken up residence on my coffee table. "I found an event."

I narrow my eyes. "An event? Like a book reading? It's after eight. My bra is off. My face is washed. I was thinking popcorn, home makeover reruns, and flannel pajamas. Bed by nine."

Viv ignores this. "It's called Rhythm & Booze."

Marin's head pops up from behind Frank like a meerkat. "Is that a band? It sounds like something people in their twenties go to."

"It's a monthly salsa night at a winery-slash-bar-slash-goat sanctuary. There's music. There's wine. There's dancing between wine barrels. There are goats. Possibly in hats."

I blink. "Goats?"

Viv grins. "It's the winery's thing. Their mascot is a goat named Kevin. He wears bowties."

Marin looks down at Frank. "I mean. That does sound vaguely spiritual."

"See?" Viv's eyes sparkle with victory. "There will be movement. There will be sangria. There will be cheese boards and middle-aged men who use the word 'divorcée' like it's sexy."

I groan, setting my mug down with more force than necessary. "Do I look like I dance?"

Viv gives me the obvious up-down and opens her mouth, but before she can answer, I add, "I'm not dancing. And if there's a drum circle, I will get in the car and drive into traffic."

Viv shrugs. "You drive a Subaru. That's what they're built for. Come on. We'll wear something flowy. You can be the moody one who sways in place and looks spiritually guarded."

Marin lifts her head from Frank's belly, either intrigued or resigned to the fact that Viv is making us do this. "Do they serve snacks?"

"From what I can see on their socials, there will be cheese boards as long as that holiday scarf you knitted for Zazzles." Viv is now up off the chair, buzzing with excitement. "We can only hope that there's a conga line, though."

Marin fidgets with her tea cozy. "Would it be a good idea to join something like that?"

"You say that like it's a choice."

Harper wanders into the room in pajama pants and a hoodie, toothbrush in hand, catching the tail end of the conversation. "Wait, are you guys going out?"

Viv throws both arms in the air. "To a winery! With rhythm and drinks and eligible men and music so loud you'll feel it vibrate through your booty. There will be goats and spiritual releases!"

Harper tilts her head. "So like, yoga for your soul with alcohol?"

"Exactly." Viv beams.

"And dancing. Not everything is therapeutic." I contribute my two cents from the corner.

Harper leans against the doorway. "Well, Mom's only got one bra that's less than five years old, and from where I'm standing, it looks like it's already off. The last time she was out past dinner was to chaperone my senior prom. Good luck getting her out the door."

"Rude," I mutter. And accurate.

Marin gets to her feet, brushing dog hair from her corduroy pants. "What's the dress code for a wine place with goats? I don't even own a pair of overalls or a dress. Much less a red tango dress. Do you think plaid works?"

Viv gasps like Marin admitted she's never heard of Beyoncé. "Marin! No dress? We need to fix that. In the meantime, plaid may work. Is it the cute kind or the 'I got lost in a pumpkin patch and gave up' kind?"

Marin scrunches up her face. "Both?"

"I think Mom has a few pieces with fringe in the back of her closet," Harper adds, ever so helpful.

Viv points dramatically. "Yes. Fringe increases mobility and distracts from hip creaks." Then she's moving down the hall toward my bedroom and telling Marin to grab her suitcase and follow her.

It looks like we're going out.

The parking lot is packed with Priuses and a suspicious number of Meat is Murder bumper stickers. From inside the barn-style bar space, a beat pulses. Latin music and laughter mix with the faint sound of bongo drums.

I freeze, one leg still in the safety of the Subaru. "Drum circle. Couldn't we go to an art gallery? There's this new artist whose pieces are quite controversial and very *risqué*. Viewing art can have a similar 'wild night' effect."

Viv stares at me. "No nude art can replace my vision for tonight. And just because you hear drumming doesn't mean there's a drum circle. It might be the sounds of a DJ dropping a beat. Drums are an integral part of any party."

Traitor.

Linking arms with me, she adds, "Now get in there. Your energy is stiff, and your aura is faded."

Inside, the winery glows like it's been filtered through a "soft romance" photo filter preset. String lights are draped across wooden beams, candles flicker in little glass jars, and a five-piece salsa band in the corner is far too enthusiastic for a Thursday night. The crowd is a mix of spiritually-liberated empty-nesters, people on their third divorce and feeling flirty, and a few confused-looking couples who clearly thought this was going to be a quiet tasting.

Viv surveys the room. Yep. She's found her natural habitat. And I'm terrified. "Yes," she breathes, grabbing my arm. "This is exactly the kind of spiritual chaos I was hoping for. Look at that man in the fedora. He's vibrating on a higher frequency."

"He's definitely vibrating on something," Harper murmurs behind me.

"Come," Viv commands, already weaving her way through the crowd. "We must find the bar before the energy stagnates."

I glance at Marin, who's clutching her purse like it contains all her earthly belongings and possibly a weapon. "You okay?"

She gives me a weak smile. "I'm not really a bar person."

"Technically you're in a winery-slash-bar."

"That's worse."

Nonetheless, we follow Viv like ducklings. She stops only to greet a woman in a cape (actual cape). Then she's doing a little shoulder shimmy in sync with the band, and muttering something about "ancestral wounds and red wine."

At the bar, Viv places both palms on the counter like she's preparing to order something that will change the course of our lives—which, to be fair, she just might be. "Three sangrias. Heavy on the merlot. We're here to celebrate being alive and having dead husbands."

The bartender doesn't even blink, which makes me wonder, if *this* doesn't faze him, what kind of crowd are we rubbing elbows with tonight?

Marin calls to the bartender's retreating muscular frame, "I'll have a Diet Coke!" But if the bartender hears her, he doesn't answer.

Instead, Viv waves a hand. "Not tonight, kitten. It's our first night together in the flesh and that demands fruit-forward undertones."

I lean against the counter, watching a man in a Hawaiian shirt attempt to salsa-spin a woman in orthopedic sandals. They nearly take out the entire cheese table but somehow stick the landing. I blink. "Viv, is this a wine bar or a retirement home dance-off?"

Honestly, I can't decide if I should feel youthful or deeply concerned, because they're both pulling off moves my knees haven't approved of in years.

"Both." Viv accepts her sangria, takes a huge sip, and sighs. "Isn't it beautiful?"

Marin takes hers with the wary hesitation of someone accepting a questionable drink at a college frat party. "I swear, if I get tipsy and start crying about my eighth-grade boyfriend, someone please cut me off."

"No promises." I take a big sip of mine.

Viv lifts her glass. "To grief, to girlfriends, and to the men we loved and lost. To the heartbreaks that taught us, the therapy that healed us, and the drinks that carried us through it all. We may be bruised, but we are not broken. We rise, we thrive, and damn it, we sparkle. We will not be shaken!"

Marin blinks, her glass poised in a half toast. "Okay, Joan of Arc."

I nod solemnly. "Truly inspiring. I think the goats saluted."

Viv grins, entirely unbothered. "Wait 'till my closing statement at dessert."

We clink glasses. At this point, resistance feels both futile and disrespectful to the moment we are trying to lose ourselves in. Somewhere behind us, the band hits a salsa crescendo, and a woman in linen pants begins an interpretive dance involving what can only be described as jazz hands and hip circles.

I have to admit, it's more entertainment than the home makeover channel was going to provide for us tonight.

Viv disappears for a suspiciously long six minutes, and just when I think she's gone off to abandon Marin and me to the salsa gurus, the music shifts. Something with a bongo beat and an aggressive cowbell starts thumping through the speakers.

Then I see her.

Viv, arms in the air, hips swaying like she's auditioning for *Dancing with the Midlife Stars*, parading around the dance stage in full formation.

"Conga line!" she shouts. And I watch in awe as people in all states of alcohol-induced disinhibition fall in line behind her.

Marin, now halfway through the drink she insisted she didn't want and already eyeing a second, groans. "Here we go."

"Birdie! It's time to release the pain and dance!"

Before I can bolt, she's at my side, Viv, not pain, though same energy.

"Up! Now!" she commands, yanking me from my chair with the strength of someone fueled by merlot and righteous heartbreak.

"I don't think I have the ankle stability for this," I protest, but it's too late.

I'm swept into the line, hands landing, regretfully, on the hips of a tan, overly confident man who looks like he's been divorced since the '90s and absolutely thriving. He gives me a wink that suggests he owns at least one timeshare and an expensive Bluetooth headset.

Behind me, Marin reluctantly joins in, muttering, "Plaid pants were not made for conga lines."

Viv leads the way like a guru on a mission, high-kicking past the cheese table and nearly taking out a startled goat on a leash.

And now I'm part of the conga line at a goat wine bar on a Thursday night, hands on a stranger's hips, questioning all my life choices.

"So," Timeshare Ken yells over the music as he sashays his hips under my hands, "you recently divorced or here for a spiritual awakening?"

I blink a few times before realizing he can't see me and yell back, "Neither?"

He winks. "Same. Love that journey for us."

I try to sidestep out of the line, but it surges forward like a merlot-powered stampede. Suddenly, we're snaking between wine barrels and bachelorette parties, and someone behind me throws glitter. Actual glitter. It sticks to the sweat at the back of my neck and itches, most likely leaving a rash.

The salsa band kicks it up a notch, drums pounding like a heartbeat gone wild. Viv shouts something unintelligible, maybe

"Liberate your hips!", and throws her hands skyward like she's channeling every ounce of joy buried deep under years of laundry and color-coordinated holiday cards. The air crackles with a kind of reckless freedom.

I don't know what comes over me, maybe it's the sangria, maybe it's the exhaustion of trying to stay stiff and collected and not sweaty in this crowd, but something in me snaps. A breath fills me, slow and steady, and I let out a sigh I didn't realize I'd been holding. A release I haven't felt for years. Then, without thinking, I lean into it. Literally.

I start swinging my hips. I mean, really swinging them. Like I'm channeling Shakira, shaking my ass in gold fringe. My arms start moving too, out of sync but passionately committed. I toss my head back and let out a yell that's meant to be carefree but sounds slightly feral.

"GRIEF ISN'T LINEAR, BABY!"

I look back to see the woman whooping behind me isn't Marin. She must've abandoned ship. Someone claps. A man in a floral shirt joins in uninvited and tries to start a second conga line, which fails, but honestly? The spirit was there.

I don't stop. I double down. I throw in a shimmy.

A shimmy.

Who even am I?

That's when I notice Viv at the edge of the crowd, casually holding her phone up with one hand, fanning herself with the other like a proud stage mom. She fixes the camera on me, mutters something about "midlife icons," and I pray to God she isn't recording this.

The conga line does another lap around the dance floor, and I feel like I'm reclaiming joy one shaky hip movement at a time. I'm laughing. Full-belly, deep-wrinkle, laugh-till-you-snort laughing. And the thing is, it feels good. It feels ridiculous, but it also feels good. I'm not sure what the hell I'm doing out here in the middle of a goat-filled bar, shaking my grief into submission, but for once, it doesn't feel heavy.

It feels free.

After a few more laps, I decide I've sweat enough for one night and start scanning the room for our table. That's when I spot Marin, perched on a wine barrel, cheeks flushed, holding a sangria, clearly her emotional support drink. The band slows down into something vaguely acoustic. She stands up, clinking her glass with a fork she's somehow acquired. When that doesn't work she loudly shouts, "Hey!"

The room goes silent as she wobbles for a moment before hoisting herself up onto the barrel. "I just wanna say something," she slurs sweetly. "To weird seasons of life. And weird friends. And a life that could be full of regret but somehow gives you exactly who you need to survive it."

There's a pause. Then someone cheers.

Viv, still on the sidelines fanning herself with a drink list in one hand and doing something with her phone in the other, pauses. "What she said!" she echoes before I hear her muttering something about, "Hashtag grief girls gone wild."

The band picks up again, something vaguely Latin-pop but with the energy of a wedding DJ who's stopped caring. I finally escape the conga line only to find Marin slow-dancing with a man in a turtleneck and flip-flops. She's swaying in a circle, whispering something into his shoulder that might be a poem or possibly the word "cabernet" over and over.

"Marin?" I approach cautiously. "You good?"

She turns, her pupils the size of quarters. "This man has opinions about jazz. We're soulmates."

"I love that for you." I gently pry her wine glass from her hand and hand her a complimentary cube of cheese. Glancing down at my watch confirms it. It's time to grab Viv and get out of here. As my mom always said, nothing good ever happens after midnight.

After making a few laps around the room, I'm about ready to call out a search party when I glance at a shadowy corner of the room, where Viv is making out, full on *making out*, with a man wearing a linen vest and aggressively white sneakers. He's got one hand in her hair and another on her waist, and they're swaying like it's prom and they're the only two people in the universe who know the lyrics to the soft indie rock song playing.

"Should we?" I motion helplessly, not expecting anyone to answer.

"Your friend?" the older woman to my right asks.

I nod.

"Leave her be. She looks hydrated and spiritually aligned. She needs this."

I hate that I understand what she means.

And right when I think the night has hit its peak weirdness, someone yells, "You! Grief lady! Come up here!"

I blink. "Me?"

"I saw you in that conga line! We need you!" He points to the poster with the glaring message: *Groove Challenge.*

I shake my head furiously. "No, thank you! I'm emotionally constipated, and it comes out in my dancing!"

But the stranger next to me is already pushing me forward. "Time for you to get hydrated and spiritually aligned. You need this too!"

The next thing I know, I'm on a makeshift stage flanked by two servers, one with bleached eyebrows and a nose ring, the other with a mullet and Crocs covered in enamel pins, both holding wine glasses like microphones and looking at me like I'm about to perform instead of panic. One of them shouts, "Okay, now, grind those hips, you got this!" and suddenly my hips are swinging in one direction while my arms go rogue in the opposite.

What they're doing looks effortless, like a metronome with rhythm. What I'm doing looks like I'm trying to ward off a swarm of bees while also bracing for a squat I may never recover from.

"Am I doing it?" I shout over the music.

"No!" Viv yells cheerfully from the crowd, apparently having broken her lip lock to record the Birdie Disaster Hour. "But it's iconic!"

Someone hands me a sangria mid-shimmy, which I accept like

a trophy for surviving this whole ordeal and perimenopause. I nearly drop it as I attempt an interpretive shoulder roll that results in an audible pop.

The crowd eats it up, and I don't know whether to curtsy or call an orthopedist.

But then I catch my reflection in the window, flushed cheeks, dark strands of hair messy and wild, arms flailing with gusto, and I realize something shocking: I'm actually having fun.

Uncoordinated, unfiltered fun, fully leaning in.

God help me, I even try a viral spin move I saw during a doom scroll.

By the time I get down, I've sweated through my blouse and might've done a jazz-hands finale I'll regret for the next decade.

"Do you think anyone was filming that?" I try to discreetly check my armpits.

Viv bounces over. "Sweetheart." She waves her phone. "You're already on all the socials. And a woman named HealingHeidi called you a goddess of grief."

I slap my hand over my face.

There it is.

My worst nightmare.

My own words ring in my ear, "grief is private."

Well, mine's just gone public. In a very embarrassing way.

Marin stumbles over with a breadstick and slings her arm around my shoulder. "We're gonna be famous. Like, widowed Spice Girls."

"More like Sangria Seniors," Viv mutters.

And then the lights dim, the band plays a slow song, and someone starts passing around a tambourine with glow sticks taped to it.

I glance at my glass, then the door. "I think we need fries."

"Fries," Marin echoes solemnly, still clinging to her cheese cube. "And maybe a nap."

We make our way toward the exit, leaving a trail of confetti from a broken party popper stuck to the back of my sensible flats.

Behind us, Viv and the magician are exchanging numbers via a crystal pendulum.

This is not how I thought healing would look.

But maybe healing wears linen and dances in public and eats fries at midnight with people who remind you that you're still alive.

We barely make it ten feet from the bar before Viv flings her arm across the path.

"Okay," she declares. "That was either the best or worst decision we've made in years."

"I haven't danced that hard since my cousin's second wedding," Marin mumbles, staggering slightly in her sandals. "Or was it the third?"

I nod, trying to guide her away from a flowerbed she looks dangerously close to falling into.

Viv, now barefoot and holding her heels, pauses to admire a man leaning against a truck in the parking lot. "Is that flannel shirt for real," she murmurs, "or am I deeply under-cuddled?"

"Oh no... Viv. Don't." But it's too late. She's already sauntering over.

"I'm going to ask him if he knows the way to the I-90," she singsongs. "With my mouth. And maybe my hands."

Marin hiccups. "Oh no. We lost her. I give it five minutes before she's either making out or making up a fake identity." Now she's leaning heavily against my side, and I'm struggling to keep us both upright. "I think she told a guy in there her name was Verona and she was a recently divorced perfume chemist."

"To be fair," I say, "she was wearing patchouli."

Viv reappears, smug and slightly disheveled. "Guess who got another phone number and a promise for a free glass of wine?"

We reach the car right as someone's phone pings, loud and aggressive.

Viv checks it, then freezes. "So, Birdie, don't freak out."

"What?"

"You've kind of gone viral?"

My stomach drops like a faulty elevator. "What?"

She turns her phone toward me. There I am. Projected in all my awkward glory, windmilling through a conga line, sunglasses on my head, my blouse slightly askew, shouting "GRIEF ISN'T LINEAR, BABY!" into the night. I look like a backup dancer in an insane asylum flash mob. It's been reposted by someone with a wine influencer handle and the caption: *"When the grief retreat goes harder than Coachella."*

"I'm going to die."

"No, you're going to trend," Viv tuts, like that's a comfort.

"Viv, I'm on the internet."

"You're welcome."

"I didn't ask for this."

"You never do." She pops the trunk and chucks her heels: a woman who's undeterred from life's consequences.

We manage to get to the car, Marin propped up between Viv and me in the backseat, Harper driving. Marin immediately starts humming to herself in the backseat, Viv's scrolling through selfies she took with random people inside, and I'm trying to help our poor designated driver navigate toward the drive-thru with the precision of a mother duck leading her drunk ducklings.

"Birdie," Marin mumbles, resting her head against the window, "I love you."

"I love you too."

"No, like, if I threw up on you, you wouldn't yell."

"I might yell a little."

"You're still my favorite."

Viv passes Marin a napkin she stole from the wine tasting table. "Just in case."

Marin sighs. "I have never been more certain we need fries."

"I need fries and an internet black out," I whisper.

We roll through the drive-thru, feeling like a clown car, and order three large fries, one chocolate milkshake, and, somehow, a breakfast burrito.

"Who ordered the burrito?" I try to toss it to Viv.

Marin raises her hand with her eyes closed. "I did. It felt like a breakfast moment."

I glance at the clock on the dash, which proudly proclaims 1:30 AM. "I guess we are getting closer to the breakfast realm."

"Time is a social construct, darling." Viv pops a fry in her mouth.

Marin moans, "I think I'm going to be sick."

———

I stand at the kitchen counter, hair in a lopsided bun, gripping a mug of coffee like it's a flotation device. I'm still wearing last night's blouse, now mysteriously buttoned wrong, and no pants. Just underwear and the unmistakable look of a woman questioning all her life choices in the harsh light of morning.

Is this who I am now? A pantless widow with raccoon eyes with only a vague recollection of a conga line and French fries?

Viv strolls in first, glowing like a woman who got eight hours of sleep and has zero regrets. She's wearing oversized sunglasses and holding a green smoothie that smells like liquified lawn clippings.

"Great night!" she sings, plopping herself onto the counter. "We laughed, we danced, Marin almost eloped with a retired orthodontist named Len."

I groan, shielding my eyes. "How are you this vertical? Did the sangria metabolize into vitamins in your body?"

Viv grins. "Chaos is my cardio."

Marin shuffles in last, her phone in a death grip. Her robe is tied in a perfect knot, hair still pinned in a tidy bun, but her eyes are wide with panic.

"I think I'm viral," she croaks.

Viv perks up. "You're welcome."

I freeze mid-sip. "You think you're viral?"

Marin thrusts her phone toward me. "Look! It's us at the winery! It's everywhere!"

Viv spins her phone around with a smug little flourish. "That's not you, babe. That's Birdie." She hits play.

There I am, front and center, conga-line-adjacent and fully committed to a dance that looks like I'm trying to swat bees with my elbows. At one point, I do a high kick. I cannot do high kicks. My brain has a foggy memory of Viv showing me this video last night.

Marin leans closer, squints at the screen, then gasps. "Wait? That's you? But I made an epic toast!"

Viv's eyes light up. "Oh, I posted that too. It's in a compilation video called 'Grief Girls Gone Wild.' But Birdie doing the conga line and then the Floss with a sangria? That's the money shot."

"So I'm the face of middle-aged emotional unraveling?" I mope.

Viv grins. "The star of it."

I wince. "No. No, no, no."

Viv starts reading the comments aloud with great enthusiasm:

"This is the kind of soft grief content I needed today."
 "Grieving and thriving. We love to see it."
 "Wine Mom Nation, rise."
 "Someone sponsor her!"

"Eighty-seven thousand likes," Marin croaks. "And climbing."

I squint at the screen. "Wait, why am I the one who went viral? I'm pretty sure Viv recorded you in the yard when you took Frank outside to potty. You told Frank you wanted to do a trust fall in a vineyard."

I've gone from the perfectly composed housewife, the kind of widow people can stomach, with her grief neatly folded between PTA meetings and silent auction donations, to a woman who dances in a goat wine bar and blurts out things like "grief isn't linear" without even flinching. Either I'm healing, or I'm unraveling.

Maybe both.

Marin groans and drops onto a stool, burying her face in her hands. "I was emotional. You try drinking half a sangria and talking about loss in public."

Viv flips her phone around and points to another comment. "This one says we should start a podcast."

"Nope." Viv barely finishes reading the comment before I protest.

She ignores me. "Healing Through Chaos. First episode: 'Dancing Away the Patriarchy.'"

"If you say 'healing energy' one more time," I mutter, pouring more coffee, "I'm putting sage in your underpants drawer."

Viv beams, toasting me with her smoothie. "And my underpants would thank you."

Frank, curled up under the table with a napkin around his neck like a cape, lets out a snort of agreement.

My phone dings, and I roll my eyes, already anticipating Harper texting me from where she's crashed out in her childhood bedroom upstairs, begging me to bring her up a bowl of Cheerios and coffee.

My hands freeze.

Noah.

> Noah: Saw the video. So, how do I join the grief society? Is there an application or a dance audition?

I stare at the screen, cheeks warming.

> Me: What are you doing on the internet, looking at viral grief videos?

> Noah: I wasn't. I was watching viral cat videos, like any normal person does on a Friday morning before work, and I saw your face.

I quickly lock my screen before anyone can peek.

Viv notices. "Was that from a handsome stranger from last night?"

"No. Worse."

"Oooh. The mailman."

I groan. "You people are feral."

Chapter Sixteen

I'm staring at the email from the Seattle Art Museum... again. Same subject line. Same blinking cursor. Same quiet sense of impending shame.

It's been sitting in my inbox like a dare. Ticking down to the deadline while I do absolutely nothing.

Every morning, I open it.

Every morning, I hover my mouse over "Start Application."

And every morning, I chicken out.

I tell myself it's timing. The laundry, the dishes, the ghost of Owen lingering in the corners of this house.

But the truth is, I'm scared.

Scared I missed my chance.

Scared I don't belong anymore.

Scared that dreaming at this age is embarrassing.

Viv appears beside me, peering over my shoulder before I even register her footsteps. "What's this?"

"Nothing."

My face flushes so fast it feels like a betrayal. I scramble to close the tab with the open email, but it's too late.

Marin walks in, nursing her late afternoon tea and raising an eyebrow. "What's nothing?"

"Still nothing," I mutter, fumbling for my mug, hoping it might somehow deflect the attention.

Viv's already squinting at the screen. "Seattle Art Museum internship?" she reads aloud. "Birdie!"

I groan and bury my face in my hands. "It's dumb. I'm too old. It's probably meant for fresh-out-of-college twenty-somethings with graphic design certificates. I have Owen's life insurance money. It's not like I need a job."

"You have an art history degree." Marin leans against the counter. "Didn't you tell me you wanted to work there once?"

"I did." I exhale, the kind of breath that comes from deep, dusty storage. "Back in college, I used to walk past the museum and pretend I worked there. I thought I'd wear long skirts and talk to people about Van Gogh's brushstrokes. Maybe write some poetic little blurbs for the wall labels. It felt possible back then."

"So why didn't you?" Viv asks the question as if the answer is simple.

It's not.

"I met Owen. Then I got pregnant. One baby turned into two, and suddenly I blinked and twenty-something years vanished into field trips, soccer games, PTA meetings, bake sales, and playdates. I was updating my résumé, telling myself that once Harper hit sixteen, I'd finally go back—start building a career, step back from being that mom who was always at the school."

"But..." Marin prompts gently.

"But then Owen died." I nod, the ache still sharp. "And suddenly, getting a job wasn't even on the table. I had life insurance, so the money wasn't the first priority. My heartbroken teenage daughter, son who just left for college and was struggling to keep it together, and a house full of grief was all I had the mental capacity for. I needed to keep everything from falling apart. I needed to hold it all together. Hold me up."

I swallow hard, the lump in my throat thick and unrelenting. "And now? Now it's just me. And this stupid email. And this even stupider idea that maybe I could still do something for myself.

But what if I apply and they laugh? Or worse—what if I actually get it, and I'm the awkward, out-of-touch intern who doesn't even know what's in style anymore?"

Marin smirks. "Then at least you'll be the brave, awkward old intern. Honestly, Birdie, what's the worst that can happen?"

"I'll look like an idiot."

"You fearlessly danced in a conga line and in a competition at a goat wine bar. You don't fear looking foolish anymore! You don't care what other people think!"

"You say that, but I feel like I'd need a translator to understand the office coffee machine. They don't want someone like me. I'm someone's mom, the person who packs snacks."

"No." Viv turns, rummaging through the junk drawer. "You're someone. Period."

"What're you doing?" I eye her suspiciously as she moves to the living room.

She rifles through a stack of books on the coffee table and returns with the pink glitter notebook raised in her triumphant hand.

"Oh no. No, no, no."

"Yup." She's already flipping to a fresh page.

"Viv, I swear—"

Too late. Her pen is already in motion, her dramatic lopsided cursive etching its decree into my paper sanctuary.

#11. Apply to Seattle Art Museum Internship. I double-dog-dare you.

I lunge for it. "You can't add things! There's an obvious theme to my dares: romance, love, human connection, remember?"

Viv lifts the notebook over her head. "This is a human connection. It's a connection to yourself."

Marin folds her arms. "Honestly, I think she's right. These dares aren't about falling in love with someone else. They're about remembering who you are. Before Owen. Before the kids. Before Noah. Before the grief."

Viv nods. "No man is going to rediscover you for you, Birdie. That's your job now."

And just like that, I'm staring at the screen again.

Same blinking cursor.

Except this time, I pull up the resume I've been editing and re-editing for years, open the link, and start filling out the application.

I'm on my knees in the garden, tugging weeds that have no business growing this aggressively. There's dirt on my cheek, a smear of something unidentifiable on my leg, and my sippy cup full of kombucha is balanced in the mulch beside me. It's the most glamorous I've felt in weeks.

The gate creaks behind me.

I don't look up.

"If you're another neighbor asking if I've 'found peace,' I swear on my begonias, I will throw compost."

Maybe it's time to take a break from my freedom filter.

A quiet laugh follows. Not the neighbor.

Noah.

Figures.

"I come in peace." His voice is warm with amusement. "And bearing flora."

I turn to look. He's standing at the garden gate, holding a potted daisy, bright yellow, cheerful, the kind of flower that has no idea the world can be terrible.

"For you," he adds. "Thought your fennel looked lonely."

My mouth opens, then closes. I stare at the plant.

"You brought me a daisy." I stand slowly, brushing the dirt from my knees. "Bold choice. Very Anne of Green Gables meets Home Depot clearance rack."

Noah snorts, pretending to look offended but failing miserably. "Hey, the Home Depot clearance rack is sacred. You once dragged me through three aisles to find a discounted pot of half-dead mums because, and I quote, 'Every sad flower deserves a second chance.'"

I roll my eyes but can't help laughing. "I stand by that. They needed love and water and maybe a little luck."

He nods solemnly, twirling the daisy between his fingers. "Exactly why I brought you this little guy."

"I love the Home Depot clearance rack."

"I know."

He grins, and something in me softens at the ease of it.

"Remember when Owen and I broke that closet handle in our dorm room and he went into a full panic spiral about getting kicked out or charged extra and what his parents would say?"

My heart aches at the memory. "Yeah. He was convinced it was a felony-level offense. I thought he was going to try to file a police report on himself."

"We both sprinted to the nearest Home Depot like it was a covert mission. Owen was combing the aisles looking for an exact match, sweating bullets, while you—" Noah chuckles, eyes bright, as though he's holding back tears.

"—while I found a box of mismatched hardware in the clearance bin and said, 'This one's close enough. Spray paint it and tell them it's vintage.'"

He points at me. "Exactly. And he was horrified. Said that would be 'deceiving the institution.'"

I shake my head, still smiling. "God, he was such a rule-follower. And you were always the middleman, trying to calm him down while also pocketing an extra handle for 'future emergencies.'"

"I still have it."

My eyes flick to his. "You do not."

He shrugs. "Top drawer. Next to my loose batteries and a lone Allen key that probably doesn't go to anything."

I laugh again, but it's softer this time, because there's a kind of ache underneath it. The kind that comes when a memory brushes right up against everything you've lost.

Noah watches me closely, the playfulness in his expression giving way to something gentler. "He was the glue back then. You know?"

"Yeah," I whisper. "He really was."

A quiet settles between us. Not uncomfortable, just full.

And then he clears his throat, nudges the daisy toward me again. "Still think it's too Anne of Green Gables?"

I take it from him, fingers brushing his. "Nah. It's exactly right."

And for a second, it feels like we're back there, college kids with broken handles and stolen daisies, before everything cracked open.

I kneel back down, digging out a space next to the lavender bushes. Noah crouches beside me, elbows on his knees, watching like he's not quite sure if he should say what he's about to say.

"I like it out here. It's quiet. You're different when it's quiet."

"Different how?"

"Softer. Like you stop bracing for the next disaster."

I pause, little hand shovel suspended above the dirt, and really look at him. The sky is shimmering with gold behind him. His beard's a little longer than usual. I wonder what it would be like to feel it against my cheek. The intrusive thought fills my mind, and I feel heat creeping up my cheeks into an obvious flush.

"Well, don't get used to it. I'll be bracing again by morning."

Noah's voice is honey-smooth. "I like both versions."

I swallow, feeling the sun-kissed dirt crumble beneath my palms. Suddenly, I feel seventeen again, skin buzzing, unsure if it's attraction or fear. Unsure of what to say.

"Where's Viv and Marin?"

I feel the smile pulling at my cheeks. He remembers their names. But then I'm remembering I'm in Owen's garden and smiling shouldn't be allowed here anymore.

"Doing a round of yoga. Viv cornered Marin into it, and I

escaped with the excuse of weeding before they started. They promised to come help me when they were done. Mostly, Viv sits with her bare feet in the earth, grounding, and giving unsolicited emotional commentary like she's narrating a documentary. 'Here we see the widow in her natural habitat, tending grief and geraniums.' Marin is really the one who digs in and will get the weeding done."

He laughs, unguarded, and something warm uncoils in my chest.

I reach for my sippy cup, stalling.

"I was actually hoping to ask you something." He starts fiddling with the small assortment of weeding tools next to me, and I try not to laugh at the sight of this strong, rugged man nervous over a simple question.

"Is this where you ask if I've tried yoga for my healing?"

"No." He smiles, small but sincere. "I was going to ask if you'd want to have dinner with me sometime. Nothing fancy or dramatic, something that doesn't involve a neighborhood potluck and a suspicious Jell-O salad."

I blink.

"You're asking me out?" That flicker of excitement barely has time to take root before guilt comes barreling after it, fast and merciless, choking the joy.

"Unless you'd prefer to call it a grief-adjacent social experiment with light appetizers."

I laugh, but it catches in my throat. The air shifts, heavier now, as excitement flutters up just in time to collide with the sinking feeling in my gut. Setting the daisy down, I wipe my palms again, telling myself I need to get the dirt off them. It's not because all my guilt and grief are trying to escape in the form of sweat.

"I haven't done this in a long time." I press my lips together.

"I know."

"I still have his slippers by the door. I yell at his ashes when the washing machine leaks. And some mornings, I cry because the coffee tastes the same."

He nods, like he knows exactly what I mean.

"You don't have to say yes. I just didn't want to walk past your fennel every day wondering if I should've said something."

My chest tightens. He's waiting, a half-smile on his face, hands smudged with my garden's dirt. There's something there. Not pressure. Just possibility.

I swallow hard. "I'm not fixed. I'm not even sanded down. I'm still rough, and some days I'm held together with bathrobes and sarcasm."

"Perfect," he says, no hesitation. "Then you'll fit in great at dinner with me."

I stare at him, all warmth and nerve and ridiculous potted daisies, and realize I'm smiling. That quiet, reluctant kind of smile that sneaks up before your brain can veto it.

"I could do appetizers." My voice is barely above a whisper. "No promises. Only appetizers."

He stands, brushing off his jeans. "One mozzarella stick. No pressure. Though if you have two, I might ask you to dance. There's no excuse about you not knowing how. Remember, I saw the video."

"Don't push your luck," I mutter.

As he heads for the gate, he pauses, glancing back over his shoulder.

"Nice flannel," he calls. "Your husband had good taste."

I press my hand to my chest and swallow.

Yeah. He really did.

Good taste in friends.

Shame he couldn't say the same about his traitorous wife.

I lean over the counter, stirring the stir-fry on the stove.

"How was the weeding?" Viv skates through the door, and Marin flops in behind after her.

"Good." I take in Viv's energized bouncy up and down and Marin's half-dead expression. "How was the yoga?"

"Revitalizing!"

Marin rolls her eyes. "Next time, I'm coming out to the garden with you. My body wasn't made to move like that."

"Well, the garden wasn't exactly peaceful this evening."

The ladies both stop and stare.

I hold up my phone, as though it's radioactive. "Noah asked me out. I might have said yes. Kind of. Soft yes. Only a whisper of a yes to appetizers."

Viv immediately throws both hands in the air, mimicking a football player scoring a touchdown. "Okay. My brain is confused. This is a good thing, but you're delivering the news like it's a bad thing?"

"It's a horrible idea. What will the neighbors think? It's too soon!"

Viv takes a dramatic sip of her chamomile, which she's added three splashes of wine to, because that's the way the "love of my life always drank it" and she's "never going back to boring tea."

"I mean, the man has the body of a superhero. If anything, you owe it to the community."

I groan and flop into a kitchen chair, hugging a throw pillow like it might absorb my panic. "It's too soon."

Viv slides me a glass of water, eyeing me like I'm seconds away from spiraling.

"Is it too soon because your heart or your guilt is saying it is? Or because you're worried about what everyone else will think?"

I stare into the water hoping it might reflect the answers back at me. "All of the above?"

But it's more than that. It's the way I still reach for a second toothbrush in the Target aisle. It's the empty side of the bed. It's the memory of casseroles and pity smiles and being told "you're so strong" when I didn't ask to be. I don't know if I'm ready, or if I'll ever be ready to love again. But I do know that moving forward feels suspiciously like leaving him behind.

I tap my phone, as if it's going to offer me an out. "I should probably cancel. I mean, what would the neighbors think? The PTA president already looks at me like I microwaved communion."

Viv leans in, voice calm but sharp enough to slice through my panic. "Birdie. Your husband's gone. You're not cheating. Also, you once mentioned you hosted a shrimp boil for the HOA. You've done your time."

I snort despite myself. "That shrimp boil had three Yelp reviews and a minor fire hazard."

Marin perks up suddenly, her phone lighting up. "Also, you're not going alone."

I blink. "What?"

Viv smirks like this has been her master plan all along. "We're making it a group date."

My jaw drops. "So many questions. First, how did you two even communicate that? Telepathically? Second, who would go with you?"

They answer at the same time.

Viv: "The guy who taught me how to twirl."

Marin: "Len. From the barrel."

Viv adds, "And good souls are able to communicate with good souls. We did yoga together. We're bonded."

I look between them like I've entered an alternate timeline. "I need to join you all for yoga because I want this superpower. You got their numbers?"

Marin shrugs. "It was a vulnerable environment."

"This is happening. You're going out. You're not canceling. And we're going to wear things that don't have elastic waistbands." Viv snaps the elastic on her yoga pants.

Before I can respond, my phone pings with a new email. The subject line alone is enough to make me break out in stress hives:

Subject: Friendly Reminder - Snack Roster Incomplete!

From: pta.party@willowridge.k12.us

I sigh and fall silent, reading as the background noise of Viv and Marin discussing outfits fills the air.

Hi Birdie!

Simply a quick nudge 😊 *to remind you we still need a confirmed nut-free, dye-free, vegan-friendly snack option for next Thursday's student council training!*

We know you always come through!

Also, could you bring cloth napkins? We're trying to be eco-conscious but still festive!

Warmly,

Your Friends at the PTA

I stare at the screen, blinking slowly. Rebooting.

The emotions hit fast and hot—anger, humiliation, something dangerously close to hurt—but habit kicks in before I can feel them all the way. Deep breath. Smooth it over. Make it look nice.

"Everything ok?" Marin places a hand on my shoulder.

Pasting on a sunny smile, I nod. "Yep. Just a little PTA trouble. No big deal."

Viv looks up, horrified. "Are you seriously still on the PTA? Didn't your daughter graduate three presidents ago?"

"Okay, not that long ago," I mutter, already starting to type a response. "I never unsubscribed. And technically, I'm an 'alumni liaison.'"

Viv snorts. "That is not a real thing."

"It is," I argue weakly. "They said I bring legacy continuity."

Marin is now several sips in and aggressively swirling her wine. "You bring Costco napkins, repressed rage, and the ability to make everyone else's life easier. I know the drill. Theo loved it when I was distracted with some PTA project. He swore it made me less 'needy.'"

Viv points a finger at Marin. "You have needs. You are not

needy." Then she grabs the phone from my hand mid-keystroke. "And you are not a legacy anything. You are not bringing kale muffins to the next fundraising bake sale. You're going on a date with the hot mailman. And you're letting the PTA figure out snacks like the grown adults they pretend to be."

I reach for the phone, but she holds it hostage behind her back. "I will write an out-of-office response if I have to."

"Viv..."

She narrows her eyes. "Birdie. Look me in the eyes and say you want to spend your one wild and precious life chasing carrot sticks for underfunded extracurriculars instead of dancing with the man who brings you flowers."

I slump back into my chair and groan. "Fine. I'm muting the thread."

Marin raises her glass in a toast. "To bold moves."

Viv clinks hers against mine. "To unsubscribing from martyrdom."

And just like that, I start to feel it—not the wine exactly, but the possibility. The tiniest shimmer of something I can do for me.

We've moved from wine to the dregs of a forgotten bottle of prosecco Marin found behind the rice cooker. Viv poured it with zero shame into mismatched mugs and declared it "festive." Things have escalated.

Viv tops off our glasses with a dramatic flourish, like she's christening a new ship. "Okay. So. Are you going to seduce the mailman or what?"

I nearly choke on my drink. "I'm going to need more wine before we even say the word *seduce*."

Viv grins. "That's not a no."

I groan, dragging my hands down my face. "I haven't kissed anyone but Owen in over two decades. I'm not even sure I remember how."

"Oh, please." Marin leans back in her chair. "It's like riding a bike. A really attractive, emotionally available bike who brings you credit card offers and Pottery Barn catalogs."

"I'm serious!" I protest. "My flirting skills are from 1994 and involve sending mix tapes."

Viv leans forward, eyes gleaming. "Have you at least thought about lingerie?"

I blink. "I've never bought lingerie."

The room goes quiet for a beat.

"Good." Viv flops dramatically onto the couch, her drink sloshing dangerously close to the faded material, although to be fair, that's not the worst thing this couch has been splashed with. "That stuff is overrated and overpriced. Who pays $80 for strips of lace?"

"Exactly," Marin agrees, swirling her drink. "Wear your birthday suit!"

I snort. "My birthday suit is white, faded, and stretched out."

Viv gasps. "Don't talk about your birthday suit that way! She carried babies and trauma and still looks hot in fluorescent lights."

"Viv, no one looks good in fluorescent lights," I deadpan.

Viv raises her mug. "Okay, hot in warm, mood lighting."

Marin cackles. "You're like one of those candlelit Renaissance nudes. Tired, gorgeous, possibly holding fruit."

"I am always holding a snack," I admit, laughing until I wheeze.

We're tipsy now. Enough for my fear to dissolve into boldness. Or maybe truth.

I trace the rim of my glass with my finger. "You want to know why I keep thinking about Noah?"

They both quiet, leaning in like we're around a campfire and I'm about to share a ghost story.

"It's not because he's hot. I mean, okay, he is, but that's not it. It's not even the way he looks at me like I'm still a person and not just... a mother, or a widow, or someone past her expiration date." I pause, searching for the thing underneath it all. "It's that—when I'm with him, I forget to brace."

Viv tilts her head. "Brace?"

"For impact. For disappointment. For the moment someone

realizes I'm too much or not enough. I've lived most of my life holding my breath, waiting for the other shoe to drop. And with Noah…" I exhale slowly. "I just breathe. I laugh without checking myself. I talk and I don't overthink. He listens, like really listens, and he says things that stick in my ribs for days."

Marin's eyes are soft now, wine glass forgotten in her lap.

I go on, voice quieter. "When Owen died, I didn't just lose my husband. I lost the only person who knew me. And I was sure I'd ever feel known again. But then there's Noah. And he sees past the polite thank-you-note me. He teases the messy, weird parts to the surface. The parts I buried a long time ago because they were too loud, or too opinionated, or too damn much."

"You're not too much." Viv's voice is uncharacteristically gentle.

"I might be." I feel my lips twist into a wry smile. "But he always could handle it. And now I'm wondering if he still can."

Marin's eyes shine. "That sounds a lot like hope."

I take a sip and nod. "It is. And that's terrifying."

Viv reaches for my phone, suddenly inspired. "Muting the thread isn't enough. Your grief dare for this week is to respond. Not with what you think you *should* say, but what you actually want to say."

"Oh no." Marin's eyes go saucer-wide.

"Do it," Viv chants, kicking her feet up. "Write the email. It's time to break free!"

"Fine." I grab my phone out of Viv's outstretched hand. "But that means you and Marin need to do a grief dare this week too."

"Deal." Viv nods toward the phone, and Marin nods in solidarity.

I thumb into my inbox and click "reply all" to the PTA thread like a woman possessed. Before I can second-guess myself, I start to type.

Subject: RE: Snack Roster

Hi everyone,

While I appreciate being considered reliable and, apparently, eternally available, I am formally resigning from all snack-related duties and emotional labor tied to themed napkins.

Please note: I am no longer the mother of a current student, nor am I a licensed chef, nor do I possess the mental bandwidth to source nut-free, dye-free, vegan options that also spark joy.

Wishing you all the best in your quinoa-forward future.

Birdie

Marin reads it over my shoulder, her alarm growing with each sentence. "Quinoa-forward future?"

"How else would one end a liberating email?" My finger hovers over the send button as my eyes skim over what I typed.

Viv leans over my shoulder, reading the emboldened words aloud. "Hi everyone...."

Marin gasps, "It sounds even more bold saying it aloud. Can you send that?"

Viv cackles. "Oh, she's sending it."

I click SEND before I can think too hard. The whoosh of the email flying off is the sexiest sound I've heard in months.

There's a beat of silence.

Then we all burst out laughing.

Viv claps. "That was poetry. I think my nipples saluted."

Marin wipes a tear. "I didn't know how much I needed that."

"I might throw up," I whisper.

"You won't." Viv hands me a tortilla chip. "You're reborn."

And honestly? Maybe I am.

"Don't think that you two are going to get out of your own grief dares this week." I get out my hot pink notebook. "Viv, you're going to let someone see you cry. Ugly cry. Because we both know how much you still miss him. Marin, you're going to tell someone a memory about your husband that doesn't have a silver lining and let it just sit there."

"Those feel worse than an email."

I level them both with a glare. "I dare you."

Chapter Seventeen

I've written and rewritten this text five times.

"It's really not that hard, Birdie. Suck it up and press send already. You've birthed two babies, unmedicated. You've survived your husband dying and that atrocious, yet no less courageous, email to the PTA. You've got this. Do it."

I hear the floorboards creak and glance up, hoping Viv, Marin, or worse, Harper, isn't going to walk into the room to overhear my less-than-stellar self-pep talk. Luckily, it's just Frank. Although, surprisingly, he's mastered the same judgy eyes that Harper nailed in high school. The two must be spending too much time together.

The text is simple enough:

So about Saturday.

I pause, my thumbs hovering over the keyboard, debating if I should send a wide-eyed emoji or carry on with the rest of the text.

Decisions, decisions.

Before I can finish typing the rest of my hours premeditated thought, my jumbled nerves cause my thumb to slip, and I accidentally hit send. He's not going to message back. Or maybe he will. Honestly, I'm not sure what would be worse at this point. Can I unsend a text? It's not even a finished text? It's half a text.

Wait... he's typing back.

He's responding to half a text.

Damn you nerves and my trigger happy thumbs.

> Noah: What about Saturday? Are you going to tell me you came down with Kuru?

Me: A prion disease transferred by cannibalism? Don't forget I was there when your last date tried that on you. She really should've read the entire Web MD article before choosing that one.

> Noah: Phew. Good cause I'm still recovering from that ego blow. So what about Saturday?

Me: Why are you answering so fast? I wasn't done typing.

> Noah: Pretend I didn't say anything. Continue.

Me: Is it alright if Viv and Marin come?

They also have dates.

Not that I don't want to spend time just us.

I do.

I think.

But it might help.

Does the block party count as a date?

I was thinking maybe it doesn't, and in that case, this would be my first official date, since, well, you know, and

I rapidly fire the text messages one after the other, the train of thought clearly derailed, wreaking havoc through my mind and transmitting out my fingertips. Too eager. Too weird. Too "what will the neighbors think?" But Noah's typing bubbles pop up. Then disappear. Then reappear. And the sight of them is enough to break my rambling. Who knew it was even possible to ramble in a text stream?

> Noah: Sounds perfect. I like your friends. Viv said I look like "someone who models flannels."

I smile, despite myself.

> Me: Do you want to pick me up?

> Noah: I do, but only if that doesn't make it feel like too much. Otherwise, I'll meet you there.

> Me: Let's meet there. One step at a time.

> Plus, I could do without Sharon's eagle eyes peeping through her Pottery Barn drapes and her commentary.

> Noah: Every great journey begins with a single step.

> Me: Quoting Lao Tzu? You didn't strike me as a man into Chinese philosophy.

> Noah: What can I say? I have layers and social media (I'm pretty hip with the groove), and an old college philosophy book around here somewhere.

Glancing up from my phone, I smile, right into the eyes of Owen smiling back at me from our wedding photo still next to my bed. The guilt hits hard.

> Me: Got to go. See you Saturday.

I set the phone down and immediately begin sweating through my shirt.

***

We arrive at the restaurant, and I briefly wonder if we look like some kind of reality show cast reunion: three women in slightly-too-tight clothes, hyped up on kombucha and nerves.

Viv walks ahead of us, all hips and high heels, swearing that the bottles of kombucha she had us all chug before walking out the door will energize us, renew our minds, and release any pent-up emotions we've been hiding deep within our intestines. Marin stumbles along behind Viv, nearly tripping over the maxi dress she found on clearance two days ago that somehow makes her look like she owns a boat.

I, Birdie "Emotionally Frazzled" Lawson, am in a casual knee-length black dress, that may or may not be inside-out, it's hard to tell with all the stretchy material, and enough concealer to spackle drywall.

Noah's already there, seated at a long table with two other men I vaguely recognize from the winery, though they look less intoxicated and slightly more nervous than I remembered.

Viv's guy is hard to miss: shoulder-length silver hair pulled into a loose ponytail, a turquoise ring the size of a small pebble, and a patterned shirt unbuttoned halfway down his chest. He's bearded, confident, and has the vibes of a man who sells hand-made guitars at the farmers market but will absolutely ghost you to go on a silent retreat.

Marin's date is the opposite: hunched posture, neat polo tucked into khakis, and socks with sandals. A man who's prepared for a casual hike and an IRS audit. He offers a shy wave when we approach and immediately drops his phone trying to pick up his water glass.

And then there's Noah, clean-shaven in a soft flannel button-down, sitting upright with that easy sky-blue eye smile that makes my ribs feel like bubble wrap. He stands the second he sees me and pulls out a chair, ever the gentleman.

I melt a little. Not a full puddle. But enough to need a breath before I sit.

"Hey," he whispers softly, like it's just the two of us. "You look stunning and slightly happy to be here."

"I am happy to be here. I think." I adjust the strap on Harper's dress, pulling it higher up my shoulder, still in shock that I could squeeze into it. "Thank you."

Marin shuffles awkwardly into a seat next to Len, fidgeting for a moment before pressing her back into the wicker, like she's never used a chair before. It's obvious she has no idea what to do with her hands or eyes. Viv is practically vibrating out of her seat, but is, for the first time since she landed a few days ago, silent.

This moment is what I'd been dreading, and hoping to avoid by adding more people to the mix, but now I'm wondering if I exacerbated the awkwardness. We all stare at each other in silence, sipping our drinks.

Noah tries to bridge the silence with some kind of group opener. "So how do you all know each other?"

It's a soft ball, really. An innocent, friendly question. And it's the absolute wrong thing to say.

Viv sets down her glass and gives a sly grin. "Oh. We're part of a club."

Marin shakes her head, eyes darting around the room as though she's hoping to be rescued by the server asking if we'd like more wine. When the silence stretches for a few more uncomfortable seconds, she finally blurts out, "The Dead Husbands Society."

Marin's date, Len, pushes his glasses further up his nose, a very uncomfortable laugh leaving his lips. "The what?" He probably thinks he misheard.

Viv doubles down cheerfully. "The. Dead. Husbands. Society."

His laughter stalls in his throat. Viv's date leans forward like he's hoping for an explanation but also questioning the universe for leading him here. There's another thick beat of silence where we all look at our menus and pretend this is normal.

Noah's shoulders shake with a quiet laugh beside me.

I want to disappear. Or dissolve. Or hide under the table where our newly appointed grief mascot, Frank, would be snoring if he were allowed in public spaces.

"Should I be worried?" Len finally asks, one brow raised, probably wondering if we meet in graveyards.

"Only if you lie about your favorite color or try to explain cryptocurrency to me." Viv's eyes stay fixed on her menu, her face a perfect composition of seriousness, and I can see her date move a few visible inches closer to his corner of the table.

Noah's arm brushes mine, and I feel goosebumps radiating up my skin. "Is this how you introduce each other regularly?"

I glance at him sideways, trying to read if he's judging me or entertained. "Only on triple dates with complete strangers. We like to weed out the faint of heart."

He laughs, low and genuine. "Mission accomplished. So, who named the club?"

I pretend to study the drink list. "Um, well, it was a group effort."

He doesn't respond, and I can feel the weight of his stare while I keep my eyes fixed on the menu.

"Okay, fine. It was me."

The others break into side conversations, presumably about our society, while Noah leans toward me, voice low. "You haven't changed."

I raise an eyebrow, peering over the menu. "I've changed a lot."

"Maybe. On the outside. But that doesn't change who you are. I enjoy all the versions of you I've seen. It's just that introduction, the name of the club..." He laughs softly. "You've always had a thing for making people wildly uncomfortable."

I glance over at him, happy to see everyone else is still engaged in their own conversations. "That's a bold accusation."

"You once hosted a mock funeral for your goldfish. Owen gave the eulogy, and you made everyone walk a candlelit lap around the dorm."

"Oh God." I cringe, smiling despite myself. "You remember that?"

"I still remember the haiku you wrote about his 'brief but slippery life.'"

"Okay, in my defense, Gil was a fighter. He survived a week in a cracked tank, and I'm pretty sure he fought to become Lord of the Underworld Sewers after I flushed him down the toilet. And it wasn't *that* dramatic." I try my best to sound serious, knowing that my statement about Gil's life adds to the evidence that I can still be quite dramatic at times.

"You made Owen wear a thrifted suit and conduct the ceremony like a Methodist minister. You had a soundtrack. There were printed programs."

"It was performance art."

Noah takes a sip of his wine before pursing his lips together. "You made me build a casket out of stolen cafeteria trays."

I snort into my wine. "I was very theatrical in college. It was the bangs."

"Or the combat boots. You were a menace." He winks.

I nudge his leg with mine under the table, and Len startles in surprise and looks at me. Whoops. "You admitted to helping build the coffin, so don't pretend you were innocent."

"I wasn't." His voice is softer. Intentional. "Not then. Not now."

I glance at him, and suddenly the restaurant feels smaller. Quieter. His gaze lingers on mine like he's remembering all of it—me, Owen, the stupid fog machine I insisted on using for "atmosphere," the black umbrellas we handed out even though it wasn't raining. The laughter. The absolute absurdity.

And something about that memory, about us, then, makes

me feel like me again. Not a widow. Not a mom. Not a ghost haunting the aisles of Whole Foods. Just a person, still strange and still here.

"Thank you."

Noah raises his eyebrows. "For what?"

"For remembering the ridiculous stuff. For not looking at me like I'm broken."

He leans in, elbow brushing mine. "You're not broken, Birdie. You're just rebooting."

My stomach flips as a memory crashes over me, vivid and sudden. I'm twenty-eight years younger, back in the dim hallway of our college dorm a few minutes past midnight. Noah and I are whispering dares, stifling laughter, plotting our mission to rescue Owen's backpack, launched into the old oak tree after too many Jell-O shots and too few good ideas. I can still feel Noah's breath warm against my cheek, see the way his eyes flicked to my lips, how he looked at me like I hung the stars myself.

Something about the memory pulls at me.

I drop my hands and look at him, that soft, serious look in his eyes doing a number on my ribcage. For a moment, it's just us. Just me and Noah. In this weird little echo of who we were before life handed us all its losses.

But before I can analyze it, Marin lets out a delighted cackle across the table, something about her date misunderstanding the word "fermentation", and the moment snaps like a stretched rubber band. The spell breaks, but the warmth doesn't leave.

Noah leans back with a slow exhale, and I wonder if he feels it.

Len pulls out a laminated cheat sheet of dad jokes from his wallet (I swear), and Viv is already halfway into her wine while explaining to her date that she doesn't believe in monogamy unless it's with carbs. He nods in full agreement before launching into an enthusiastic discussion about her aura, and Marin starts explaining to her date why she no longer drinks things she can't pronounce.

Meanwhile, I pick up my wine glass and take a long sip,

because if this is what dating looks like in your 40s, I might need a bottle.

By the time our dessert arrives, we've polished off three bottles of wine and enjoyed learning about Len's latest dermatologist visit. I shove another bite of chocolate torte into my mouth and savor the way the tart raspberry coulis balances out the rich dark chocolate. It is utter perfection in a single bite. I must be making an embarrassingly blissed-out face, because Marin bumps me with her elbow, grinning.

"We need to use the bathroom." Viv grabs Marin's arm and hoists her up before shooting me a pointed look. "All of us."

I try not to look back wistfully at my little slice of chocolate heaven as Viv tugs us all toward the ladies' room. But the second the bathroom door closes behind us, I hiss, "You better have a fantastic reason to have pulled me away from dessert. It's the best thing I've tasted in years!"

"I pulled you in here to talk about dessert! That man out there is the final course. Not the cake."

"Okay, yes, dinner was lovely, but I don't want to ruin our friendship. Noah and Owen were friends for years, and we've been friends a long time. It might be better to keep it that way."

"Friends don't look at friends like they want to devour them like pieces of chocolate cake." Viv raises her eyebrows in pure skepticism before sashaying into the stall and closing the door.

The bathroom lighting is merciless. Too bright, too reflective, and far too honest. I try not to cringe as I touch up my lipstick, feeling like a woman who's acting half her age.

I tug at the straps of my dress, wishing it were a little looser. "Fine. There has been a bit of chemistry." I shudder; even using the word sounds ridiculous. "I feel like I'm seventeen again. Do I kiss him? Do I wave? Do I fist bump?"

Marin is dabbing her lip gloss on, looking very serious. "I think you should be polite. Maybe a hug. A respectable, non-romantic hug. Never a fist bump. I'm not even sure what that would even look like."

Viv emerges from the bathroom stall looking horrified. "If you hug him, I will take your phone and text him your pap smear results to spice things up. Kiss the man."

"Shouldn't he kiss me? Me kissing him seems much too forward. And maybe he likes being in the friend zone. He's been there for years. It's cozy. He probably has a stack of comic books in the corner and his favorite chair dialed in. It would be tragic to move him now."

"Girl. You have spent the last decade being appropriate. Let this be your Roman Empire moment. Make the first move. Kiss the damn mailman."

We all go quiet for a second.

Marin blinks.

I blink.

Viv lifts her chin before leading the charge back to the table.

"We've got it all covered, ladies." Len smiles, stuffing a card back into his wallet while Viv's date grumbles something about it being the 21st century and halfsies are an acceptable and even feminist choice to make.

Noah's waiting near the curb, one hand stuffed into the pocket of a worn Carhartt jacket, the other dragging along the back of his neck like he's trying to decide what his next move should be. You and me both, buddy.

"Can I drive you home?" He sounds almost sheepish.

I nod before I can overthink it. "Yeah. That'd be nice."

Behind me, the others are waving a final farewell. Viv mouths "Empire moment" and does a very committed hip thrust before Marin elbows her with surgical precision.

I pretend not to notice as Noah opens the passenger door for me, reminding me that some things never change.

Once I'm in and buckled, he slides behind the wheel and glances over, a half-smile playing at his lips.

He looks at Viv waving and smiling with some kind of "knowing" look on her face. "Your friends are subtle."

"Oh yeah," I deadpan. "They specialize in quiet dignity and zero public embarrassment."

He laughs, low and warm, before pulling his large pickup truck onto the road.

We drive in silence for a few seconds, just enough to make me hyper aware of everything: the heat in the car, the way his fingers drum lightly against the steering wheel, the smell of soap and something woodsy that's definitely not cologne but still unreasonably attractive.

"So." He glances sideways. "You survived your first group date."

"Barely." I fidget with the seatbelt strap, trying to look casual. "There was pre-game kombucha, that's what Harper said the kids are calling it these days. Marin ordered calamari and had no idea it was squid. I was emotionally unprepared."

"You didn't seem unprepared."

"I was bluffing. The key is to say 'hmm' a lot and pretend you've had squid before."

He grins and taps the turn signal. "I was impressed."

"Really?"

"You made three different men laugh. Not at the same time, but still, pretty solid odds."

I glance at him. "You keeping score?"

He shrugs, but there's a flicker in his eyes, something warm and a little... possessive?

"Maybe."

That one word is doing a lot of heavy lifting.

We stop at a red light, and he finally turns to fully look at me —a look that lingers.

"I like that dress. It reminds me of one you wore in college to the first frat party we went to. But I think you paired that one with Converse, not nude heels."

I exhale, a little too loudly, and look down at my lap because, apparently, it's fascinating. "You clean up nice too. I wasn't sure you owned anything that didn't say USPS on the chest."

He chuckles. "This is my off-duty look. For special occasions and mild flirtations."

My eyebrows lift. "Mild?"

"Well, I didn't want to overstep."

I meet his gaze again. His eyes are steady, playful, with something deeper simmering below.

"You're safe," I whisper. "I'll let you know when it's too much."

The light turns green. He doesn't move right away. Just watches me for a second longer. Then his hand tightens ever so slightly on the gear shift, and he accelerates, turning down my street.

Finally, he clears his throat. "I didn't expect to have this much fun tonight."

The words are simple. Sincere. A little reckless.

I don't know what to say, so I don't. I let it settle, warm and aching somewhere in my chest.

We pull into my driveway, the porch light casting everything in a soft glow. He shifts into park and kills the engine. Turning toward me, he drapes one hand over the steering wheel, the other resting near the console, inches from mine. "I'm glad you came out tonight. I've been wanting to see you outside of mailbox territory again ever since the block party."

I unfasten my seatbelt, and the click it makes is much too loud. "Well, you've officially seen me at my worst and medium-best now. Next stop: Costco, where I really shine." Reaching for my purse with one hand and the door handle with the other, I pause. "Thanks for tonight. For driving. For being good company."

He turns toward me again, his expression unreadable but focused.

"You want me to walk you to the door?"

I shake my head. "No. I mean, yes. I mean, I think if we stand too close, I might forget that I'm supposed to be sad."

Noah's grin falters. "And that would be bad?"

"Potentially. For my reputation. For the HOA."

He chuckles, but it's quieter now. He gets out of the truck and walks around to my door, opening it for me and offering his arm. I take it, and he laces his fingers with mine—warm, steady, a little hesitant.

As we head toward my porch, he says softly, "What if I'm a little afraid of forgetting too... but I still want to try?" He leans a little closer, and before I can process it, his fingers reach up and brush a loose strand of hair behind my ear. It's a small touch. Barely a touch.

But my body responds like it's everything.

And then, before my brain can shout *what are you doing*, I lean in.

Just slightly. Just enough.

He meets me halfway. "May I?"

My voice is a whisper. "Yes."

The kiss starts tentatively, testing my reaction. His lips are soft, careful, like he doesn't want to scare me off. But when I don't pull back, when I press in, enough to let him know I'm still here and I want this, his hand finds my jaw. His thumb brushes against my cheek, and something in me splinters open.

The kiss deepens, slow and hot and aching, like he's been thinking about this longer than he'll ever admit. Like he's memorizing it.

My fingers find the front of his jacket, searching for something to hold onto, something to tether me while my heart does gymnastics in my ribcage. He slants my chin higher, and his tongue gently brushes along my lips.

And then, too soon, he eases back. Gently. Reluctantly. As though it's the hardest thing he's had to do all night.

His forehead rests against mine for a breathless second before his voice cascades down my back, husky and broken. "I should probably go."

My whole body protests, but I nod. "Right. Yeah. Of course."

He lingers for a second longer, eyes searching mine, looking for a reason to stay.

God, I want to give him one. I want to reach out and say, *Come inside. Let me get lost in you. Make me forget, just for tonight.*

But grief is sticky. It clings to you even when no one's watching. And is it ever alright to forget the person you loved?

So I do what I've always done.

I smile. The same smile I've worn my whole adult life: Polite. Polished. Appropriate.

His gaze drops for half a second—like maybe he's carrying something too. Maybe he knows what it's like to want something and feel guilty for wanting it.

He opens the front door for me and steps back. "Goodnight, B."

And then he disappears into the night like some tortured rom-com antihero with excellent posture and self-control I deeply resent.

I sit there in the silence for a moment, pulse racing, lips still tingling, trying to remember how breathing works. I attempt a smile, pretending I'm calm and unbothered, not internally spiraling about what I did wrong or whether my lips taste like breadsticks.

I watch his taillights fade, feeling equal parts flushed and feral.

"Stupid perimenopause," I mutter, unlocking the door and stomping inside.

But even as I kick off my shoes and lean against the door, I know better.

This isn't hormones.

It's *him*.

And now I have a real problem. Because I want him to do it again.

But longer.

Without stopping.

Chapter Eighteen

"Grape Goodness or Guava Goddess?" Viv punctuates her question with the fizzy pop of a kombucha cap twisting loose. A jet of bubbles fizzes over the rim.

My kitchen looks like the party aisle at Party City had an emotional breakdown: glitter, catalogs, metallic fringe curtains, inflatable flamingos, and about four hundred sample napkins, most of which are either sequined or themed around being "over the hill."

"Is water still an option?" Marin eyes the bottle with the suspicion of someone about to lick a subway pole on a dare. "I'm not sure my intestines have recovered from the last round of this stuff."

"Girl, water was never an option," I half-whisper behind my hand as Viv waves two wine glasses in our direction.

"Is it supposed to sound like that?" Marin asks, wincing.

"Is it supposed to smell like that?" I wrinkle my nose.

"Yes," Viv declares, pouring with flair. "That's the sound of fermentation and gut magic. Don't question the gut magic."

"When you said you'd grab drinks, I thought you meant a classic bottle of red. You know, something with a cork. Not this fizzy foot juice. You sabotaged us with it last time, and I'm not falling for it again."

"Too much alcohol kills your liver and your aura," Viv says serenely. "Fine for a wild night or a steamy romance novel binge, but you can't live off the stuff. We're here to restore, not rot."

The three of us clink glasses. Marin sips.

Her face does things. Regret. Confusion. Possibly betrayal.

"Tastes more like vinegar than last time," she mumbles.

"That's the gut biome calling you to the dance floor." Viv's already half-finished with hers. "Bottoms up."

I raise my glass. "To Owen's fiftieth. And breaking every PTA rule in the handbook."

We clink with dramatic flair, like warriors before battle. My table is a war zone of party supply catalogues, glitter swatches, and a spreadsheet Marin made color-coded by *cheesiness level*. There's a sticky note stuck to Viv's sleeve that says *Confetti cannon? Tasteful?* One of Owen's old ball caps perches on the back of a chair, and it makes me feel like he's overseeing the entire circus. There's a notecard that reads "Piñata or fire dancer?" and another that says "YES TO BOTH" in Viv's handwriting.

"Okay." I pull up the catering site again. "So, we've narrowed it down to 'Sandwiches and Sips' or 'Nacho Explosion.'"

"I vote nacho." Viv takes another big swig of her drink. "Nobody cries with cheese in hand."

"Agreed." Marin's face pinches as she takes a reluctant sip of her drink. "Speaking of cheese, do you still have that brie in the fridge? It would, um, pair nicely with this grape situation."

She says "grape situation" like it's been court-ordered.

I try not to laugh. I've already caught her subtly trying to offer some to Frank, who sniffed it once and walked away like the bougiest stray ever.

Viv's off on a tear now, passionately defending her case for making a life-size cardboard cutout of Owen in his '90s karaoke glory.

"Or," Marin's voice is as dry as a cracker, "we could honor

him in a way that doesn't scream backyard haunted house meets dollar store memorial."

"Okay, first of all, rude." Viv flips her hair to emphasize her offense. "Second of all, it's what he would've wanted."

"How would you know? You've never met the man." Marin leans over to my potted fern, attempting to subtly pour her drink into it.

"I know his *soul*, Marin."

My phone pings. I glance down, expecting a text from Noah—maybe something flirty, maybe something about the piñata size he offered to handle (which, now that I say it, sounds inappropriate).

Instead, I see:

From: Jill

Subject: Re: Snack Roster

Hi Birdie,

I wanted to follow up on your email. A few of us read it and, well, we're a little worried. It didn't quite sound like you.

If you're feeling overwhelmed, please know it's okay to step back quietly. We've all been there. No need for dramatic declarations. Just take the time you need, and maybe avoid replying-all next time? 😊

We're all here if you ever want to talk through anything.

Wishing you peace and perspective,

Jill 🤍

I read it aloud. The "🤍" makes me want to throw my phone into the compost bin.

Marin snorts. "She means well."

Viv leans in. "She means be quiet and polite and please stop being publicly unhinged in front of the gluten-free cupcake moms."

"Oh, please." I set my drink down. "She's worried I'm

mentally unraveling because I finally said no to being the designated snack serf."

"I don't know." Marin sighs. "Sometimes I wish I could be that honest. Say the thing. Do the thing. Stop worrying what people will think."

Viv grins. "Then let's do it. Let's say the things we've never done because we were scared of being too much. Or not enough. Or offending the other cookie cutters out there."

"Viv." I hold my hand up in protest. "I am the other cookie cutter out there."

"Exactly." She winks. "Okay, I'll start. I've always wanted to pole dance. Not professionally. More recreationally. Like, climb it like a sexy fireman and spin dramatically."

Marin nearly chokes on her kombucha. "You want to become a Cirque du Soleil stripper?"

Viv smirks, unbothered. She shifts in her chair and crosses one leg over the other, swirling the last bit of her drink with intention. "I want to reclaim my core strength *and* my narrative, Marin. And one day I will float down from the ceiling wrapped in silk scarves, and you will *weep*."

Marin raises her cup in a mock salute. "Have you found a class near you?"

Viv shrugs, suddenly studying her nails. "Yes. But I haven't signed up. I've always chickened out."

Marin leans forward, propping her elbows on the table, her tone suddenly earnest. "Fine. Your grief dare is to find a class and sign up when you get home."

I blink. This is the first time Marin has dished out a dare. "You're giving dares now?"

"Yep. It's time for me to step up and join in. And I'm even giving myself one." She hesitates, watching the bubbles rise and settle. "I've always wanted to make an online dating profile."

I straighten at the same time I feel Viv turn her full attention to Marin.

She hesitates. "But I never did. I met Theo in college, and that was that. Then I blinked and it was twenty years and two kids later and now I'm a widow who's never even swiped on a stranger. And then I went on a date with Len, so can I really make a profile?"

Viv's mouth hangs open. "Marin! It was one date. You aren't exclusive!" She's already got her phone out. "Well, tonight is the night. We're building you a profile and you're going to fall in love with a decent man, or at least get a drink with someone who owns pants without drawstrings."

"I don't think I have any pictures that scream 'I'm ready to flirt.' Is this one okay?" Marin turns her phone toward us with the hopeful look of someone holding up a half-burned casserole.

Viv recoils. "Not unless your goal is to attract a serial killer who collects Civil War memorabilia."

"It was from my niece's graduation."

"You're wearing orthopedic sandals and holding a meat tray, Marin."

Marin huffs. "Well, I have other photos, somewhere."

Viv points dramatically toward the hallway. "You have five minutes to go change into something that says 'I might kiss you on a second date' instead of 'I teach Sunday school and my hobby is structured silence.'"

"I'll see what I can do." Marin disappears toward the guest room-slash-costume-closet with the resigned sigh of a woman about to make poor decisions in borrowed sequins.

Meanwhile, I'm back at my laptop, staring down the PTA queen's passive-aggressive email, clearly coated in shame. I crack my knuckles and start typing.

Subject: Re: Re: Snack Roster

Hi Jill,

Thank you for your concern. I'm touched that you're worried about my mental state after I dared to step away from napkin duty.

Please rest assured, I am doing well, but I will no longer be volunteering with the PTA. I wish you all the best with prom this year.

Warm regards,
Birdie

I read it aloud with the kind of pride typically reserved for standing up to homeowners associations or getting out of a timeshare.

Marin snorts from the other room. Viv pumps her fist in the air. "Hit send," she says, "for all the moms who've been emotionally blackmailed by the juice box mafia."

I do. And it feels like exhaling after holding my breath for years.

Marin reappears in one of Viv's old glitter tank tops and black jeans that somehow both fit and stun. Her hair's fluffed, her lips are glossed, and she looks alive.

"How's this?"

Viv clutches her chest. "You're a MILF with boundaries. You're a divorced Renaissance woman. You're a kombucha-fueled goddess of second chances."

"I'm a woman who borrowed a tank top from a friend who owns four crystals and an erotic candle shaped like Mr. Darcy."

"Potayto, potahto." Viv shrugs and starts snapping pictures. "Now give me brooding. Now give me accidental joy. Oh, look like you saw your high school ex, but you're hotter than ever."

Marin laughs, which turns out to be the best photo of the bunch.

Within minutes, Viv's got a profile built with an opening line that reads: *Recovering snack mom seeking man with sense of humor, respect for boundaries, and a working knowledge of composting.*

Viv's already swiping like it's an Olympic sport. "Okay, this one has a fish, so *nope*. This one's holding a baby tiger, either emotionally unstable or vacationing in Thailand in 2013. Pass."

Marin leans over. "What about that one?"

Viv zooms in. "He's holding a sword and calling himself a 'dragon of desire.'"

I squint at the screen. "That feels like something you pick up in a humid renaissance fair tent, not a life partner."

Marin laughs nervously and does her first real swipe. Right. Then another. And another.

"Okay, okay!" Her cheeks are pink, and she's beaming. "This one looks normal. He's got a beard, and I don't know, something about his flannel is speaking to my inner suburban lumberjack."

Viv nods solemnly. "That beard could solve at least two-thirds of your emotional issues."

"Swipe right," I call from the other side of the kitchen where I'm prepping popcorn.

"You should look at him, Birdie. He looks like he owns tools *and* listens when women talk."

"Popcorn calls and I believe you!"

We fall into a rhythm. Every profile comes with a mini roast session.

"Too many mirrors in the background. He lives at a gym."

"Is that a python? Swipe left before he invites you to his 'reptile room.'"

"Oh no. This one has a quote from *The Wolf of Wall Street*. Left, left, *LEFT*."

Marin claps her hands over her mouth and gasps.

"What?" I almost drop the popcorn seasoning, preparing to fight whatever intruder has broken into my kitchen.

"I think I matched with the hot flannel guy."

We crowd around the screen.

Viv squints. "Ohhh. He's hot *and* local. We love a responsible king."

Marin stares at her screen. "Do I message him? What do I say?"

Viv snatches the phone and types. "'Hey, what's your go-to comfort meal?' Boom. Flirty *and* practical."

She hits send before Marin can protest. And Marin stares frozen at the screen, a small smile pulling across her face. "Viv!"

"I accept your hatred and your future wedding invite," Viv replies.

My phone dings with an updated delivery notification, and I remember the party.

"Back to business, ladies. Owen's piñata isn't going to design itself."

We start tearing open glitter packets and paper fan decorations with renewed energy. Marin's still holding her phone gingerly between her fingers, but there's a little sparkle in her eye now. We mock up an invite with glitter borders, the phrase LET'S GET LIT (FOR OWEN) across the top, and a quote from Owen's favorite karaoke song in Comic Sans, because I'm still salty.

I click *send* on the invitations, and not two minutes later, my phone buzzes.

> Harper: Comic Sans? Are you trying to get exiled from society? You're lucky I love chaos.

> Also, this is the most unhinged invite I've ever seen.

> 10/10. Don't change a thing.

I lift my kombucha. "To dead husbands, dating apps, and glitter bombs."

Viv clinks her glass to mine. "And to you, Birdie. For finally telling off the snack mafia."

"Honestly." Marin raises her phone in a toast. "I think we're all a little wild tonight."

"Probably buzzed on probiotics," I mutter.

The phone pings on the kitchen counter, wedged between a

half-eaten granola bar and a crumpled grocery list that says "milk?" in three different handwritings.

I wipe my hands on my pajama pants and answer without checking the number.

"Hello?"

"Hi, may I speak with Birdie Lawson?"

My stomach drops. The voice is young and crisp, someone I don't recognize.

"This is her." I already regret my tone, which somehow comes out like I'm either answering a census or being interrogated.

"This is Callie from the Seattle Art Museum. I'm calling about your application for the Exhibition Curator Internship. We'd love to schedule an interview if you're still interested?"

Still interested? I choke on air.

"Oh! Yes! I'm very interested. Enthusiastic, even." I sound like I've never spoken to another human before.

"Great!" I can hear the smile in her voice, but she otherwise seems unfazed by my exuberance. "Does tomorrow at 10 AM work?"

"Absolutely."

"Wonderful, I'll email you the details shortly."

We hang up, and I stare at my phone, still not entirely sure I didn't just make up that whole conversation in my head.

Chapter Nineteen

Marin is upstairs doing what Viv calls "final date prep" and what I call "light panic grooming." Viv swore she had a foolproof plan—lip gloss, highlighter, and a touch of cleavage.

"We're going to manifest love through power lipstick and spiritual contouring." She's already pulling out a makeup bag the size of a carry-on.

Marin blinks. "Is that a real thing?"

Viv ignores her. "You've been cloaked in beige cardigans and widow energy for far too long. We're opening your aura with bronzer and unleashing your inner hot girl."

By the time she's done, Marin is barely recognizable. Fake lashes that won't stop peeling at the corners are pasted onto her eyelids, lip color that could stop traffic pops off her lips, and a flowy floral kimono is giving her a "mystical but accessible" vibe.

Marin tries to act cool, but the minute she attempts to leave, her sleeve gets caught in the doorframe.

"Jesus," she mutters, trying to wriggle free while also keeping her lashes intact.

Harper, naturally, is filming the entire thing on her phone from my bed.

"For posterity." She doesn't look up. "The masses demand it."

Marin finally yanks herself loose and spins, breathless and exasperated.

"I don't know how I feel about this outfit."

Viv beams. "You're welcome."

That's when it hits us—none of us actually know what this man looks like. Not really. Just a possibly altered profile picture where he's holding a golden retriever and standing in front of a suspiciously majestic mountain that may or may not be Photoshopped. He's also wearing a very flattering flannel, which frankly could be doing most of the heavy lifting.

"Birdie!" Viv hisses, eyes wide. "Go stand guard!"

I freeze mid-sip of my iced tea, lowering the glass slowly. "Why me? I'm the only one here who hasn't even seen the profile picture. How am I supposed to know if it's the same guy?"

"You've got great Mama Bear energy." Marin's already peeking through the blinds from my upstairs window like she's in a rom-com stakeout. "You'll feel it in your gut if he's a serial killer."

I stare at her. "That's so much pressure."

Viv waves a hand dismissively. "Trust your instincts. If your hackles go up, run."

Seeing I'm getting nowhere, I stand and can't resist muttering, "My hackles haven't been activated since 2009, but sure, let's roll the dice."

So I'm sent outside to "casually monitor the perimeter," which is how I end up crouched in a flower bed with no actual flowers, pretending to weed in the dark, like I'm part of a poorly budgeted spy movie.

It's not even a real flower bed. It's mostly bark mulch and a weed-blocking mesh that's holding on for dear life. There's nothing here to weed. I tug at invisible stems anyway, doing my best to look casual while blatantly staring at the road. If Marin's mystery date turns out to be a murderer, I will at least get a good look at his face first. That's friendship.

I glance at my phone. No messages. No sightings.

Inside, I can hear Viv coaching Marin through a second outfit change. Something about the first blouse being "too stepmom at curriculum night." I try not to laugh.

I've started talking myself down, telling myself this is all ridiculous, that serial killers don't want to drive for dates into idyllic suburban neighborhoods, when a silver Prius glides up to the curb.

I straighten up instinctively, brushing nonexistent dirt from my jeans. The Prius eases to a stop, and the door opens.

Out steps a man in a tucked-in polo shirt and khakis. He's holding a single rose and wearing an expression that's equal parts hopeful and terrified.

And then I see it. The bumper sticker.

Floss Like a Boss.

Oh. Oh no.

"Hi." His voice is warm, deep, and familiar. But it comes out all warbled, coated in nerves and an awkward smile. "I'm looking for Marin?"

I squint at him, stepping slightly closer. "Dr. Reynolds?"

He blinks, clearly surprised. "Birdie? Oh, right, the crown. No, cavity! Lower left molar. Number 18. Great enamel, by the way. What're you doing here?"

My mouth opens and closes, and I'm pretty sure I look like a confused goldfish. "You're here... for Marin?"

"Yeah, we matched on this dating app." He flushes, shifting from foot to foot, and I wonder if he's also nervous. "She said to pick her up here? I brought a flower. I didn't realize this was your house."

Just as my brain is short-circuiting with this new information, the front door creaks open.

Marin steps out, moving slowly. She's now wearing dark jeans, a soft blue button-down blouse that says "responsible citizen" more than "available bachelorette," and the unmistakable face of a woman who's nervous for a first date.

Viv follows her out, kombucha in one hand, popcorn in the

other. "You're welcome!" she calls out to Marin's date as if she's delivered her to a red carpet instead of my cracked concrete stoop.

Marin's eyes widen when she sees Dr. Reynolds.

Dr. Reynolds waves the rose with a hopeful little jiggle. "Hi again! I brought coupons."

"Of course you did," Marin murmurs.

And just when I think the scene can't get any more absurd, a familiar rumble echoes down the street.

Noah's truck.

Of all the times for him to show up.

His headlights spotlight the entire uncomfortable scene before Noah cuts the engine and steps out slowly, eyebrows already knitting as he surveys the situation. His gaze moves from me, still half-squatting in the mulch, to Dr. Reynolds with his flower and tucked-in optimism, then to Marin, and finally to Viv, who gives him a little wave like this is the most normal thing in the world.

"Everything okay?" His voice is low and careful.

Dr. Reynolds steps forward. "Hey! I'm picking up my date."

Noah's eyes snap to mine.

"Your date?"

"Not me. I'm not dating my dentist," I immediately protest.

"This isn't a date," Marin says at the same time.

We all blink at each other in the awkward silence.

Marin straightens up, shoulders back. "You know what? Fine. This is a date. I'm going to dinner. I'm going to talk about knitting, and apparently floss, and probably order dessert."

She walks toward Dr. Reynolds. He beams, clearly thrilled to be part of whatever this is.

Viv raises her kombucha. "A gentleman and a saver."

As they drive off I realize Noah hasn't moved. He's still standing at the curb, hands now tucked in his jacket pockets.

"I gotta say," he says, finally, with a crooked grin, "I didn't have 'dentist love triangle' on my bingo card for this year."

I cross my arms, heat blooming in my chest for no good reason. "It's not a love triangle."

"No?" His smile widens, slow and infuriating. "Because I could've sworn there was a bit of a swoon there."

I narrow my eyes. "You're jealous."

"I'm just saying, if I'd known your type was men in polos who come bearing floss-related pickup lines..."

I swat his arm. "Stop. He has a gentle touch. For root canals."

He laughs, and something soft flickers in his eyes before he's clearing his throat and stepping back.

"What brought you by anyhow?" I smooth my hair in an attempt to look casual and not like I've been half-crouched in a mulch bed pulling weeds that aren't even real.

He leans against the porch railing with all the nonchalance of a man who does this every Tuesday and is definitely not thrown off by the scene in my front yard or the dirt smudges on my face.

"Mrs. Stevens, three houses down, was convinced her CBD dog treats had been stolen. Panic attack incoming. Turned out, she misread the tracking info and they're not even out for delivery until tomorrow."

"That explains the siren of anxious barking I heard earlier."

"Yeah." He nods. "She was spiraling, so I dropped off a 'care package' of mint tea and melatonin dog biscuits to keep her from calling the mayor. Again."

"How civic of you."

"And then," he adds, narrowing his eyes at me, "as I was being the neighborhood emotional support human, I looked up and saw you crouched like a Navy SEAL in a flower bed that I know is bark mulch on top of a plastic Home Depot screen."

"This is espionage," I say with mock seriousness, gesturing at my gloves. "I'm surveilling a date in progress."

"Ah. Spycraft. Of course."

"High stakes. Very classified."

Before he can retort, Viv steps onto the porch dramatically, draping an arm across her stomach. "Birdie, darling, I hate to interrupt your leaf patrol, but I'm suddenly not feeling so great. A touch of the vapors. Possibly food poisoning. Or moon allergies."

Harper follows, gently rubbing Viv's back with all the sincerity of a kid who helped stage the crime scene. "She really doesn't look well. And Marin's out with your dentist, so I think I should stay home and nurse her back to health."

I turn, slowly, already feeling my eyebrows knit in suspicion.

"Viv, we both know you ate two slices of pineapple pizza and a mango sparkling water."

Viv puts a hand to her forehead. "And now I feel faint."

"Wasn't tonight the poetry reading? At that little art boutique you love so much?" Harper chimes in innocently. "Mom's been talking about it all week. But she can't go alone, right?"

I glare daggers at them both.

Noah straightens up, interested. "Poetry reading?"

Harper's eyes go wide with weaponized sweetness. "It's local. Downtown. Very cool, very angsty. She was so excited. I would hate for her to have to experience it by herself now that Viv is sick. Art and poetry truly pair beautifully together, you know."

"I can absolutely go al—"

"No," Harper cuts in brightly, placing a hand on my shoulder. "No one should go listen to sad poems by themselves. That's how people end up writing their own sad poems at a coffee shop while it rains."

Viv nods solemnly, still clutching her chest like she's seconds from swooning. "She needs a date."

My brain short-circuits for a second and then reboots mid-panic. "I'm sure Noah has far better things to do with his evening. Like saving more neighbors or reorganizing his spice rack alphabetically."

But Noah gives a slow, amused shrug. "Actually, I'm pretty free tonight."

I freeze. Like, full-body, statuary-level freeze. This was not on my dare docket for the week.

He smiles, the kind that feels like a challenge. "Let me go change, and I'll pick you up around eight?"

Before I can answer, Harper jumps in. "She'll be ready!"

Viv coughs delicately. "By eight-oh-five, max."

I'm still trying to form words as Viv yanks me by the elbow toward the porch, and Harper makes a show of waving goodbye.

Noah ambles off toward his truck, tossing a wink over his shoulder like he's got all the time in the world. Like this isn't a trap sprung by a meddling houseguest and a daughter with dangerous matchmaking tendencies.

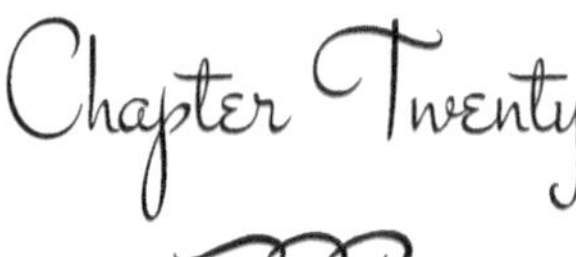

Chapter Twenty

I'm standing in front of the mirror, smudging liner under my eyes like I'm twenty again and about to fall in love to some pop song in someone's old Chevy. I haven't worn eyeliner this dark since Owen died. I haven't worn it on a date since, well, let's just say my mascara hasn't flirted in a very long time.

There's a knock at the door. Not a knock, exactly, a rhythmic tap, like someone trying not to seem eager but failing.

I glance at the clock. 8:00 PM on the dot.

Of course, Noah would be punctual. The man probably sets alarms to water his plants. In college, he used to show up to study groups five minutes early with color-coded notes and a mechanical pencil he referred to as "Old Reliable." Meanwhile, I once showed up to a final exam wearing two different shoes and a shirt that may have been inside out.

I think of my punctual self, showing up on time to everything wearing a piece from my beige, neutral, striped boring color-coded closet and wonder what happened to that version of myself.

I breathe in. Out. My house is actually quiet.

It hasn't been quiet like this in weeks, and I'm not sure how I feel about the familiar silence being back.

At least it won't be quiet for long. Matt texted me this morning to say he and one of his college teammates were coming to the big 50th bash this weekend. Which means I should probably hide the emotional support wine by Friday morning.

Viv, who made a miraculous and not-at-all-suspicious recovery the moment Noah left earlier, had insisted on overseeing my outfit like a deranged fashion fairy godmother. After rejecting seven potential tops for "lacking romantic tension," she'd poured me into a dark green wrap dress that "brought out my latent sex appeal." My hair was curled in loose waves that screamed *I woke up like this* (I did not), and a swipe of berry lipstick had been declared "powerful yet kissable."

I'd drawn the line at stilettos, opting instead for ankle boots that gave me enough height to fake confidence without risking a twisted ankle and a viral moment. I looked like someone who'd read *Eat Pray Love* twice but still paid her taxes on time. After a final nod of approval, she disappeared with Harper to "work on RSVP logistics" on the back patio. Translation: drink canned sangria and spy through the window like two underpaid P.I.s. They had a full night of espionage ahead of them with Marin due back from her date soon.

Now it's me and the ticking of the kitchen clock and the knowledge that my date is with someone who has known me since the era of Avril Lavigne and microwave ramen.

I do one last check in the entryway mirror. Not bad. The curls are keeping their form in my stick-straight hair. My mascara is doing the Lord's work. I give myself a firm nod and open the door.

Noah stands there in a navy button-down that fits his body like it was personally tailored by someone who specializes in sculpting forearms. The sleeves are rolled up the perfect amount to make me press my thighs together, Lord knows why. He's holding two to-go cups, and I swallow hard as I stare for much too long at the way his long fingers wrap around the drink.

"I brought caffeine." He holds them up. "Or poetry survival juice. Dealer's choice."

I laugh before I mean to. "I can't drink coffee after four. Not after I hit forty. But I appreciate you coming prepared."

"Good thing I brought an herbal tea back-up." He grins. "I remember college. I came emotionally prepared for a night of metaphor and regret."

"Metaphor and regret is the name of my memoir."

He chuckles, then leans in slightly, his arm brushing mine, and it's entirely unfair how fast my nerve endings notice. My skin is a traitor, a teenage traitor in a very uncool mom body.

"If I remember correctly," I lock the door behind me as we walk to his truck, "you used to drag Owen to those same poetry nights and then immediately undercut the vibe by trying to impress whatever girl you were dating with a hot take about modern verse being 'culturally overindulgent.'"

"I did not." He presses a hand to his chest, mock-offended.

"You said spoken word was just therapy with an audience."

He winces. "Okay, that one sounds familiar."

"And you said enjambment was an 'emotional crutch for people who don't believe in punctuation.'"

"Wow," he mutters, opening the passenger door for me. "I was kind of a tool."

"Oh, honey." I climb into the truck's cab. "You were a handsome tool. Which is why it worked."

He nods toward the center cupholders where another mug sits. "Your tea." He shuts the door, and I let myself grin at the sound of his footsteps rounding the front of the truck. I sip the chamomile. It has a touch of honey and is steaming hot, just how I like it. This whole thing feels absurd and charming and oddly normal, which is somehow even scarier than it being a total awkward disaster.

He gets in, starts the engine, and glances over at me with a smile that doesn't feel like a joke. Not a performance. Something soft and maybe slightly hopeful.

"Ready to enjoy poems about heartbreak and seasonal affective disorder with me?" I ask, tilting my head as I lock my seatbelt into place. "Nothing like existential dread echoing through a converted art gallery. Honestly, I might be more excited about the gallery walls than the open mic. Last time, they had this whole series on rusted bicycles and abandonment. It was incredible."

Noah shoots me a sideways smile, the kind that says he's both amused and mildly alarmed. "Define 'ready.' Are there snacks? A panic button? A safe word?"

"You could've said no, you know." I nudge him with my shoulder as he pulls out into traffic. "This was a volunteer mission."

He shrugs with exaggerated martyrdom. "Nah. I figured if I was going to spiral into existential dread, I might as well do it next to someone pretty."

I roll my eyes. "Charming. Is that on your dating profile?"

"First, how do you know about dating profiles? Should I be worried I have competition? Second, I don't have one."

My heart flutters at his worry over competition. "Oh, please. You once tried to impress a girl in college by quoting Death Cab for Cutie."

He gasps. "Low blow."

I grin, trying to hide it behind a sip of tea. "You're right. They weren't even your best sad-boy band."

Noah's eyes remain fixed to the road, his voice nonchalant. "So, if there's an open mic, will you be reading something from your emotionally-repressed college journals?"

"Absolutely not."

Noah gives a sad shake of his head. "Then it's not a real poetry night."

We move into downtown, and as Noah starts hunting for a parking spot, I lean back in the seat, already bracing myself for questionable rhymes, overzealous finger snapping, and the possibility that this night might mean more than either of us planned.

I haven't been to a poetry reading since college, and my heart is battling with my brain. I should be guilty, going to an event with another man. But lately, I'm tired of feeling guilty and sad.

The streetlights cast a warm glow in the truck's cab. The windows are cracked and there's no music, just the soft creak of old shocks and the occasional sigh of wind. I surprise myself by feeling a strange sense of calm. Like this isn't a date-date. Like I didn't spend an hour in front of the mirror, changing three times.

It's just Noah.

My friend, my husband's college roommate, our mailman, the man who pruned the butterfly garden.

The gentle smell of sandalwood and something else—soap or cedar or whatever scent they bottle to make you think men who fix trucks also read Virginia Woolf—makes me breathe deep, and wonder if Noah changed three times too.

We arrive at the poetry reading, and I pause just inside the doorway, drawn immediately to a large mixed-media piece, charcoal and fabric stitched across raw canvas, layered like it was trying to say something its creator couldn't quite put into words.

"God, I love when a piece feels unresolved," I murmur, half to myself, half to Noah. "Like it's still becoming."

He leans in, studying it with a furrowed brow. "Looks like a haunted quilt to me."

I laugh, and we move farther in. The gallery glows under the warm, uneven light of mismatched lamps and string lights draped across the ceiling in lazy zigzags. Someone's brought a tray of vegan brownies, and there's a self-serve tea bar labeled *Steep Your Feelings*. The room hums with people trying very hard to seem unfazed by metaphor—lots of dramatic scarves, purposeful eye contact, and the occasional aggressive snapping.

Noah surveys the crowd with a kind of fascinated horror. "I forgot that we don't clap. We snap. So this is where irony comes to die."

"It's been a long time since I've been a part of this world," I whisper, nudging him with my elbow. "It felt weird and wrong to go without Owen."

"Should I be worried?" he murmurs. "You look like you're one poem away from resurrecting your 'all pain is beauty' college phase."

I smirk. "Don't tempt me. I still have a spiral notebook somewhere full of poems about the color gray."

He shudders. "Did they rhyme?"

"Not even a little. It was all freeform despair. I wore a lot of turtlenecks."

He lifts his coffee cup in a solemn toast. "To your recovery."

I clink his cup. "To your survival."

We settle into two creaky folding chairs in the third row. The vibe is somewhere between open mic night and religious ceremony. Everyone looks ready to Feel Something.

The first poet is introduced as "Blaze."

Noah leans over and whispers, "That's either a first name or a threat. Wasn't that the name of a horse in a children's book?"

I choke on my tea. "Maybe. Or the name of a monster truck."

"Pretty sure it's a horse too."

I turn my head, fully prepared to argue that Blaze is a monster machine name, and he turns his head, presumably to argue his case. His eyebrow lifts. My lips twitch. It ends with my shoulders shaking in silent laughter while I pretend to sip the tea.

Blaze begins a poem titled "Soul Drain: An Ode to Late-Stage Capitalism." It is exactly as earnest and deeply felt as it sounds.

He compares Amazon to "a leech feeding on the marrow of our collective dreamscape."

Noah leans closer. "How many leech tattoos do you think he has?"

"Three. Minimum."

"Do they have names?"

"Oh, for sure. Envy. Greed. And Jeff Bezos."

He snorts. "You've still got it, you know."

I pretend not to notice the way his voice softens on the word *you*.

We spend the next few readers snickering into our sleeves,

pretending we're back in college, whispering behind the backs of more earnest souls. It's easy. Fun. Like muscle memory. Like we never stopped being whoever we used to be around each other, before we grew up and life changed and we remade ourselves.

Then the next poet steps up, and everything shifts.

She's older, maybe in her sixties, with soft gray curls tucked behind her ears and a worn flannel button-up over a flowing skirt. She grips the mic stand as though it's steadying her. Her voice is sandpaper smoothed by time.

There's no puff or pomp to her introduction. "For anyone who has ever outlived someone they loved."

Beside me, Noah stills. His arm brushes mine.

Her words are gentle but devastating. Grief as the echo left in your bones. Grief as the shape of someone who used to breathe beside you. Grief as a house you still live in, even after all the furniture is gone.

She talks about the way people stop saying their name. The way silence grows teeth. The way the world keeps turning like nothing broke.

By the third stanza, I'm crying.

Not a dramatic, cinematic cry. Just quiet, steady tears. My cheeks are wet. My breath comes uneven. My throat closes around something sharp and familiar. His name. Countless memories—the ones I've forgotten, the ones I'll never let go. A weight I've carried for so long, I stopped noticing how much it was crushing me.

I don't make a sound, but I feel Noah's hand move behind me, slow and tentative, resting gently on the back of my chair, then sliding to my shoulder.

Warm. Steady. Not pushing.

Just there.

I don't lean in.

But I don't pull away either.

When the poem ends, the room exhales with a single lung.

I do too.

Noah doesn't say anything at first. He watches me, his eyes soft and unreadable. He's letting it breathe, instead of trying to fix anything. Like he knows better than to offer words when none will do.

After a beat, he murmurs, "She reminded me of Owen's mom."

I glance at him, surprised.

"She used to write poetry." His eyes are fixed on the now-empty stage. "Mostly in her garden journal. After he died, I went to check on her. She handed me a bunch of notes tucked between seed packets. Little lines. Tiny griefs. Stuff about how he used to hum when he washed the dishes. How she'd give him a drink of water when he skinned his knee on his bike to distract him from how much it hurt. How no mother should have to outlive her child. It wrecked me."

I swallow. "I didn't know that."

He shrugs, the movement small. "You were carrying your own wreckage."

I stare at my hands, folded in my lap. "I think I still am."

"I know."

We sit in silence for a minute, surrounded by strangers who are all still pretending they didn't cry.

"I miss him." My voice cracks on the last word.

Noah nods. "Me too."

He leans closer, enough for his shoulder to press against mine. "He would've loved this night."

"He would've roasted Blaze within an inch of his life."

"And made us sit through the whole thing anyway and snap at the end. Out of respect."

I glance at him. "He always made you tag along with us, didn't he? He'd guilt-trip you into bad college poetry."

"I didn't go for him." His voice is so quiet, I almost don't hear his response. "I went for you."

I look at him then. Really look.

And that's when it hits me: this isn't new for him. This feeling. This care. He's been carrying it for years. Quietly. Without condition.

And I wonder how long he's known. How long he's waited without saying a word. Without needing anything from me but my presence.

My healing.

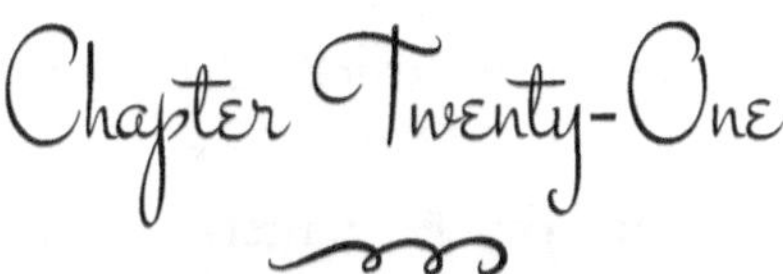

Chapter Twenty-One

The rest of the poetry reading passes in a blur.

I hear words, yes, snap judgments and metaphors about bees and moonlight and someone's extremely complicated feelings concerning their stepfather's saxophone, but none of them land. Not really.

All I can feel is the weight of Noah's hand on my shoulder. The press of his knee against mine. The echo of that poem ringing in my chest like it found something hollow and struck it just right.

When the last poet takes a bow and the crowd disperses toward the door, I stay in my seat for a beat longer.

"Ready?" Noah's hand is still on my shoulder, sending fire down my spine.

I nod, but I'm not. Not really. Not for whatever's buzzing under the surface.

We walk out into the night, cool air brushing against skin still flushed with leftover emotion. The streetlights hum. Someone down the block is playing jazz from a second-story window—a saxophone, weirdly enough.

Noah opens the car door for me, and I give him a look but slide in anyway.

The ride home is quiet, but not awkward. It's charged. Like

something alive is pacing between us. He drums his fingers on the steering wheel at red lights, and I watch his profile, how his jaw tightens, how his throat bobs when he swallows hard.

I wonder if he's going to say something.

When we pull into my driveway, neither of us moves.

He kills the engine, but the truck still ticks faintly.

"You okay?"

"Yeah." I clear my throat, acutely aware of the warmth pooling between my legs and the guilt pooling in my chest. "It's just—"

"I know."

A pause. A breath.

"Noah."

He turns to me.

"Do you want to come in?"

Something flickers in his expression. Hunger, maybe. Or relief.

But he still doesn't move.

So I do.

I lean in, slow. Measured. Until our faces are inches apart. I can smell the faint trace of his cologne, clean, warm, familiar. He closes the distance with a quiet sound, not quite a groan, not quite a sigh. Just need, barely contained.

The kiss starts soft. Like the one on my front step all those weeks ago, tentative, reverent.

But then it changes.

He cups my face with both hands and deepens it, like he's been holding this in for years and finally has permission to want out loud.

And I let him.

Because I want it too.

God, I want it too.

We barely make it to the front door. My keys fumble in the lock. He's behind me, hands at my waist, lips at my neck. I gasp, the sound catching somewhere between a moan and a laugh.

By the time the door swings open, we're already tangled up in each other.

He kicks it shut behind us, and I stumble backward, pulling him with me, both of us breathless with something half-wild.

That's when I see it.

A note on the counter written in Viv's aggressive cursive:

We're staying at Harper's friend's house tonight (in case things escalate).

Marin's neat, tidy block letters follow in smaller letters:

(Viv means we're getting a younger generation's perspective on party details. And can't wait to hear how your date went and share details about mine. Hint: he's dreamy.)

There's a drawing of a condom wearing a glitter hat in the corner of the note.

Of course there is.

Noah picks it up, reads silently, and lets out a low chuckle that sends goosebumps dancing up my spine. He sets his keys beside it with a little clink. "Well. That's not subtle."

I shrug, trying to look unbothered. "I have very supportive friends." Then I lean in toward him, rising slightly on my tiptoes, practically begging for his lips to send fire through my veins again.

But he doesn't meet me.

Instead, he steps back, eyes lingering on my face.

A shadow flickers across his features—hesitation, guilt, something heavier than just nerves. And I wonder if he's weighing what this means not just for us, but for the memory of someone else.

"How are you?" His voice is low, sincere. "After the poem."

I blink, thrown for a second by the tenderness.

"It felt like someone opened a window in my chest." I try not to elaborate, because I'm not sure what to say, and I don't want this newfound feeling of desire to end with a long talk over chamomile tea, grief, and poetry. "And everything flew out."

He nods, seeming to know exactly what I mean. "It was beautiful. Hard. Honest." His jaw tenses. "He was my best friend." His voice is soft, and I wonder if the words are slipping out without permission.

"Me too."

I squirm a little in the silence, under the weight of his stare.

Then, finally, he says it.

"I've wanted this for longer than I should," he murmurs, his voice thick with conflict. "But I never wanted to be the reason you moved on. Or the thing you regretted."

My heart stumbles over itself. "I don't know what I'm ready for," I whisper. "But I want this. I want tonight."

"Are you sure?" His eyes bore into me, intense and searching.

"Yes."

That's all it takes.

He's kissing me again, hungrier now. Like he's been starving for this.

His hands slide down my back, anchoring me to him. My fingers dig into his hair, pulling him closer, needing something I can't name. We fumble toward the couch, bumping into furniture, laughing breathlessly between kisses that grow deeper, more desperate.

He leans over me, weight balanced on his forearms, and brushes my hair back from my face with a gentleness that steals my breath.

Then he says it, barely audible, his lips ghosting my cheek:

"I can't believe this is actually happening. After all this time."

I freeze. Just for a second.

"What did you—?"

But I don't get the whole question out.

Because he's kissing me again—slow, open-mouthed, full of fire and something heavier, and whatever part of me registered his words can't seem to process them anymore. Not when his hands are on my waist, moving up toward my aching breasts. Not when his mouth trails down my neck like a prayer.

My skin is hot. My pulse, a drumbeat in my ears. And I can't think past this moment.

I don't know what this is yet. Or what it means. Or how we get from here to whatever might come next.

But I know this:

I'm not alone.

I'm not numb.

And for the first time in a very long time, I don't want to stop feeling.

Not with him.

Not tonight.

We stumble down the hallway, drunk on each other.

My back hits the wall with a soft thud, and his mouth is on mine again before I can gasp. His hands are everywhere, my waist, the small of my back, the curve of my hip. I arch into him, hungry and half-unraveled.

We make it to the bedroom, leaving Noah's jeans somewhere lost on the stairs. The bedroom door barely closes behind us before I'm yanking at the buttons on his shirt, cursing softly when I fumble the middle one. He covers my hands with his, stilling them.

"Hey." His voice is thick with need, rough and gasping. "We've got time."

Something in my chest pinches, like he reminded me I deserve not to be rushed.

So I slow down.

We undress each other the way people do when it means something. When the fabric is less an obstacle and more a ceremony. When every layer removed feels like revealing a story.

I hesitate as he peels the green wrap dress from around my

body, every muscle tight with the instinct to cover up. The light feels too honest, too unforgiving. I've spent years learning how to dress around my body, how to flatter, distract, conceal. I never learned how to simply *be* in it.

But then he looks at me.

Really looks.

When he sees me, there's no flinch, no pause. Just reverence. His mouth trails kisses over my stretch marks like they're constellations, his hands mapping all the soft parts I've spent years trying to fix with pilates or hide beneath PTA-appropriate blouses. He kisses my stomach like it's sacred. He touches the hollow beneath my ribs like it's a secret only he's allowed to know.

My breath hitches.

"You're killing me," I whisper.

He looks up and murmurs, "Good."

When he peels off my bra, he stares before taking a breath, the sight of me seeming to undo him in some fundamental way.

"God, you're beautiful, B."

His voice is husky, low, and under his gaze, I feel seen. And not the kind of seen where someone says you're pretty to be polite, but the kind where their voice catches and their eyes darken and you feel worshipped, a little.

We fall into bed in a tangle of limbs and laughter, our kisses growing deeper, hungrier, until there's nothing left between us but skin and heat. His hands move over me, memorizing me, knowing every inch of me before he claims it.

Then he slides one hand between my thighs, his touch slow and deliberate, coaxing my body open with gentle strokes that make my breath catch. He watches me the whole time, his gaze dark, focused, reverent. My pleasure is a prayer he's committed to answering.

Each movement builds on the last, and soon I'm arching into him, my thighs trembling, my fingers curled into the sheets. My voice breaks on a plea, low, desperate, honest.

"Please. I need you."

He doesn't tease. Doesn't make me wait.

Instead, he leans in close, brushing his mouth against my jaw as he murmurs, "You have me."

And then he pushes inside, slow and steady, filling me completely.

As he enters me, he exhales my name, a deep moan that feels as if it's been lodged in his throat for years.

And when I finally let go, of the fear, of the past, of everything that's kept me frozen, his name is the first thing I say too.

My hands are on his back, tracing the shape of him, relishing in the rise and fall of muscle. His mouth finds my neck, my collarbone, the soft dip of skin between my ribs and hip.

"You okay?" he murmurs.

I nod, throat too thick for words. "More than okay."

He moves slow. Anchored. Like he wants me to feel every second of this.

And I do.

It's not fireworks and moans and drama. It's breath and sweat and skin and knowing. It's me whispering his name like a secret I've remembered. It's him telling me I'm beautiful with his mouth on my jaw and his hands on my hips until I'm tightening around him and he's pulsing inside me.

Later, when the air is thick with sleep and we're bare limbs and tangled sheets, he runs his hand lazily over my side, his fingers whispering along the curve of me.

"Was this weird?" I murmur into his chest.

He presses a kiss to the top of my head, his lips soft against my hair. "I hope not."

I let out a quiet laugh, one that catches in my throat.

Somewhere in the back of my mind, I know I'm supposed to feel guilty. Like I've crossed some line I promised not to.

But all I feel is warm. Anchored. Alive.

And this time, I don't apologize for it.

Not to him.

Not even to myself.

Chapter Twenty-Two

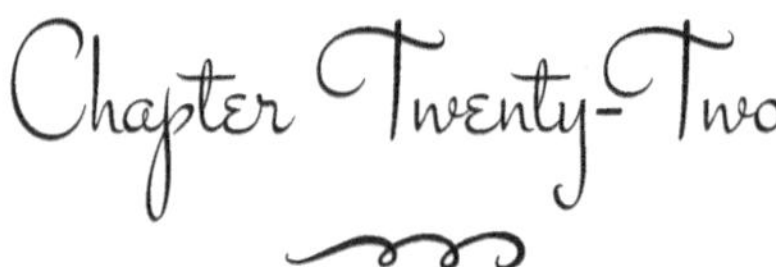

"Birdie! Time to rise and shine!" Viv's voice bounces down the hallway, her voice all cheer and singsongy.

I jolt awake, nearly rolling off the bed, my arm flailing until I manage to smack myself in the face. Elegant. I groan as consciousness sets in and I realize three very concerning things in quick succession:

1. My mouth is glued shut by my own dried drool.
2. The beachy, care-free curls I went to sleep with abandoned me overnight and now hang like limp linguine against my forehead.
3. Noah.

Noah's still here.

Sprawled gloriously across the mattress like a Roman god slumming it in suburbia. He's on Owen's side of the bed, because of course he is, and he's shirtless, the sheet barely covering enough to keep this scene PG-13. His dark hair is mussed, his body warm and solid, and I hate how much I want to crawl back under the covers and continue doing what we did last night.

I also hate that I'm about five seconds from being caught by my friends with a literal mailman in my bed.

"Um, hang on!" I shout toward the door, scrambling like a raccoon caught in kitchen lights. I smack Noah's bare back with pure urgency. "Get up."

He groans, groggy and infuriatingly unconcerned. "What's going on?" His voice is thick with sleep, and there's a dreamy little smile on his face.

"I forgot to have you sneak out before the crack of dawn," I hiss, yanking the sheet off him and tossing it toward my feet. "Viv and Marin and Harper are back, and if they see you here, I'll have to explain, and I'm not sure I'm ready to explain."

I blink at him, taking in the warm, gloriously male shape taking up Owen's side of the bed, which feels both symbolic and mildly sacrilegious, and my stomach does a weird lurch. Guilt, lust, panic, maybe gas. Too early to tell.

"Shit, shit, shit," I whisper, scrambling to untangle myself from the sheets. "You weren't supposed to still be here."

Noah groans and rolls onto his stomach. "So? Didn't we already establish they're fine with this? It's not like we're teenagers and I left my boots on the porch for your parents to find."

"So?" I throw on my T-shirt and gesture wildly. "There's a picture of my dead husband staring at us from the nightstand, and you're lying there like you own this bed. I'm emotionally compromised, Noah."

He pushes himself up on one elbow. "Birdie—"

"I haven't moved that picture since the funeral," I snap. "I'm not ready to explain what this is or how I feel about any of it, because the truth is—I don't know. I just know it's too soon to be caught with you in Owen's spot. And I don't want to hash it out with them over scones and kombucha."

The hallway creaks.

"Window. Now."

Noah blinks. "It's the second floor."

"You deliver mail. You climb porch steps for a living. You can handle one measly trellis."

"Again, I thought they were fine with this?"

"Yes." I pull on yesterday's T-shirt and try to flatten my hair with the palm of my hand. "But they've been fine with a lot of things lately, and I haven't had coffee yet, and I'm not awake enough to deal with Viv's face when she walks in here and sees you half-naked in Owen's bed."

He frowns, finally sitting up. "It's your bed."

I pull my hair into something that might resemble a ponytail in certain lighting. "It is and it isn't. I'm not—God—I'm not ready to have a post-hookup brunch while my dead husband's toothbrush is still in the drawer."

Noah sits up, rubbing his face. "B…"

"I like you." I press my palms into my eyes. "And that's the problem. It felt good. Too good. And I'm scared that if I let it keep feeling good, I won't have room for the grief anymore. I'm scared that if you stay for coffee, Owen will disappear completely."

A beat passes.

Then, he places a gentle hand on my back. "Take a breath. You're okay. This was a big step. It's grief, and it's normal. But he's not disappearing."

I flinch like he's touched an open wound.

"Don't—" I pull away, wrapping the sheet around myself like armor. "Don't try to make this neat. It's not normal. It's not okay. I woke up with you in his spot, Noah, and I couldn't breathe."

He's quiet for a long moment. Then he exhales through his nose and scrubs a hand through his hair. "I know. Believe me, I know."

He stands, gathers his clothes in one hand like they're shame made cotton, and walks to the window with a stiff sort of grace.

"You're not cheating on your grief, B." He's not looking at me. "You're surviving it."

"Don't do that," I snap. "Don't give me permission to feel

better. Don't offer some bumper sticker wisdom and pretend this doesn't change everything."

He turns, finally. His eyes are tired, and there's something raw in his voice now. "You think I don't feel guilty about it? He was my best friend. He trusted me."

"And I was his wife."

The words slice through the room, and for a second, neither of us moves. The morning light turns everything soft and golden, and I hate how beautiful it is in here. Clearly, the world should pause while I try to untangle what the hell I've done.

Noah swallows hard. "I know."

"No, you don't." My voice is barely more than a whisper. "You can't. Because if you did, you wouldn't be standing there looking like you want me to say it was okay."

His jaw tightens. "I don't want you to say it was okay. I wasn't supposed to fall in love with you." He presses a hand to the windowsill. "I was supposed to protect you. That's what you do with your best friend's girl, right? You keep her safe. You hold the line. And instead... I crossed it."

Silence. It roars between us.

"I didn't mean for this to happen," he adds, almost to himself. "But that doesn't make it better."

Viv's footsteps are coming down the hall now. "Window."

Noah stares down at the dew-slicked roofing. "No."

"Yes," I whisper-shout. "You're going out the window. If you hurry, you can sneak down the trellis and be halfway over the yard before she makes it to the door."

"I'm not a squirrel, B."

"No, but you are a man with an incredible ass and no pants. One who was born to go down this trellis to save me from having to explain to my daughter why her mother is having sex in her dead dad's bed with the mailman."

That gets him moving. He shoves both feet through his boxers, before stuffing his arms into the shirt discarded on the floor. After searching for a few more seconds, he whispers, "I can't find my pants."

"Do it without pants."

He raises both his eyebrows, gripping the window's edge with mild suspicion. "This feels dangerous."

"You bike in traffic for fun."

"I also wear a helmet."

"Great, next time, I'll leave one by the window."

As he starts inching his way onto the roof like an overgrown cat burglar, I scramble to gather the only sock I can find, tossing it out the window like a dramatic ex in a romantic comedy.

Noah's head pokes back through the window. "This is ridiculous."

"Noah," I beg, "Please."

He sighs, but I watch him inch his way further out onto the roof, the dew-slick shingles gleaming in the early morning light.

That's when I hear it, the unmistakable bark of Frank losing his mind on the back porch.

I rush to the window in time to see Marin and Harper standing on our back porch below, coffee mugs in hand, staring straight up at Noah mid-treacherous descent.

They say nothing.

Just blinking. Watching. Like spectators at a weird, sad Cirque du Soleil performance.

Noah looks down. "Morning."

Marin raises a hand in an awkward half-wave. Harper sips her coffee slowly, then murmurs, "Bold strategy."

Frank is barking so hard he's spinning in circles.

Noah loses his footing slightly, flails, grabs the gutter. I yelp. Viv barrels into the room behind me.

"Good morning, gorgeous!"

Viv is in full performance mode, holding a steaming mug of coffee. She doesn't even turn her eyes toward the open window or the unmistakable thump, followed by an "ow" with a casual "I'm fine!" tacked on at the end.

"I want to hear everything about how it went last night."

Before I can physically shove her out or pull the comforter over my shame, she strolls right to the window and removes something from behind her back.

Is that—

Oh, God.

It's Noah's jeans.

"You forgot your dignity! Want me to toss it down with your pants?" Viv sing-songs as she flings the denim projectile out the window.

"It's a shame to cover up such a fine specimen," she calls after him, "but we can't have the HOA getting involved."

"Uh, thank you," Noah's voice rings through the window.

Viv sips her coffee. "Next time, leave a tip on the nightstand and call it even."

I groan and cover my face with both hands.

Viv sits down on the bed beside me, resting a hand on my shoulder. "Don't worry, honey. The first pancake is always a little messy."

Chapter Twenty-Three

Why, why, did I pick last night of all nights to have sex for the first time in two years? And not just sex. Sex with someone who isn't Owen. Sex with his best friend.

Yep. I'm going to widow hell.

What was I thinking?

I cannot do an interview today. My body is still confused, and my brain feels like it's been lightly scrambled. I should cancel. Would it be rude to back out with only two hours' notice?

I can already hear Viv's voice in my head lecturing me about self-sabotage and my dare: Don't talk yourself out of the interview.

I've changed my outfit four times. First, a blazer that made me look like I manage a dental office. Then a dress I wore to a PTA fundraiser last year. Then a floral blouse that whispered "Pinterest mom," followed by the same floral blouse with a black cardigan to tone down the whisper. Now I've settled on a pair of high-waisted black, dress pants that may or may not be back in style, a tucked-in boat neck top that keeps trying to untuck itself, and a pair of nude pumps.

I stare in the mirror. I look like a woman who is trying really, really hard not to look like she hasn't worked in two decades.

Viv pops her head in the bedroom door. "You good?"

"Nope."

Marin's head pops in under Viv's. "Too bad. You're gonna be great."

I pull at the hem of my top. "You don't think this screams 'please give me a job, I swear I'm still relevant'?"

"Nope." Marin shakes her head. "But even if it does, you are. Now go. Be dazzling."

"Do I look like I know how to use Google Docs? Is that even something you can convey with an outfit?" I'm panicking, and Viv sees it.

Crossing the room, Viv rests her hand on my arm. "Woman, you survived the PTA elections in 2009 and the HOA statue debacle in 2012. You could take Google in a cage match."

Then Viv reaches down to lift my leather briefcase. Technically Owen's lucky leather briefcase, the one I found in the back of the closet and tried very hard not to cry over.

"Good God, what do you have in here? A small anvil?"

"Just the essentials." I straighten my blazer. "A few copies of my résumé, backup hairbrush, gum, tissues, granola bars."

Viv sets the case on the bed and pops it open with the suspicion of someone diffusing a bomb.

"A few résumés?" She rifles through the stack. "Birdie, there have to be at least twenty in here. Are you planning to hand them out to tourists on your way through the lobby?"

She pulls something else out: two enamel pins.

One says, "Van Gogh Hard or Go Home."

The other: "I Was Framed!" with a tiny gilded frame illustration.

She holds them up like she's caught me trying to smuggle contraband.

"Birdie. Please tell me you were not going to pin one to each boob and stroll into your interview like a walking Etsy cart."

"No..." I stretch out the word because that's exactly what I was going to do. "They're for luck."

Viv narrows her eyes. "How about they stay here for luck, far, far away from your top."

She sets them gently on the dresser and buckles the case shut.

I smooth my pants, glance at the mirror, and give myself a shaky nod before heading towards the door.

Right before I push out into the hall, my hand stills on the doorknob. "I got this?"

"No question. You got this."

Viv and Marin both raise their fists triumphantly at me.

Yep. I got this.

Right as I pump myself up enough to walk out the door, Viv calls, "Don't you think that we've forgotten about this morning! Once the interview is over, we want all the details. And I do mean *all* of them!"

I'm ten minutes early, which feels both responsible and tragic. I've been sitting in the lobby trying to pretend I'm not sweating through my teal blue shirt. The museum is all sleek lines and clean light. Everyone passing by looks like they've never spilled coffee on themselves. Or cried in the Target parking lot.

I'm led into a conference room with big windows and mid-century chairs, and I try not to feel like I'm deflating as I lower myself into its embrace. A young woman rocking a cropped green blazer and a chic blonde bob greets me with a smile. Callie, the program coordinator, I think. She's wearing loafers without socks, which feels bold.

Next to her is an older man with a beard that says "jazz playlist" and a sweater vest that makes me miss Owen in the worst way.

"Thanks so much for coming in, Birdie." Callie nods. "This is Greg. He's one of our art exhibition curators and will be sitting in on our interview."

"Wonderful. Pleasure to meet you both." I put on my

sunniest smile, even though my mouth is dry and I'm fairly certain my voice is doing something weird and squeaky.

"So, tell us what drew you to apply for this internship."

I take a breath, mentally reciting all the answers I'd prepared.

"Well. I majored in art history. Years ago, I actually dreamed about working here, at SAM, back in college."

They nod, so I keep rattling off my script.

"I used to imagine myself writing the little wall placards next to the exhibits and pretending I knew everything about 18th-century brushwork. It was a fantasy version of me."

Wait, that last bit wasn't on script. What am I doing?

"Then I got married. And pregnant. Not necessarily in that order. And I blinked and twenty-something years went by in a blur of juice boxes and paper mâché volcanoes."

Now we're entirely off script, and I'm having a weird out-of-body experience where I can't seem to get my mouth to stop moving.

"And then my husband died. Which is not what this interview is about, I promise, but it sort of cracked my life open. And I'm trying to figure out who I am now. I mean, I know who I was. I was excellent at running PTA fundraisers. And crafting center-pieces. And convincing local businesses to donate baskets for silent auctions. I can also plan an event on a dime, set up a gallery wall with no budget, and redirect a room of sugar-high children without crying."

What happened to sticking with the basics? Nope. Here's the highlight reel of my personal life.

Callie is writing something down, which somehow makes me more nervous, and when no one answers for half a second, my nerves go into overdrive, so I keep talking. The rational part of my brain is holding up a large stop sign and dramatically falling to its knees going, "why?"

"I guess what I'm saying is, I may not know all the right terms anymore. Or be fluent in Excel. But I know how to tell a story. I know how to make people care about things. And I know what it's like to love art so much it kind of saves you."

Callie's smile softens. Greg leans forward.

"On your resume here, I see you mention you run a grief support group?"

"Yes." I straighten up. Why did Viv insist I add that? "It's, um, small. Informal. We call it the Dead Husbands Society." Greg's eyebrows shoot up. Stop talking. Stop talking. "Terrible name, I know. But it's kind of become this sacred space. For women to be messy and honest and lost together. We started challenging each other to reclaim our lives with these weekly dares."

Callie looks up from her notes. "You know, curating isn't only about the art. It's about framing a story people can step into. Making them feel something. What you described, that's the heart of exhibition work."

I blink. "Oh."

"I mean it. It's important to bring life experiences and perspective. It's something we don't always see enough of in candidates. You've lived quite a bit of life. That matters here."

Greg nods. "There really is no substitute for life."

I nod too, mostly to stop myself from crying.

They shift in their chairs, smiling politely, then Callie leans forward. "Okay, a few rapid-fire questions, if that's alright?"

"Only if I can give half-thought answers," I try for a joke, and Greg smiles again.

"What's your favorite art period and why?"

"If I had to choose? Late 19th-century Impressionism. The women were finally painting the inside of life—the domestic, the quiet, the overlooked. Mary Cassatt made me feel seen before I even knew I needed that."

They nod, and Greg adjusts his tortoiseshell glasses before scribbling something down on his own notes.

"What would you do if we gave you a weekend pop-up gallery to highlight local artists?"

"I'd turn it into a community night." I don't hesitate. "Local wine, coffee, cheese, and chocolates, local musicians, maybe a kids' table with coloring pages of the art on display. I want people to feel like art is for them, not something they have to whisper around."

"Love that." Callie smiles.

The rest of the interview is a blur of questions and what I'm convinced are awkward answers. At one point, I'm pretty sure I hummed my response.

There's a beat of silence. "Thanks for coming in, Birdie. We'll be in touch."

I nod, grip Owen's lucky briefcase a little tighter, shake each of their hands, and beeline toward the door.

By the time I leave, I'm convinced I bombed it. I made a weird joke about hashtags, overshared about my obsession with symmetrical desk setups, and probably came off like a walking Pinterest board with anxiety issues. I even admitted I can't focus if my office chair isn't perfectly centered on the rug. I probably talked too much about dead husbands.

Still, I was real and candid.

That's new.

I'm halfway through stress-eating popcorn and dissecting every awkward thing I said (Why did I bring up the importance of a good leavening agent in cupcakes? Why did I say 'moons ago' like I'm a Middle Ages wizard?) when the phone rings.

Unknown number.

I freeze.

"Hello?"

"Hi, Birdie? This is Callie from the Seattle Art Museum again."

My heart dives straight into my stomach.

"We'd love to offer you the internship position, if you're still interested."

There's a pause.

I forget how to speak.

"Birdie?"

"I'm here," I finally manage to squeeze out past the lump of emotions in my throat. "I really gave it my all."

"We know and we loved you. Your experience, your presence, your humor, it's exactly what we're looking for. You're going to be an incredible addition to the team."

I blink back tears.

"Thank you," I whisper. "Thank you so much."

"You'll be receiving an email in the next few days with details about your start day, hours for the week, and an orientation. Do you have any questions I can answer for you?"

Viv walks in mid-call, sees my face, and mouths, "Well?"

I nod, unable to speak.

She lets out a whoop loud enough to shake the spice rack.

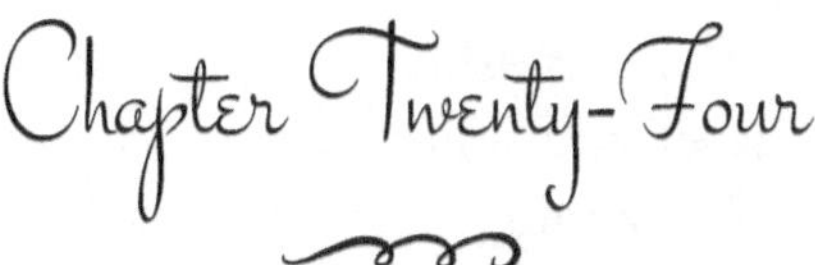

Chapter Twenty-Four

There's glitter on the ceiling.

How it got there, I don't know. But it shimmers at me like a disco ball as I teeter on a chair with a roll of crepe paper in one hand and a half-empty glass of kombucha in the other. I'm not going to lie... It's grown on me, but I can't let Viv know that. If I admit to it, I won't have any excuse not to have her drag me off to an early morning goat yoga class.

Somewhere behind me, Viv's arguing with Harper about whether the balloon arch is "whimsically festive" or "a desperate attempt to outrun mortality with latex."

Marin's laughing, actually laughing, which feels like a minor miracle considering how few times I've heard her let go and allow a smile to slip through her tough exterior the past few months.

"It looks great, Mom!" Harper's arms are crossed, and her critical eye is scanning the living room like she's judging a baking competition and I'm the sad, undercooked scone. "I think between the backyard and the abundance of glitter and the karaoke machine, it's going to be the party of the year."

I add another piece of tape to the balloon arch. "Are you only saying that so I don't cry?"

She shrugs. "Yeah, but also it looks great. Like, impressively not tragic."

I hop down from the chair and nearly take out the huge "50th" piñata hanging from my ceiling fan with my face.

"Your glue gun work is really improving." Viv nods toward the banner that Marin finished hanging. "You're only mildly hazardous to yourself and others now." Then she side eyes my mostly empty glass of kombucha. "Dare I say you liked the cranberry flavor?"

I try to shove the glass behind my back. "I admit nothing."

Marin flops dramatically onto the couch, giggling like a teenager as she pulls her constantly dinging phone out of her pocket.

"So, Marin, three dates in three days. Things must be going well?" I flop down on the armchair beside her.

"When are we going to get the details of what's happening with Mr. Floss Boss?" Viv wiggles onto the end of the couch, shuffling so her lap's under Marin's feet.

Marin throws a pillow over her face. "It's been good? Weird? He told me I have good looking tonsils," Marin mumbles from under the pillow. "Which was surprisingly sexier than one might think because the kiss that followed was perfection."

Viv cackles. "Honestly, I'd take nice tonsils. Some guy at the grocery store told me I had 'heart stopping earlobes.'"

"Resilient enamel? Are we dating or getting a dental cleaning?" Harper raises an eyebrow and tosses a streamer roll at Marin.

"But you're into him?" Viv kicks her feet up on the coffee table, brushing aside the pile of "50th" napkins.

"He's... nice. Predictable. Comfortably boring." Marin pulls the pillow off her face and sets it on her lap, her expression suddenly less amused and more thoughtful. "But, well, he's not just boring." Her voice is soft, almost as though she's talking to herself. "I mean, he is. He's the human equivalent of a Subaru, no offense, Birdie. But the other night, he kissed me and I just —" She pauses, blinking. "I felt something. Like my body remembered I was allowed to feel good again. That I'm still in here."

Viv leans forward, suddenly very sober. "Marin."

She nods. "I know. It sounds dumb. But it's been years since I felt that, even before the accident. There was so much silence in my marriage. Not fighting. Not closeness. Just this growing echo of nothing."

Viv reaches out and taps Marin's shin with her hand. "It's not dumb. It's huge. Good-for-you huge."

"I almost forgot what that flutter was." Marin swirls her own glass of kombucha, cheeks coloring. "It made me feel like I might still have a future. Like there might be something on the other side of all this guilt."

"You do have a future." I set my empty glass on the coffee table and lean close. "You're not frozen in place because everything stopped for a while."

Marin sinks deeper into the couch with a groan. "I swear, I used muscles I didn't know I had trying to remember how to flirt. I didn't think I'd feel anything again. Especially not on date three with a dentist who complimented my enamel." She lets out a short laugh.

"Let's hope that next time he gets to see more of you to compliment." Viv winks. "Is he coming to the party?"

Marin wiggles her phone. "That was him confirming that he'll be there."

I almost expect her to let out a girlish squeal with the announcement.

"I did something much more intimate than sex last night." Viv's statement is casual, as though she's declaring that she decided to give oat milk another try.

We both turn to her.

"Viv!" Marin's eyes go wide. "You finally let someone see your belly button?"

"Hell no!" Viv grabs her chapstick off the end table and dabs her lips with it. "But thank you for reminding me I'm overdue for a pedicure. I'm talking about real intimacy. The terrifying, soul-baring kind."

I raise an eyebrow. "Who are you and what have you done with Viv?"

Harper, who's sitting cross-legged on the rug, eating a Pop-Tart like she's watching a daytime talk show, chimes in. "She's not lying. I was there. I have emotional whiplash."

Viv rolls her eyes but doesn't deny it. "I was out back hanging fairy lights last night, and I got hit by this wave of sadness. You know that kind that sneaks up and punches you in the throat? One second you're yelling at a knot of extension cords, and the next you're grieving your whole damn life."

We're quiet now, the joking gone still. Viv's voice drops softer.

"Danny would've fixed the lights in thirty seconds and then made fun of my taste in disco ball garland. And I missed him. But not in that nostalgic, 'aw, memories' kind of way. In the gut-level, 'how do I still breathe without you?' kind of way."

Viv glances at Harper, her eyes shinier than usual.

"And then Harper came out with tea. No lecture. No awkward questions. She sat next to me while I ugly cried about the fact that I loved my best friend so deeply that I don't think I know how to let him go. And I don't know how to love anyone else because I keep measuring them by a man who doesn't exist anymore. And I can't stand to sit in the silence because the silence is where I drown, and if I fill it with enough life, then death can't touch me."

Harper puts down her Pop-Tart and moves beside her on the floor, resting her head on Viv's shoulder. "You're not broken because you loved him well. You're grieving honestly. That's brave."

Viv snorts, blinking rapidly. "If this turns into an after-school special, I'm out."

Marin nudges her. "Too late. We're already planning the commercial break."

I smile at the two of them, the way Harper leans into Viv, the way Viv doesn't flinch. "That's beautiful, Viv. That you let someone see you like that. And Harper's the perfect person. She's a good reminder that life can and does go on."

Viv lifts Harper's hand and kisses the back of it dramatically. "Don't make a habit of being emotionally supportive, Harper. It'll ruin your sarcastic brand."

Harper smirks. "I've got range."

Marin sighs, mock-wiping a tear. "I love us. We're like a Hallmark movie, but with better boobs and trauma."

Viv laughs and tosses a pillow at her. "That's going on our group text bio." And then Viv's eyes narrow in my direction. "Alright, your turn."

I blink. "My turn for what?"

Marin shifts to sit upright, suddenly alert. "We haven't properly unpacked the whole Noah on the roof with no pants and the post-coital glow you were rocking. You want to talk about *your* thing with Noah or should we assume he was looking for his mailbag up there?"

"I'm sure I have no idea what you're talking about," I mutter, pulling a throw pillow into my lap like it's emotional armor and wondering if it's possible to die of embarrassment talking about sex with my daughter in the room.

Viv grins. "So. You and Noah. How are we feeling?"

I take a deep breath, staring at the piñata because it's easier than looking at their knowing faces.

"I don't know. I mean, it was good. *Really* good. Better than I expected. But now I'm scared it was a one-time, post-repression explosion and I've opened a door I don't know how to close."

"You don't *have* to close it," Marin says gently. "It doesn't have to mean anything right away."

"But that's the thing." My fingers pick at the edge of the couch cushion. "What if it does? What if it already means something and I've completely upended my brain and my grief and my kids' image of their father's best friend because I couldn't stop myself from falling into bed with a man who's been orbiting our lives for two decades?"

They're both quiet for a moment. "You didn't fall into bed with him," Viv whispers. "You *chose* to. That's different."

"And you haven't uprooted my entire image of Noah, Mom. You're a woman with needs, and Noah's a great guy." Harper's thoughtful response shocks me. How did I raise such a good one?

"Yeah," Marin adds. "And maybe the world didn't explode because of it. Maybe it's the next thing."

I nod slowly, biting the inside of my cheek. "It's complicated. Noah was always Owen's. His best friend. His shadow. His right hand. And then he was both of ours. And now I'm seeing him in this whole new light, and it feels like betrayal and safety all at once."

Viv nudges me with her foot. "That's grief, babe. It rewrites all the rules."

We clink glasses, Marin with her honesty, Harper with her thoughtfulness, Viv with her progress, and me, clinging to the edges of this strange, healing mess.

Mid-sip, I hear the front door swinging open and the telltale sound of heavy footsteps pounding into my front entryway. "Mom?"

I know that voice. That voice has yelled "MOOOOM" across more gymnasiums and soccer fields and fast food drive-thrus than I can count.

"Matt!" I dart up, glass abandoned, and race for the door like the house is on fire.

There he is—six-foot-four of pure athlete, with a duffel slung over his shoulder and a smirk that hasn't changed since kinder-garten. He catches me mid-run and lifts me off the ground in a hug that makes me forget every ache in my joints.

"You didn't warn me you turned into a full-blown adult," I exhale into his sweatshirt.

"You didn't warn me you turned the house into a party store." He leans back, grinning.

He sets me down and gestures behind him. "Mom, this is my teammate, Jalen. We flew in together. He didn't have plans this weekend, and I figured he could use a party."

Jalen steps into the house, the same tall, athletic build as Matt. Stretching out his hand, he nods. "Nice to meet you, Mrs. Lawson."

Before I can reply, Viv steps forward, previous emotional healing apparently forgotten.

"Well, *hellooo*, Jalen." She extends her hand. "I'm Viv. Widow. Former dancer. Frequent flirt."

Jalen takes her hand and flushes crimson. "Um. Nice to meet you?"

"God help you," Marin mutters behind her glass of kombucha.

"Don't mind her." I try to ease the discomfort and shoot Viv a look. "She gets friskier around other people's adult children."

Matt groans. "Mom, can we *not*?"

"Just a little hazing," Viv says sweetly. "You want to be part of the Lawson family vortex, you need to survive innuendo and small batches of kombucha."

Jalen glances around the room, at the balloon arch, the piñata, the streamers, the glitter, and does what I can only assume is a mental risk assessment while he runs his hand through his dark hair. "It's a really nice house."

"Thanks." I nod toward the kitchen. "It was nicer before glitter happened. But we're celebrating my late husband's fiftieth tomorrow."

"Yeah. Matt told me." Jalen's voice is instantly serious, his eyebrows knitting together. "I'm sorry."

I wave it off. "Don't be. He'd have loved this circus. Especially the karaoke machine."

Matt slings an arm around my shoulders. "I told him there'd be pulled pork and old people dancing. He still came."

"Brave man." Viv raises her eyebrows and does a little sashay in Jalen's direction. He looks at me, wild-eyed, and I step in to rescue him.

"Come on. You guys hungry? We've got Thai food and more vegan cookies than anyone needs."

As the boys trail into the kitchen, Viv leans toward Marin and whispers, "I call dibs on Jalen's therapist in ten years."

"I'm pretty sure that's not how that works," Marin mutters.

"So, Mom, is your date going to be here tomorrow?" Harper wiggles her eyebrows before stuffing a large bite of Pad Thai into her mouth.

"Yeah, Mom. Will I finally get to meet this mystery man? Between practices and classes and gym sessions, I've only gotten a few cryptic texts from Harper about him. Need to make sure he treats you well."

I haven't told Matt who the mystery man is, and apparently, Harper's been waiting for the right moment. "Are you two really okay with this? Me seeing someone?" My fingers twist into each other, my right hand moving to work the wedding band on my left finger out of habit. Except it's not there anymore.

Matt's eyes flicker down to catch the movement. "We want you to be happy. No one's ever going to replace Dad, but that doesn't mean you need to be alone forever. I mean, you're not *that* old."

"Thank you?" It comes out as a question, as I have no idea if I've been complimented or insulted.

Matt takes another big bite of curry. "So, like I said, I'm lacking details. Who's the lucky guy?"

I don't have a chance to answer before Harper's blurting out, "Bro! You're never going to believe it. I'll give you three hints."

I guess this is Harper's right moment.

Matt leans forward like he's about to get the best secret he's heard all year.

"One: tall, dark, and handsome."

"Well, that doesn't really help me out. You could be describing twenty percent of the Seattle area."

"Two: someone we've known for a long time."

Matt shifts back, his eyebrows knitting together.

"Three: he delivers our mail."

Now Matt's fully back in his chair, mouth set in a firm line. "Oh."

"Oh? That's all I get? It's romantic! I don't expect you to swoon, but a little 'awe' wouldn't kill you," Harper continues, but I can't take my eyes off Matt and how suddenly his reaction has changed.

"Yeah. Romantic." He takes a long swig of the kombucha Viv's placed in front of him. "So, need any help with party details?"

The obvious change in subject doesn't go unnoticed.

Later, as the house winds down and I'm rinsing wine glasses in the kitchen, I catch a glimpse of Owen's old watch on the counter; I'd found it when I was rummaging through the drawer for an extra roll of tape.

My heart tugs, confused and aching.

Tomorrow, I'll stand in front of everyone and try to celebrate a man who's gone, while trying not to fall apart in front of the one who's somehow still here.

Chapter Twenty-Five

The backyard smells like fresh-cut grass and citrus candles. Tacky plastic tablecloths, Viv's idea, flutter over the tables, printed with tiny piña coladas that feel more party store than paradise. Somewhere behind me, the grill sizzles, filling the air with barbecue smoke. I couldn't decide between tropical beach vibes that reminded me of our honeymoon in Hawaii, or the smoky comfort of a Texas steakhouse—like that roadside diner we stumbled into on our road trip, the one with the pulled pork sandwiches we talked about for years. Two of Owen's favorite memories. Two of mine.

I hover by the drinks table, trying to remember how to breathe without hiccupping on my own nostalgia.

I raise my glass after most of our guests have poured into our backyard. Harper pauses the music, and I clear my throat loudly a few times, trying to get everyone's attention. Their murmurs quiet as they turn to face me.

"Thank you all for being here tonight. I know it's a little unconventional, throwing a party for someone who isn't here to enjoy it." A soft laugh rises from the group, and I press on, voice steady despite the lump in my throat. "But Owen and I made a promise. Every decade, we'd celebrate big. We haven't missed one yet, and I wasn't about to start now."

I pause, swallow, and smile through the tears building behind my eyes.

"Tonight isn't about loss. It's about love. It's about all the joy Owen brought into the world, and the way it still lingers in every ridiculous story, every laugh, every one of you."

My gaze sweeps the backyard, the twinkle lights, the photo wall, the karaoke machine already humming to life, and I roll my eyes a little at my own overused, cheesy request.

"So please, sing like you mean it. Dance like nobody's filming. Be a little too loud and a little too sentimental. Because if Owen were here, he'd be the first one on the mic and the last one off the dance floor."

I lift my glass a little higher.

"Here's to Owen. And to making the most of the birthdays we get."

Laughter. Clinks of glass. Someone sniffs a little too loudly.

I smile, but my throat tightens.

Because there's a hole in this night shaped exactly like the man I loved.

Off-key karaoke drifts in from the backyard, someone absolutely murdering a Bon Jovi song. There's laughter, clinking glasses, the occasional screech of a chair dragging across the deck. Someone honks into a tissue like a foghorn, then immediately starts laughing again.

The kind of night that smells like summer and spilled beer and cheap citronella candles working overtime.

Near the firepit, someone's trying to balance a flaming marshmallow on a plastic spoon while the crowd chants "CHUG IT." The tables are a mix of dollar-store luau kits and leftover Fourth of July decor—tiny American flags shoved into pineapple centerpieces. Viv brought matching koozies that say Resting Birthday Face. Harper made jello shots shaped like tiny beach balls. The whole thing is has no rhyme or reason, no clear theme, and it's perfect.

I duck into the kitchen for a breather, fanning myself with a paper plate that says "Over the Hill and Hot as Ever" in glittery script. But before I can make it to the fridge for a cold drink, the photo wall catches my eye.

It's a tradition, one Owen and I started years ago, where we have a wall of Polaroids and snapshots that guests can add to, along with a stack of neon sticky notes and glitter pens for jotting down memories. This year, Harper outdid herself, framing it all in mismatched wood like a scrapbook exploded on the wall.

There's one of Owen covered in silly string from his 30th, and another of us in our twenties, wearing matching party hats and tipsy grins. Someone's written:

"Owen once dared me to sing 'SexyBack' at karaoke and ended up joining me with a tambourine."

Another says:

"He showed up to my birthday party in a banana costume. No one had invited him. It was perfect."

I laugh, touching the corner of the whipped-cream-smeared photo from his 34th, right after I smashed the birthday pie in his face. Of course it wasn't an official party. He hadn't let me do anything big that year. He said all he wanted was for me to bring him a birthday pie in my birthday suit. I remember how he looked at me, like I was the whole party.

The ache comes quick and sharp, but not enough to knock the smile off my face. Because this? This is how Owen would've wanted us to celebrate. Loud. Ridiculous. With a little chaos and a lot of cake. After all these years, I finally threw the party that he would've loved—imperfect, unpolished, not color coordinated.

And he's not here to enjoy it.

And just as I turn to head back out—

"Birdie!"

I look up at the sound of the familiar husky voice.

And there he is.

Noah.

Looking like he walked straight out of one of the Polaroids.

He's standing at the door to the back patio, framed in gold light and shadow, holding a bottle of wine and wearing the expression of a man who feels he walked into a moment he shouldn't have.

He's a little late. And for a moment, I remember that this must be hard for him too.

He steps in and sets the bottle on the table next to me. "You look... beautiful."

I swallow, running my hands down the yellow butterfly patterned sundress. "It's Owen's favorite."

He nods. Doesn't touch me. Doesn't push. Just stands beside me for a long moment, watching the way the breeze catches the edge of the photo wall.

"I still expect him to walk in and take over the grill." He nods toward where Jalen and Matt have taken up Owen's post.

I close my eyes. "Me too."

It's quiet.

And then slowly, quietly, his fingers brush mine. I don't stop them.

Not yet.

"Want to go check out the rest of the party?"

He nods.

I lead the way out into the backyard. It's strung with twinkle lights, the good wine is flowing, and Harper is blasting the playlist that she spent hours putting together last night. It reminds me way too much of my college frat party days. Neighbors, friends, and family are laughing. Dancing. Singing.

Marin's actually smiling at her phone and keeps glancing at the door. The dentist should be here any minute now. Viv is two margaritas deep and flirting with someone's cousin who owns a paddleboard business while also sending the occasional smirk in Jalen's direction. I think she likes to see him squirm.

It's perfect. But it isn't.

The soft yellow halter-back sundress is pressing in a little too close. And I'm trying not to overthink the fact that Noah is holding my hand.

Like it's no big deal.

Like this is normal.

Like I'm not two inches from a panic spiral.

Like it's okay that I'm celebrating a 50th birthday party for my dead husband while standing much too close to his best friend.

Like I'm not the scum of the earth.

Okay, deep breath. The guilt is apparently stronger than usual tonight.

He leans in close to murmur something, and his breath tickles my ear, and I laugh, because it's easier than saying, *this is the first time I've ever gone with someone to a party since Owen asked me out freshman year.*

But it's not only someone.

It's him.

Noah.

And then it happens.

Someone taps my shoulder.

"Oh, Birdie, I was just saying how much you and Owen used to light up every party you went to together. You always danced to that song. Wasn't this it? I swear some of the neighborhood party planners would put it on there to help the rest of us cynics see that you could still be madly in love after twenty years of marriage."

I freeze.

Because yes. Yes, it's playing right now.

Owen and my song.

The only slow song that played at our first college party on our first date.

It's floaty and sweet and God, the kind of thing that doesn't feel like *just a song* when your dead husband used to hum it while doing the dishes or while holding your crying baby boy.

Noah follows my gaze, and his face shifts, like he understands something has changed in me.

"Birdie?" His voice is low. "You okay?"

I shake my head. "It's fine. I'm fine."

But it's *not*.

Because now every laugh feels like betrayal. Every inch of skin we're touching feels like a lie. Every happy flutter in my stomach feels like I'm dancing on Owen's grave in wedge sandals. Honoring his memory? Ha. I'm rubbing it in his face that I lived and he didn't.

I pull my hand away.

"Noah, I need a minute."

He watches me, uncertain. "What's going on?"

The words fall from my lips before I can stop them. "My heart is exploding," I whisper.

I walk toward a quiet corner of the backyard, out of the merry glow cast by the twinkling fairy lights, needing air, space, time— something to unstick this grief from my lungs. I hear Noah behind me, his voice gentle.

"B. Wait."

I spin around, eyes burning. "This was a mistake."

The words fall out too fast.

"What was a mistake?"

"This party. You. The other night." I inhale sharply. "I can't keep pretending this doesn't feel like cheating."

He flinches. Not dramatically. But enough.

And I hate myself for it.

He nods once, stiff. "I see."

I reach for him, already wishing I could pull back the hurt my words have placed on his features. "Noah—"

"It's okay." He bobs his head a few times. "You're not ready. I get it."

"I want to be."

"But you're not."

"I don't think I'll ever be. We get one great love in our life-time, right? It would be cruel and selfish to think I deserve two. I lost mine. And that's it."

"Birdie..." His voice is calm, gentle. "What's going on?"

"This feels wrong," I whisper. "All of it. Laughing. Touching. *You.*"

He steps back as though I verbally slapped him.

And I wish I could take the words back.

He swallows hard, blinking at the ground, and lets out a slow, careful breath. "Well. Shit." He gives a sad laugh.

The silence stretches as we both stare, shoulder brushing shoulders, into the darkness.

"Owen used to love dares too, you know. Could never resist a challenge."

The statement comes out of nowhere, but it still makes me smile, my heart aching a little more. Yes. We always were daring each other to do some outrageous thing. It's how I ended up in the Puget Sound in December pretending to be an orca.

"It's all because of a stupid dare."

I pause. "What?"

"That you ended up with him and not with..." I turn to look into his deep blue eyes, already seeing the answer swirling there in the way he looks at me.

He rubs the back of his neck, eyes not meeting mine. "That night you met. I dared Owen to ask for your number before you left. Thinking you'd turn him down and we would date, and I could avoid an awkward love triangle with my new roommate."

I stare at him, heart thudding.

"Owen told me to dare him to do it, and that's when I knew

he had already fallen for the same girl I'd fallen for weeks ago. I thought there was no harm in it. Figured he'd chicken out or bomb or something and then there would be no hard feelings when I asked you out." He exhales, a wistful kind of smile tugging at the edge of his mouth. "But he didn't."

I feel the air go out of my lungs.

"He got you talking about art, made some cheesy joke. And you laughed, and then that was it. It was pure chemistry." Noah finally meets my eyes. "You two were perfect together. And I never blamed him for that."

I don't know what to say.

"Noah..."

"I watched him fall in love with you. And I tried to fall out of love with you while he fell harder."

The words split something in my chest.

"I never told him. But he figured it out. He could see it every time I looked at you. I never told *you*. Because he was my best friend and you were his, and I would've rather cut off my own hand than hurt either of you."

Silence swells between us, aching and terrible.

"I thought maybe, after all these years... maybe this was something. But now it's your song playing, one that's seared into my brain too, and you're looking at me like I'm a mistake. And I feel like a mistake. Like all these years of wanting you were wrong, and maybe some part of me wondered what it would be like if Owen was out of the picture, and now he is and I hate myself all over again for it."

"I didn't mean—"

"I know." He smiles, soft and devastating. "You're grieving. And I'm not trying to take his place. I couldn't. But I can't pretend I don't feel what I feel."

I cover my mouth with my hand, holding back a sob.

He shakes his head gently. "I never fully got over you, B. Not even when I tried."

And then, just like that, he turns and walks back toward the house.

I stand there shaking, still clutching a plastic cup of chardonnay, the sound of Owen and my song dissolving into the night.

The thoughts swirl in my head, making my stomach clench. Was I really that blind all these years? How could I not have seen this?

This isn't only grief.

This is love, too.

And I have no idea what to do with both.

Chapter Twenty-Six

I hold it together until the party is over, until every last neighbor and friend has either claimed their casserole dish or offered me a gentle squeeze and warm smile.

"Great party, Birdie!" One of Owen's old colleagues beams. "I know your parties are notoriously perfect, from the color-coordinated napkins to the hand-calligraphed menu cards, and I've enjoyed every last one of them. But this, well, this was by far the best one."

I smile, resisting the urge to tell him that four-years-ago Birdie would've broken out in hives. Nothing matched. Nothing was coordinated. It was a riot of colors, clashing themes, and a playlist that swung wildly between Sinatra and Lizzo like it couldn't decide if we were sipping champagne or body rolling in the kitchen. It was perfect.

The door bangs shut behind us, and I wave from the porch until his headlights are out of sight. Making sure no one else is lurking behind the lavender bushes, I sigh before slumping against the door. The sounds of Viv, Marin, Harper, Matt, and Jalen cleaning up in the backyard and kitchen break the otherwise quiet late summer evening.

I should go back inside, but part of me wants to sit and listen

—to pretend Owen's in there too, stacking red solo cups on his head, making everyone laugh while he pretends to help clean. If I stay out here long enough, the memories feel less like the past and more like something still unfolding in the backyard. Like maybe, maybe, he'll still be there waiting to kiss me goodnight when I finally get up.

"Don't act coy. I *totally* saw you making out with mom's dentist in the corner when that 80's love song came on," Harper crows.

Viv's high soprano adds in, "I told you to play it. I knew that one would do the trick!"

I can practically feel Marin blushing from here.

"Do you think anyone else noticed? I don't know what came over me. I haven't made out at a party since junior year of college." Her voice drops lower and I strain to make out whatever confession she's sharing next. "I blame Viv's kombucha. It's doing something to my senses."

"You can blame the kombucha or your renewed sense of womanhood! Either way, it's good for the gut and the guilt." Viv's voice fades, and she must be moving toward the kitchen, presumably to pour Marin another cup of liberating kombucha.

"I forgot how early an old people party ends. It's only 11! Your favorite old haunt, the BeatWave is still pretty good. Should be starting to pick up in about an hour," Harper's voice calls out across the yard.

"Sounds promising." Jalen's deep voice bounces off the porch. "Matt, you up for round two?"

"There's no 5 AM practice tomorrow so I can party all night. Hey, has anyone seen Mom?"

I hear a few murmurs and presumably some head shakes and I sigh, bracing myself to stand. But my body won't budge, my arms refuse to listen. I'm not ready to walk back in and face that wall of memories, those frozen frames of the man who was supposed to grow old with me, captured forever at forty-eight. Like time ran out, and no one told me we were on the clock.

Then Matt's voice echoes down the hall, followed by the tell-tale sound of his heavy footsteps. "Mom, you out here?"

It's quite obvious that I'm slumped against the front door so I don't bother to lie as Matt pushes against it and shifts my whole body across the rough wooden porch. "Mom? What're you doing? You ok?"

I nod, and then shake my head, and then nod again. No one wants to break down in front of their child.

"Does this have something to do with Noah ducking out of here early?"

I shake my head, then nod, then shake it again—like my body can't decide what story to tell. Matt gives me a look that would've made his dad proud. It's the same one Owen used to master, half patience, half "I'm not buying a word of it."

"Are you dating him?"

"No. Well, maybe. I thought I was. I don't know. I'm not sure that's going to work out." My voice is barely above a whisper.

"Oh?" Matt crosses his legs and sinks down next to me, leaning his shoulder back against the wall. He's trying to act casual, but his brows are knit together.

Something in the way he asks, the way his arms are clamped tightly together. My mom senses are tingling. "You knew... didn't you?"

"Knew what?"

"Matthew Theodore Lawson." I raise an eyebrow. "Don't play dumb with me."

He sighs, running a hand through his hair. "Remember when I used to have trouble sleeping as a kid, so Dad set up that little basketball hoop in the backyard so I could shoot around and wear myself out?"

"Yeah." A soft smile touches my lips. "You used to be out there for hours."

"Well, one night, must've been after one of your PTA meetings or something, you got home late. I was already outside, shooting free throws with that little foam ball, and I saw Dad and Noah out on the porch. They didn't know I was there."

I shift slightly. "What happened?"

He pauses, staring at the floor. "I heard Dad say, 'I see the way you look at her.' And Noah said something like, 'You don't have to worry. I'd never do anything. You two are it. I'd never mess that up.' And Dad, he didn't yell or anything. He didn't really say anything. After Noah left, he stood there, staring out into the backyard, playing that one sad Sufjan Stevens song on repeat like he'd done something unforgivable."

A silence blooms between us.

"Noah kinda stopped coming around after that. I didn't know what it meant until years later. And even then, I tried to convince myself it wasn't a big deal. Just a weird one-off thing. But now?" Matt's jaw tightens. "He promised."

I exhale slowly. "He did."

"I've always liked Noah." Matt's voice is soft in the night. "I mean, he was part of our family. He was around all the time, holidays, school stuff, even movie nights where he'd bring popcorn with, like, five different seasonings."

He swallows, his brow tightening. I reach for his hand instinctively, and to my relief, he lets me take it.

"I know that probably sounds petty," he mutters. "And I know it's not fair to him. He *was* a good guy. I mean, he's still a good guy. But this, this version of him? The one who's with you? I don't know where that fits yet. I guess I'm still figuring it out."

"I am too," I say softly. "I didn't plan this, Matt. I never in a million years thought I'd feel anything again, let alone for him. I wish it were simpler."

Matt doesn't speak for a beat. When he does, his voice is quieter. "I know it's not my place. You're allowed to live, Mom. You are. And I want that for you. But part of me still feels like it's, well, I don't know. Disrespectful. Like he waited long enough to feel justified. And maybe that's unfair, but it's how I feel."

I nod, throat tight. "It's not unfair."

He looks at me then, his eyes softer. "I need to know one thing."

"What?"

"Do you want it to work out with him?"

I hesitate.

"I don't know," I admit. "I thought I did. I think maybe I still do. But tonight, I kept thinking about your dad. About how happy he would've been with all of this. About the damn song. And I felt like I was betraying him by being happy."

Matt nods. "You know what Dad used to say?"

"What?"

"'Some shots are ugly as hell, but they still count.'"

I blink at him. "What does that even mean?"

He smirks, sitting back on his heels. "It means sometimes you throw something up from the wrong angle, with bad form, and zero finesse, and it still goes in. Not because it was perfect. But because it mattered enough to try. Maybe this thing with Noah. It's messy. Maybe it always will be. But if it ends up being real, then maybe that's enough."

I press my lips together, overwhelmed.

He looks at me, eyes clear now. "I'm not saying I'm okay with it yet. But I'm not gonna stand in your way. You loved Dad. We all did. That doesn't mean you don't get to love again. And Noah is a good guy. Maybe we shouldn't always have to keep decades old promises to the dead. Maybe Dad wouldn't have wanted it that way."

I pull him into a hug, burying my face in his shoulder.

He hugs me back tightly, his voice muffled in my hair. "Please, Mom... if you're going to do this, don't do it halfway. Either give it a real shot, or let it go. No one wants to be someone's backup plan."

"I know." And I mean it.

Because I'm starting to wonder if maybe this whole thing, the grief, the guilt, the what-if of it all, isn't something I have to figure out *before* I love someone again.

Maybe it's part of *how* I learn to love someone again.

Chapter Twenty-Seven

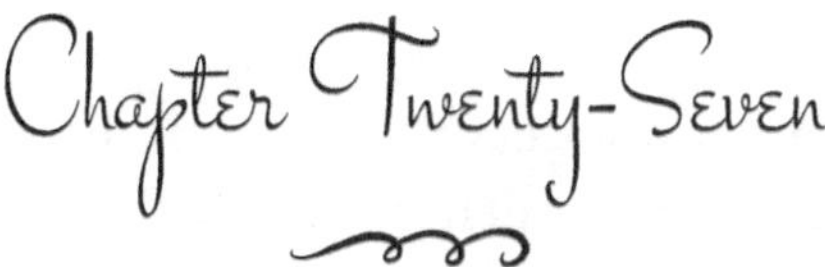

I inhale deeply as the wind rolls up Queen Anne Hill, sharp with salt from the Sound. The bench is warm beneath me, the fading afternoon sun sinking into the warped wood. This is the view—the one you see on postcards and social media and the back of ferry brochures. But none of them ever quite get it right. Not like this.

The Space Needle stands like a toy in the distance, proud and strange, perfectly framed by the glass-and-steel thicket of downtown. Below, the bay shimmers, dotted with ferries carving slow, patient paths across the water. Mount Rainier stands guard over it all, soft and surreal.

Tourists murmur and shuffle around me, angling for the perfect photo, but I don't hear them. Not really. I sit. Let it all soak into me. The city, the salt, the memory of Owen's hand brushing mine in moments just like this.

We used to come here when life was too loud. When a decision needed clarity or the day had simply swallowed us whole. We'd sit side by side, saying nothing, waiting for the twilight to hush everything into stillness. In those quiet pauses, it felt as though time was folding in on itself. Like we were infinite.

"I should probably go to your grave for this," I whisper. The breeze tugs at the ends of my braids. If I close my eyes, I can almost believe it's Owen, tugging like he used to, teasing, gentle, so alive. "But it never feels like you're there. You're here. In the wind and the skyline and that mountain. The ground doesn't suit you. Not even in death."

I glance at the thermos beside mine. His thermos. Still dented from that camping trip where he tried to fight off a raccoon with it.

"I brought you coffee. I know, I know, you'd prefer something stronger, but I still can't drink whiskey without crying, so this'll have to do."

I take a shaky breath.

"Noah and I kissed." The words fall out, fragile and loud in the space between me and the mountain. "Well... more than kissed. And I'm not going to give you details, because if you were here, you'd tease me until I turned redder than this stupid thermos about the fact that I still don't like to say the word *sex*. But it happened. And it felt confusing. Right and wrong and real all at once."

My throat tightens. "And I don't know who I'm more afraid of hurting, him, or me... or you."

I stare out across the Sound, waiting for a sign that won't come.

"After you died, I came here every night," I whisper. "Sat on this bench, playing that last voicemail. Over and over. Every breath, every pause etched into my chest. Like if I listened enough times, I could hold onto the way it felt to be loved by you."

The sound of a family packing up their picnic fills our silence, and I inhale deeply.

"Is it okay that I kissed him? That I felt something? I'm not really moving on. I don't think I ever could. But is it possible to reach for something new without letting go of you?"

A throat clears behind me.

I don't jump. I know who it is before I turn around.

Viv and Marin are standing behind me, arms crossed against the wind. Viv's in a leopard print shirt that clashes with everything around us, and Marin's hair is in a ponytail that's already giving up against the breeze.

"We figured we'd find you here." Viv settles beside me like she owns the bench.

"Or the overlook," Marin adds. "Harper and Matt gave us a list."

I smile faintly. "You guys really didn't have to—"

"We wanted to," Marin interrupts. "Besides, Viv made me promise we wouldn't leave without finishing all our grief dares." She pulls out the three pink, glittered notebooks.

"Which you haven't." Viv raises an eyebrow at me.

I groan. "It was a stupid idea. I don't know what I was thinking."

"I'll tell you what you were thinking. You were struck by brilliance!" Viv jabs a thumb toward herself. "I mean, come on. A grief dare book? Who else could've made mourning feel like a chaotic scavenger hunt through emotional trauma and karaoke bars?"

I shake my head, but I'm smiling now. "You two really did it, didn't you? You actually finished yours."

Marin nods. "Every last dare." She tilts her head, eyes thoughtful. "I thought I'd be relieved when I checked the final box the other night. But really, it cracked something open."

"Same." Viv's voice drops low, uncharacteristically serious. "Like I'd been holding my breath for years. And somewhere between leading a conga line in a wine bar full of strangers and telling Harper I don't think I can do this life without him, I realized I was finally exhaling."

Marin folds her hands in her lap. "It didn't make the grief disappear. It just stopped being the only thing I carried."

Viv nods. "Yeah. I think I used to think moving forward

meant leaving our husbands behind. But now it feels like we've brought them with us. Just in a different way."

I feel that in my bones.

Viv shifts on the bench to face me more directly. "Which brings us back to you."

I groan again, dramatic this time. "You guys are relentless."

"You're welcome," Viv says cheerfully. "Now finish your last dare."

Marin raises her eyebrows in gentle encouragement, opening the book to the big circle around the final item on my list.

"Tell the truth about what you're afraid of," Viv says simply.

I look down at my hands. "I'm not afraid of replacing Owen. I know no one could. I'm afraid, if I let myself move forward, really move forward, I'll lose him again. That letting someone else in means erasing him."

There's a long pause. The wind tugs at the edges of the moment.

"You're not erasing him." Marin rests her hand on my shoulder. "You're carrying him forward. But if all you carry is grief, you're not really carrying him—you're carrying the weight of losing him."

Viv nods. "Owen wouldn't want you stuck in a loop. He'd want you to be happy. You know that, right?"

I wipe at my eyes. "We never talked about moving on or not moving on if one of us died. And he died so suddenly there was no time to process."

Marin nods. "But knowing Owen, knowing how much he loved you, would he want you to be alone the rest of your life?"

My voice is small. "No."

Viv leans forward. "Do you love this guy?"

I open my mouth, fumbling for the kind of answer that sounds balanced and responsible—grief-approved, widow-appropriate, emotionally nuanced.

But before I can get a single word out, Viv holds up a hand, and Marin taps the page of my grief dare book.

"Truth," she reminds me gently.

I exhale, my chest tight. "Yeah. I do."

Marin draws a soft half-checkmark. "And how does that make you feel?"

"Terrified. Excited. Guilty. Overwhelmed."

"Yep. She's in love." Viv gives a satisfied nod as Marin completes the checkmark with a flourish.

"We could sit here and tell you a thousand times that you deserve love and happiness, and that Owen would want you to find joy again." Marin's voice is quiet but sure. "But none of it matters if you don't believe it too."

"I..." My voice wavers. "I wish there was a sign."

Viv shrugs. "This isn't the movies. Sometimes there's no perfect sign. No lightning bolt. No rainbow or raven. Sometimes it's just this. Your favorite bench, a sunset, and the quiet reminder that life keeps going. That we carry them with us, not behind us."

There's a beat, then Marin gives a little sigh. "I might be moving here."

"What?" I blink.

"Let's be honest. I'm not exactly in my thirties anymore. I know what I want and what I don't want and what I need and don't need in a man. After my last failed marriage, I swore I'd never fall in love again. But things are going really well, really fast with Dr. Dentist. If they keep going the way they are," she pauses, blushing, "and if I can find a rental that doesn't smell like wet carpet, I might move here. The great benefit of working remote."

Viv claps her hands. "See? Everyone's out here making big moves! And we've got two days left before our flights, which means you've got about 48 hours to either make up your mind about Noah, or make out with him again."

I laugh through my tears. "That's your advice?"

"It's what Owen would've wanted," Viv deadpans.

I look out at the sky, begging the universe for some kind of sign that this is true. A few more minutes of silence pass as the sun dips lower in the sky.

Sighing, I start to rise. This is life and there are no signs to make moving forward easier. "Alright, let's go home." I turn to move down the path, Viv and Marin behind me, when a splat of white, grey seagull poop lands squarely on top of Viv's head.

Owen would've loved that.

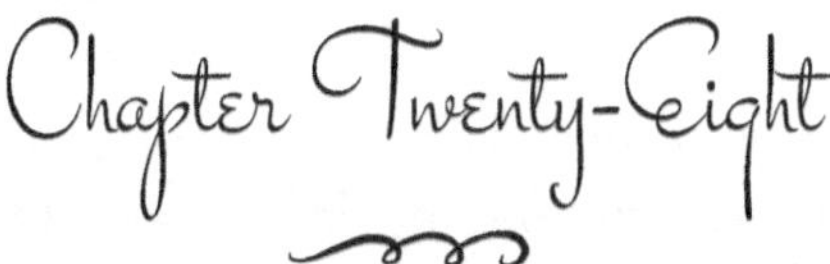

Chapter Twenty-Eight

Viv and Marin left two weeks ago, and much to their dismay, I still haven't worked up the nerve to talk to Noah. Instead, I've perfected a very sophisticated routine: hide out in the back of the house, peek through the blinds when he drops off the mail, sprint back inside, study the current art showings at the museum in preparation for my internship starting next week, then spend the rest of the day marinating in guilt and confusion. Rinse. Repeat.

But this morning is different.

This morning, Harper is perched at the kitchen counter, her long legs tucked beneath her and her laptop open, a half-empty mug of coffee sitting beside her. She's been home more, and the house doesn't feel quite so cavernous with Viv and Marin gone. I love having her here. It anchors me. Reminds me that not everything is changing at once.

Sunlight streams in through the window, catching the glittery cover of my pink notebook, my grief dare book, casting sparkles all over the wall like a disco ball for feelings. Frank, clearly unimpressed, narrows his eyes at the sparkle display and pads toward the porch, desperate for his morning constitutional.

I open the door for him, then glance at the table. "What's this doing out here?" I haven't opened the book in over a week, and I have plenty of excuses why. I've been helping Marin find a rental, trying to convince Viv to move here too, busy with the upcoming internship.

Harper looks up from her screen and shrugs. "Viv and Marin texted me. Said to add one last dare and make sure you saw it."

I groan, already suspicious before crossing the room, flipping open the notebook, and finding Harper's unmistakable handwriting:

We double-dog-dare you to take the honesty you brought to yourself and bring it to Noah, preferably before breakfast.

Frank lets out a sigh from the porch that's somewhere between judgment and gas.

I raise an eyebrow at him. "Don't judge me, sir."

Behind me, Harper clears her throat. "Actually, there's more."

She turns her laptop toward me. On the screen is Matt, bleary-eyed and definitely calling from a dorm room that looks like it smells faintly of Axe body spray and poor choices.

"Hi, Mom." He gives a little wave before stifling a yawn. "Harper said this was urgent."

I blink. "Isn't it noon over there? Why're you still in bed? Is someone dying?"

"Nope." Harper's all sunshine. "Just your love life."

Matt grins. "Late night. Look, I know we had that whole heavy talk, and I meant every word. But I've been thinking. And talking to Dad, well, thinking about Dad. And I want you to be happy. For real."

Harper nods. "You don't have to carry grief like it's the price of loving someone."

"You'll never replace Dad," Matt says gently. "But that's not what this is. This is about not wasting a second chance. If someone makes you laugh, and brings you coffee, and goes to poetry readings with you—"

Harper smirks. "—even when those poetry readings are truly awful."

"—then maybe that someone deserves to know how you feel," Matt finishes.

I swallow. "You two rehearsed this, didn't you?"

"Obviously," Matt deadpans. "Now, what are you waiting for?"

"You never turn down a dare." Harper pushes the book closer to me, like it's a fact etched into my DNA.

I stare at the screen, heart thumping. Then I glance at the notebook again. The pink sparkles daring me to find my own spark again.

"You guys are the worst," I mutter, wiping my eyes.

"And yet," Harper's already standing up, "you're reaching for the leash."

Frank lets out an excited yip, practically vibrating with anticipation. He may not know what's happening, but he's fully committed to the idea of a walk.

"Fine." I grab a doggie bag. "But if this goes terribly, I'm blaming both of you."

"Chalk it up to part of all of our healing journey." Matt nods. "But also, go get him, Mom."

Harper gives me a thumbs-up. "Before breakfast. That was the dare."

I glance down at Frank, who's already nose-first at the door like a tiny, overdramatic herald of fate.

I sprint up the stairs and run my hairbrush through my long, stick-straight strands before glancing in the mirror. Should I go for a little mascara? Heart check. Will there be any emotional meltdowns or crying that will cause it to run? I think it's a safe bet to put some on. With that decided, I swipe a few coats of mascara on my lashes, clip Frank's leash, and push open the door.

Noah should be turning onto Beecher Street a few blocks up

right about now. If I hurry, I can hopefully do this whole thing away from the prying eyes of my own neighbors.

We're halfway down the block when the dark, looming clouds that've been hanging around since late last night decide now is the ideal time to unleash their fury.

Perfect.

The deluge comes on fast and hard, easily soaking through my long sleeves and yoga pants. The thin, sky-blue shirt is now translucent, and I'm pretty sure the soggy material is doing little to hide my braless nipples.

I fold my arms across my chest, but it's too late. The damage is done. I look like a woman on the verge of a nervous breakdown who's also trying to seduce the postman.

Which, ironically, isn't far off.

I consider turning back. Dry clothes. Dignity. Sanity.

But no. Viv and Marin double-dog-dared me. You can't ignore a glitter notebook and a double-dog dare. Not when you're the founder of the Dead Husbands Society. Our glitter notebooks are basically binding legal contracts.

So I do what any slightly damp, mostly mortified woman would do: I square my shoulders, wipe mascara from under one eye, and keep walking toward my fate.

Because nothing says ready to be honest about love like showing up braless, soggy, and racoon-eyed in the rain.

That's when I see him.

Shit.

He must be moving fast because of the rain, because we aren't out of my neighborhood territory yet.

Mailbag slung low over one shoulder, forearm flexing under the weight like it's nothing. There's a bit of scruff on his jaw, enough to be dangerous, and his hair is a little damp from the rain, dark strands clinging to his forehead in a way that reminds me entirely too much of *The Notebook.*

That familiar crease sits between his brows, the one that always made me think that he's the kind of man who could handle other people's nonsense and still have room to hold yours, too.

My heart stumbles, and for one completely irrational second, I wonder if the rain has been building to this all along. Like the universe needed drama. Mood lighting. A shirt that clings perfectly to the muscles under it.

God help me, it's working.

And that's when Frank decides now is the perfect time to start scooting his bum across Mildred's perfectly trimmed yard.

I freeze before going into hyperdrive and tugging on Frank's leash like an insane person trying to get him to remove his bottom from the grass.

And that's when Noah notices me. The rain is running over his mail baseball cap, creating little streams of water along his jawline, and in a moment of brief insanity, I wonder what it would be like to run my fingers along that same spot and follow their path down. Of course, he's wearing a rain jacket and entirely prepared for the weather.

"Well. This isn't something I was expecting to see today." Noah's voice is equal parts warm and husky and does not help the peaked nipple situation.

In my desperate attempt to separate Mildred's prize-winning grass from Frank's very determined butt, I've somehow tangled myself in the leash. Which is how I'm twisted like a pretzel, with Frank perfectly centered between us, tail lifted, eyes locked with mine, just as Frank starts pooping on the neighbor's lawn.

Because of course he does.

I shift my weight, trying to draw attention away from Frank's business. "So, this is your route." Why did I say that? Of course this is his route. Shouldn't I have gone with, 'does walking by my fennel plants devastate you because I couldn't even look at them the last few weeks?'

"Yep." He lifts the bundle in his hand. "Same route that it's been for the last fifteen years. Mail waits for no man."

Or woman with a rogue mutt and boundary issues, apparently.

I wrack my brain for the perfect speech that I'd been writing and rewriting in my mind and on my notes app for the last few weeks. Something that didn't seem desperate, or in love, or too eager, but also lets him know I really am able to move on. But standing here, the rain pounding the pavement between us, shivers working their way up my arms, all I can think of is,

"Rain looks good on you."

"I'd say the same." Noah's eyes move over my body, fixing on my pebbled nipples. "But, uh, you also look a little cold." Before I can protest, he's pulling off his rain jacket and closing the distance between us to drape it over my shoulders. It's warm and smells like him.

There's a weird silence. Like neither of us knows who we're supposed to be now. We were friends. Then not. Then more. Then very much not. And now?

He clears his throat. "So, uh, how've you been?"

"Good," I lie. "You?"

He nods. "Also good. Lots of envelopes. Got a few scented ones the last few days."

My heart beats. Once. Twice. Truth. I promised honesty with myself. With Noah. "I'm not good. I didn't think it was possible to be more miserable but I am."

Noah raises an eyebrow. "You are?"

The air shifts. The silence stretches again—tight, uncertain.

I look at him, and I see it. The thing he's trying not to show. The hurt. The guilt. The hope, still flickering behind his eyes even though he's trying to smother it.

I take a breath, then another. My hands are ice in his sleeves, and I decide I need to own up to my dare. "You weren't my first love. But you're the first person I've wanted to love since. And that has to mean something."

His face, his whole body, goes still.

"B…"

"I know. I'm late. Like, comically late. But I needed time. And a glitter notebook. And two friends with no boundaries."

He looks down at his shoes. "It's not only you. I've been holding back, too."

"Because of Owen."

He nods. "I made a promise to him. I loved him. He was my best friend. And I—there were years where I wondered if I screwed it all up by feeling something for you. Like I'd broken some sacred code. Or that me wishing that we could be together caused something catastrophic to happen in the universe. Like checking on you, wanting to comfort you, was the ultimate act of betrayal."

The rain is drumming harder now, creating little rivers in the street. "I can't speak on behalf of the universe, but you didn't. You were there. You took care of us. You were you."

Noah's face twists into a grimace, and I wonder if the words splinter his heart like they have mine. "I don't want to replace him. That's never what this was." He pauses, dragging a hand down his face. "I went up to our old fishing spot last weekend. Brought his favorite sandwich, sat on that rock where he always used to yell at me for tangling the lines."

A quiet smile ghosts across his lips, then fades.

"I talked to him. Like he was sitting right there next to me." He swallows hard. "And I don't know, maybe it sounds crazy, but I felt like he was listening. Maybe he gave me his blessing or something. Like, he was okay with this. With me trying to keep living and loving the one person he'd do anything for."

I swallow. "I'm not promising anything except honesty. I'm not fixed. I still cry in the laundry room sometimes for no reason."

"I once teared up a bit in the frozen peas aisle." His voice is husky and low.

"Yeah. Owen used to hate peas."

"You don't owe me love," he says quietly. "But maybe you owe yourself the chance to try. Whether it's with me or someone else."

That's when I step closer. Close enough to see the lines at the corners of his eyes and the hope he's still trying to bury.

"I am trying," I whisper. "Right now. And I wouldn't want it to be with anyone else."

And then I kiss him. The water cascades down our backs and faces, the scent of rain mingling with his warm cedar smell and minty taste. My body pushes into his, instinctively craving his touch and the brief thought runs through my head: I have to tell Viv that I did it.

Yep. I rain-troped the mailman.

I had it worked out in my mind that it would be sunny and sweet, but it's not. There's the faint smell of Frank's poop that's now running down a river in Mildred's lawn, and the water is dripping down my pants into my underwear. It's not neat or choreographed. It's real. The kind of kiss that tastes like laughter and tears and too much time spent pretending we didn't want this.

I step back before tilting my chin up. "I'm still scared, and a little guilty, and not entirely healed."

"Me too."

Frank snorts.

We both look down at him. His tongue flops out of his mouth, and he looks at us like he's above all this emotional nonsense.

"Want to walk my route with me?"

I glance up at the still thundering sky and then over at Noah's already soaked shirt.

"I mean, I'm not wearing a bra, but sure."

He grins. "Neither am I."

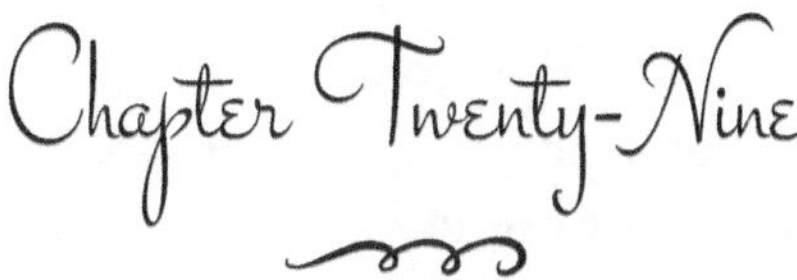

Chapter Twenty-Nine

As we finish walking his route around my neighborhood, he turns toward me, wiping the still falling rain out of his eyes. "Can I come over after I finish for the day?"

I nod, hoping he means what I think he might.

He presses a gentle kiss to my forehead. "I can't wait."

After closing the door behind me, I shimmy, because after Viv's night out I'm apparently a shimmier, while Frank drips dirty rain water all over the floor.

"I take it that things went well?" Harper leans against the doorframe, brows raised over a steaming cup of tea, and takes in the sight of my disheveled, rain-soaked self.

I don't need more prompting before I word-vomit the entire incredible moment to Harper who immediately dials Viv and Marin over a video chat.

"You rain-troped the mailman! I knew you would do it!" Viv crows.

Harper, never one for subtlety, declares, "So, I'll be staying at Maddie's tonight. You're welcome. Don't be weird about it."

Before I even fully swing the front door open, he's pressing into me. "B... Can I kiss you?"

The college nickname whispered on his lips, his eyes burning with longing, it all undoes me, and my "yes" comes out as a desperate moan. It doesn't look like he even took the time to go home and change. Rain drips from his hair, and this time, I don't stop myself from tangling my fingers in the damp strands.

Noah's mouth finds mine before the door is fully shut behind us. His jacket hits the floor, soaked through, and I'm reaching for the hem of his shirt, pushing it up over muscles slick with rain. He's all heat beneath the chill, his skin flushed from the cold, his breath ragged like he ran here.

He presses me up against the hallway wall, the old wood cool and rough against my back. I gasp, the sharp contrast making my body arch, my nipples tightening instantly under the damp cotton of my shirt. His mouth is on mine again, urgent, claiming, tongue sliding past my lips like he's starving for the taste of me.

There's nothing slow about this. No tiptoeing, nothing tentative, no easing in. It's heat and hunger and decision. This time I've given myself permission to want him, need him, to give myself to him entirely. The passion I've been holding back breaks like a fever.

His hands are everywhere—sliding under my shirt, over my ribs, down to the waistband of my leggings. He groans when he feels how ready I already am for him. I don't need to speak. I'm all need, dripping wet, all yes.

"You need a shower," I whisper, the words catching in my throat.

He doesn't hesitate. "Only if it's with you."

We barely make it that far. Somewhere between the hallway and the bedroom, we lose layers, socks, pants, inhibition. The air is damp and thick with the scent of rain and skin and that faint woodsmoke from the candle I lit earlier to set the mood.

He lifts me easily, my legs wrapping around his waist in pure instinct, like my body knew how to fit to his before my brain caught up. Then we're in the shower, the hot water pounding down my back while Noah cups my breasts, circling my nipple with his tongue before one hand is moving down between my legs.

I grip his back tighter, gasping, aching for him. He plunges a finger inside me, curling his finger, pressing deep, causing little shivers to race up my spine as I clench around him, my nails digging into his shoulders, trying to stay upright.

He pushes in and out, running his thumb over my pulsing need until I'm begging, "Please, Noah. Inside me. Now."

"Not like this." His mouth is against my ear and then he's turning off the water, wrapping me in a towel, and carrying me, still dripping wet to the bed. He lays me down gently, drying each part of me, before stepping back, admiring every inch of my body. When he finally pushes inside me everything quiets. There's nothing but this—his breath in my ear, my name on his lips, our bodies moving like we're trying to memorize each other from the inside out.

I feel my need building until I'm clenching around him, and he's pulsing deep inside me.

His arms wrap around me, pulling me close, his fingers tracing slow, lazy circles on my bare hip, his touch featherlight now—reverent in a way that reminds me he's loved me for a lifetime.

I reach up and push the damp hair off his forehead. "I don't know if that shower counts as you getting clean."

"It shouldn't." His grin is wicked and boyish all at once. "And my mind's filthy. Already replaying all the ways I'm gonna make you beg like that again."

I laugh, breathless, still catching up to my own heartbeat. "Careful. That sounds like a dare."

He kisses the tip of my nose, then my mouth, slow, possessive, sealing a promise. "Good." His voice is low and warm against my lips. "I double-dog dare you to love me like that every day for the rest of our lives."

"Noah..." I breathe out his name, half a protest, half a laugh that cracks right through my chest. "You can't say something like that unless you mean it. You know I always follow through on a dare."

He leans back, that soft, crooked grin that has wrecked me since college curving at the corner of his mouth.

His hand cups my jaw, thumb sweeping over my lip. "Good. I'm counting on it."

Epilogue

The screen flickers to life, and there they are—Viv sipping what I assume is some frothy soy milk abomination and Marin with her kombucha. It's clear. She's hooked on the stuff. My Wi-Fi is a little glitchy, the images are a little blurry, and the sound cuts out every few seconds, but honestly? It feels like home.

I give Noah a quick peck on the cheek before moving my laptop off the bed and padding in my pajamas down the hall toward the living room.

"Is that Noah?" Viv's voice breaks out through the speaker loud and clear. "Tell him I'm not there to toss him his jeans if he forgets them while trying to crawl out onto the roof again."

I hear Noah's deep chuckle from the bed. "Hi, Viv. Birdie doesn't make me sneak out of the window since she invited me to move in with her."

Settling into my favorite corner of the couch, I adjust the screen in time to see Viv stare pointedly through the screen. "Someone really needs to ask Marin about her love life."

"No one needs to ask." Marin's voice is serious, but she's smiling.

Viv ignores her. "He picks up his socks off the floor, Birdie. *Unprompted.* I almost proposed on the spot."

"You say that like it's not the bare minimum," I chuckle.

"Sweetheart." Viv swirls her coffee like it's wine. "Believe me, a clean floor is not the bare minimum. We're in the past forty club. The bare minimums have changed."

I shudder and write myself a mental note to thank Noah for his good hygiene habits later.

Marin snorts. "He also owns real bedsheets. Not polyester. I checked the tag."

Viv winks. "Thread count is foreplay now."

We all burst out laughing.

"Also, your daughter is quite the love guru."

"Harper?" It comes out as a question that I'm a little scared to get the answer to.

"She's terrifying," Marin says immediately. "She's already texted me twice with dating suggestions."

Viv nods solemnly. "Yesterday, she told Marin to 'trust her womb wisdom.'"

I choke on my tea. "Her *what*?"

Marin throws up her hands. "Apparently, my dusty old uterus has more insight into my love life than my brain does."

Viv's voice turns serious. "That's the best advice anyone could ever give. Your body knows."

"She actually said something that stuck with me," Marin adds quietly. "That maybe it's not about finding someone who fills the space they left. Just someone who reminds you that you still deserve to take up space, period."

I blink at her. "Harper said that?"

"She *texted* it. In lowercase. No punctuation. But yeah."

Viv nods. "That girl's an old soul in a Gen Z wrapper." Then she's waving a perfectly manicured hand and adding, "And I did it. I posted a video last week, me, in full face, dancing to a Lizzo song with my wine glass, and guess what's not in the background?"

Marin lifts an eyebrow. "A tragic montage of your dead husband?"

Viv's grin holds only 10% sadness. "Exactly. No candlelit tribute corner. No black-and-white slow-mo. No cut of him dancing with me. Just me. Laughing. Being ridiculous. I didn't even mention him. And I finally changed my username."

I raise my eyebrows. "No more ThisIsUs?"

"Nope. Now it's ThisIsMe."

"Wow." I set my cup down. "How did that feel?"

"Sad, but also weirdly good. Like I'm allowed to take up space again without wrapping everything in a grief bow first. Like I'm still me, even if I'm not us anymore. I even signed up for my pole dancing class, and because of all your nagging, I am looking into the possibility of apartments in the Seattle area."

Marin and I let out a few squeals. "Join me! My move-in date is next week and finding a decent apartment wasn't *that* bad. We could be roomies!"

Viv stares before quirking an eyebrow. "Don't lie to me, lady. It was awful, and we both know it, but you were fueled by love... or lust."

Marin's face turns a thousand shades of red.

Then I take a breath. "I've been thinking about something."

Viv pauses. "Always dangerous."

"What if we didn't stop? The dares, I mean. What if we kept going? Made new ones. Not because we're broken or grieving or healing from loss, but because life doesn't stop asking us to be brave."

Marin leans in. "You mean make this a thing?"

"Not like a brand or a business. A way to keep showing up. For ourselves. For each other."

Viv grins. "Birdie, that's not only a good idea. That's kind of the point, isn't it? When are we ever really done daring ourselves to live fuller, deeper lives?"

"I mean, we dared each other to get out of bed and into the world again." Marin sets down her knitting needles. "What's next? Daring each other to write a poem? Take a pottery class? Start a business? Actually take the full-time position at the museum?" Marin shoots me a pointed look. The internship was every-thing I imagined and I excelled. So much so that they offered me a permanent place on the team.

"I have been wanting to get into vegan cupcakes." Viv pauses as though she's already pondering the logistics of such a venture. "Not that I don't love my work as a yoga instructor, but moving to Seattle and starting a business is always a possibility."

"I'm in." Marin raises her kombucha-filled mug. "To grief dares and life dares and making a little magic out of our mess."

"To more," I echo. "Always to more."

———————

@GinnyHotFlash1945 Please gather Betsy and Helen. (I even found a coupon for half off a pair of Birkenstocks, so Betsy won't be too disappointed.) Your Reddit post, and two friends I didn't know I needed, kind of changed my life. Or at least helped me see it wasn't over.

This is for you. And maybe someone else too.

Post Title: The Dead Husbands Society: Grief Dares (Inspired by The Romance Checklist)

Hi.

This is Birdie.

This post is inspired by The Romance Checklist by Helen, Betsy, and Ginny—three women with sharper minds and dirtier jokes than anyone is giving them credit for.

The Dead Husbands Society and I wrapped up something we called the Grief Dare Challenge. Well, wrapped up is generous. Because grief doesn't end, it shifts. It softens. Sometimes it ambushes you in the freezer aisle because you saw his favorite frozen waffles. But it doesn't go away. And maybe it's not supposed to.

Helen, Betsy, and Ginny changed their main gal's life with a romance checklist. While I needed a list, it wasn't a checklist. We're perimenopausal women. We needed a list of dares:

→ Tell the truth.

→ *Do something scary.*

→ *Wear red lipstick to the post office.*

→ *Say his name without crying.*

→ *Laugh.*

→ *Flirt.*

→ *Let someone hold your hand.*

→ *Let yourself be happy, even if it's only for five minutes.*

What's the Dead Husbands Society? It's nothing fancy. Just three middle-aged women whose husbands died too soon and who realized they might have lost themselves long before that. We met online. We bonded over grief. We stayed for the healing, and the snort-laughs, and the group texts where Viv tried to convince us to get matching tattoos. (Still pending.)

Here's the thing: we got tired.

Tired of guilt.

Tired of walking around like love was a museum full of pieces we weren't allowed to touch anymore.

Tired of being scared of wanting anything more than survival.

So we dared each other to start small.

My first dare? Let the mailman trim my fennel plants. (No, not a euphemism. Though, in hindsight...)

Your first dare might be:

→ *Make breakfast and eat it while sitting down.*

→ *Wear the earrings he bought you.*

→ *Call the friend you've been avoiding.*

→ *Let someone see your messy house, and your messy heart.*

If you want to see our dare lists for inspiration, we'll share them. But your dares won't be ours. And your life? It's yours. That means you get to decide how to hold it, and how to let in joy and sadness alongside it.

So if you're stuck in grief. Or perimenopause. Or a chapter of your life that you didn't ask for, but you're reading through anyway, here's our invitation:

Dare yourself to live a little louder. Write the dare list.

You're not done.

You're beginning again.

Now if you'll excuse me, I'm going back to snuggle up next to a man I love—without any guilt. Because healing doesn't mean forgetting. And it's okay to be happy.

— Birdie (founding member of The Dead Husbands Society, recent griever, future joy-darer)

Freebies

Read on for an excerpt from *This Is Not A Romance*, book 2 in the *What Comes Next* series. What happens when three elderly matchmakers armed with a trope-filled romance checklist take over your love life? Emma Clark is about to find out...

CHAPTER 1

His mouth traces soft kisses along my skin, and my body pushes up to meet him, aching for more...

"Emma, you're not supposed to read ahead in book club."

I slam the book shut at the sound of Ginny's voice, already feeling the hot flush of embarrassment warming my face. Ginny crosses her arms over her thin frame. She's wearing her usual: tailored slacks, a neatly pressed cardigan, and an air of authority, as if she's running the whole assisted living facility instead of living in it.

"You might want to calm down, dear. You look like you got a sunburn." Betsy parks her walker before lowering her ample bottom into the chair next to mine.

"Ladies, not that I don't adore your company, but I still have —" I glance down at the faded break room table before feeling around in the pockets of my oversized scrubs. "—Um, has anyone seen my phone?"

"Honestly, Emma, you're worse than Geraldine," Ginny tuts, perching on the edge of her chair like a debutante at high tea.

"And we all know she's losing it. You really need a watch. Or some kind of zipline device to attach important items to your person."

"Oh! That commercial with the heartthrob who looks like Denzel Washington? I think he was selling one of those thingamajigs. Of course, I have no need for it, but it was tempting. I'd buy anything that man's selling. He's a looker." Betsy sighs wistfully.

"Is someone talking about Tom Cruise? He's such a nice young man." Helen shuffles across the faded grey carpet to join us.

Does no one respect the assisted living facility's *employees only* break room sign?

Betsy shakes her head, and her bifocals bob with the movement.

"You know, I once dated a man who looked a lot like Denzel." Ginny takes out her signature compact mirror, running a hand over an imaginary out-of-place strand of hair.

While they've been talking, I've successfully rummaged through the pockets of my scrub pants and sweater, and am now working on my jacket. I don't bother masking my eye roll before I shout a triumphant "Aha!" as I pull my phone out of my jacket pocket. "Now, as I was saying, I still have..." I check the time on the screen. "Well, I would've had three more minutes on my break, if I hadn't been interrupted. So I'm taking those three minutes now." I open the book, trying to appear mildly annoyed, but the truth is, I've grown to love their slightly intrusive company more than I'd ever admit.

His mouth traces soft kisses along my skin, and my body pushes up to meet him, aching for more...

"Unacceptable." Ginny snatches the book out of my hand, the red of her manicured nails flashing with the motion. "We said we'd read till chapter eight, and I can see from here that you're on chapter ten."

"Ginny, believe me, reading this is not for my own enjoyment. I'm trying to come up with the discussion questions for tomorrow. Do you know how hard it is to spark meaningful conversation with *this* type of book?" I drop my voice lower. "They're about to do... the deed."

Betsy snorts. "You mean sex? You can say sex. I've had enough of it being a taboo term my whole life. Now, I just want to be free to utter it whenever I darn well please."

Much to my horror, Betsy begins warbling, "Sex. Sex. Sex!"

Then Ginny starts to chant, adding an accompanying melody to Betsy's erotic song. Helen is trying to melt into her chair, clutching at her signature pearls. I grab the book out of Ginny's hand and wave it around, trying to get both of their attention.

Which is when Mr. Rhodes walks through the door. The fluorescent lights radiate off of the top of his balding head, and I wish the floor would swallow me whole.

Betsy and Ginny finish one more chant for good measure before they both snap their mouths shut. I assume they're trying to look contrite, but it's a poor attempt considering their chagrined smiles don't budge.

"Ladies, we've talked about this. You can't be in the break room." Mr. Rhodes takes in the scene before him, his eyes lingering on the muscular male chest adorning the novel's cover. Helen makes a move as though she's hoping to snatch it from me and stuff it under her floral cardigan or hide it in her impressively large crocheted handbag. I set it down on the table, hoping she does.

Ginny gives an exaggerated eye roll before turning her attention to her nails.

Mr. Rhodes ambles over to the table. "What're you reading? Looks like something on nutrition? Reminds me of myself back in my younger days."

Betsy and Ginny try to cover their snickers with coughs. Helen's fingers stretch closer to the offending book.

"It's actually our book club's pick for this month." Ginny sounds proud, but Helen is trying to toss one of her embroidered doilies over the cover. Ginny gives her arm a gentle slap. "Don't be ashamed, Helen. It was a great choice."

"You're interested in body building, Helen?"

"Something like that," Betsy titters, while Helen fiddles with her long pale grey braid, looking like she also hopes the floor will swallow her whole. "It had, how did you put it?"

Betsy turns to Helen who manages to mumble, "Rave reviews." Her Southern drawl is even more pronounced when she drops her voice.

Mr. Rhodes walks over to the coffee pot, pouring the stale brew all the way to the brim of his *I Brake for Rare Coins* mug. "You all know that we are advocates of health and longevity here."

I think Ginny might lose it as she presses her fingernails to her cinnamon red lips and shakes her head. *Please, Mr. Rhodes, for all of our sakes, retreat now. Save yourself!*

"Maybe when you're finished, I'll give it a try. I bet Mrs. Rhodes would appreciate me putting a little more effort into the old physique." He gives his protruding stomach a pat for good measure.

And that's when Betsy loses it, doubling over in a fit of laughter, while Helen stares in horror. Meanwhile, I'm desperately trying to erase the mental image of my boss reenacting the very explicit scenes from this book with his very conservative (and probably sex-starved) wife.

I shoot Ginny a stern look before turning back to Mr. Rhodes. "I actually had a few questions about my schedule next week, if you have a minute? I'm starting my last semester, and there's an orientation for clinical rotations that will conflict with my shifts. I might need to cut down on my hours for a few weeks."

"Of course! Why don't we step into my office?" As Mr. Rhodes turns to leave and walk down the hallway, he tosses one final grenade over his shoulder. "Oh, and be sure to send me the title of that book, ladies! The missus and I sure would appreciate it."

Dear God. If that book ends up in their hands, I'll need to find a new job.

"Emma! Don't forget you're doing our hair in five minutes!" Ginny's little silver mirror is back in her hand, and she doesn't bother looking up as her fingers smooth her bangs.

"How could I ever forget your hair, Ginny?" I snatch the book off the table before racing to catch up to Mr. Rhodes.

"Emma, I'm concerned about the schedule you're keeping." He powerwalks down the hall, and I lengthen my stride, attempting to keep pace. "Burnout is so high in this industry, and as the director it's my job to mitigate it as much as possible with employees."

"I'm not burning out. It's only two jobs. Well, three if you count the evenings volunteering in the salon." Which I can't be late for. I fight the urge to check the time on my phone.

Mr. Rhodes lets out a weary sigh, opening the door to his tiny office and gesturing for me to follow. "I know we're short-staffed, but it's not your responsibility to keep everything running. That's my job. It's the nature of the beast that we call assisted living." He shakes his head before offering a tired smile. "That said, I really appreciate you stepping up as our temporary activities director on top of your CNA work."

"Honestly, working as a certified nursing assistant, doing all the hands-on care is better preparing me than any of my nursing courses so far. Really, you're doing me the favor."

Probably knowing he won't change my mind, Mr. Rhodes sends me a gentle smile. "I've heard nothing but great things about that book club you started. You have Ginny, Betsy, and Helen in it, correct? How's it going?"

I debate giving an honest answer. Yes, Southern Belle Helen, who blushes at every spicy line; Ginny, the ex-fashion-store owner and resident fashionista, critiquing every outfit; and sweet Betsy, who keeps trying to order matching 'Smut Sister' hoodies online with her never-ending coupon collection. I clutch the novel tighter to my chest and summon a smile so bright and fake it would stun an infomercial audience. "Yep. Just the four of us for now. It's been educational."

Focus, Emma. Get his attention off of this atrocious, completely unrealistic novel. "About my schedule..."

"Of course. Send me an email with the dates you need rearranged, and I'll make it happen." Mr. Rhodes settles into his saggy office chair. "Now about book club—"

I'd rather eat my own shoe than rehash book club, but my brain short-circuits when searching for an escape route. Desperate, I flick my gaze to the clock. "Oh no, would you look at that? I'm late for, uh, salon night! Gotta go save some perms from disaster."

His expression goes flat. "Emma."

I slap on my best innocent look. "Yes?"

He falls back into his office chair and the cracked leather moans under his weight. "Again, we appreciate you, but you don't have to wear so many hats around here."

I flash him a cheeky grin as I edge toward the door, reaching for the doorknob. "I know. But I like being busy." Busy means no time for a personal life.

His voice stops me right before I slip out. "Just don't burn yourself out."

"Me? Never. I'm *thriving*." I throw the statement over my shoulder, already speed-walking down the hall because Ginny is going to kill me.

I fish my phone from my pocket, check the time, and yep, I'm six minutes behind schedule. Which, in Ginny's world, means I've been declared legally dead, and she's probably rallying the other residents to avenge me.

I barely dodge a rogue walker in the hallway, muttering an apology over my shoulder as I half-jog toward the assisted living home's small salon. I burst through the door right as Betsy— seated in the stylist's chair, hair in foils, looking like a very stylish and very angry space alien—turns her glare on me.

"You're late. Ginny was worried we wouldn't have time for her hair so she already started on mine."

I cross the few feet between us. "I know. I was detained."

Betsy narrows her eyes. "Mr. Rhodes keep you?"

"Maybe."

She lets out a slow, exasperated breath. "If he talks to me about that damn 1946 *rare* penny one more time, I'm launching his entire coin collection into a koi pond."

I stifle a smile. "Noted."

I grab an apron, tie it around my waist, and prepare for the chaos that is salon night, because if I don't redeem myself, I will be paying for my lateness in bingo sabotage for the next month.

I peek under one of the foils, half-expecting disaster. "Betsy, is there anything under these foils?"

"Oh, these?" She squirms, trying to get a look at herself. "Just a test run for placement. Ginny went off to find some dye."

"How about we stick with a shampoo for tonight?" I start taking the foils out, her dark grey peppered strands falling back into place. I massage her scalp as I go, and she relaxes back into my hands with a hum of approval.

As I reach for the shampoo, Ginny glides into the salon, plops down in the chair beside Betsy, and waves a brush at me like a scepter. "Emma, first, I thought I told you to order more bleach. I can't find a box of dye anywhere. Second, you're undoing my work."

I smirk. "First, you're on bleach probation after the last incident. Betsy almost lost half her hair. Second, please, refer to my first point."

Ginny leans over to whisper in Betsy's ear. "Can you order some off that site? You know the one that has *everything*." Ginny turns toward me. "It's like an online Ames Department Store."

Betsy grins. "I did find a coupon..."

I run shampoo through Betsy's hair, watching out of the corner of my eye as Helen tries to subtly sink into the final cracked salon chair. "There will be no ordering!"

Ginny huffs. "How about you, Helen? Your hair's so pale we wouldn't even need to wait for Betsy to find her coupon stash and order the bleach." She turns toward Helen.

Helen holds her braid as far away from Ginny as possible. "Absolutely not. That hair dye is full of toxins, Ginny. *Toxins.* The government puts chemicals in everything nowadays, and I won't be part of their experiment."

Ginny lets out a sigh. "Here we go."

Helen straightens, her voice dropping to a dramatic whisper. "You do realize they put fluoride in the water to control us, don't you?"

Ginny snorts. "Yes, Helen, the government is out here using fluoride to control an eighty-six-year-old woman's decision to color her hair."

"I wish the government would use fluoride to get Emma to start dating again." Betsy taps her fingers against the armrest. "Your love life's fizzled out."

Ginny nods in agreement, apparently happy for the subject change. "You used to come in here with a new tale of flirting and passion every week." She sighs dramatically. "Those were the days. I didn't even have to watch any soaps. Then you met *him*. And he ruined it all."

"Those *weren't* the days, and it's for the best they ended," I mutter. "If it hadn't been him, it would've been some other man in the near future."

I can still feel the sting of the concrete steps outside the courthouse beneath me, cutting through the thin fabric of my white sundress. We weren't doing anything fancy—his words, not mine. Just a simple civil ceremony, no fuss, no flowers, no crowd. Only the two of us and a lunch reservation after.

Except it wasn't the two of us. It was me. Sitting there. Waiting.

He texted six hours later to say his online gaming team had made it to the end of some quest. A *quest*. Not a job interview. Not a family emergency. A digital dragon or a virtual sword or something equally absurd had been more important than saying "I do." And the worst part was I wasn't the least bit surprised.

Ginny waves a manicured hand like she's batting away a fly.

"Well, men are always late to something. That one just happened to be your wedding. Tragic, yes, but hardly original."

She adjusts her silk scarf with the poise of someone delivering a TEDTalk on heartbreak and high fashion. "Now, if you'd had the good sense to schedule your nuptials at Neiman Marcus, at least you could've returned the dress while you waited."

I don't remind her that the dress was a thrift store original and that she was the one holding the tissue box while I tried to laugh through the tears. She knows. They all do.

"It's been a year, dear," Ginny continues. "We've held your hand, passed the tissues, and pretended that thrift store dress was couture. But mourning, like white after Labor Day, has an expiration date. It's time to pull yourself together and move on. Preferably in heels."

Betsy perks up. "Have I mentioned my grandson is supposed to stop by tomorrow?"

"The one who still lives in your daughter's basement, plays video games, and has a steady online girlfriend from Canada? That grandson?"

"Well, when you put it like that," Betsy grumbles.

I lift my eyes to the heavens, grateful Betsy can't see.

"The Lord isn't going to help you get a boyfriend," she adds.

Damn. How does she always know?

I take a deep breath. "Betsy, I'm sure your grandson is a wonderful person with many admirable qualities. But I've officially retired from dating. Turns out, I'm not interested in being a man's second-favorite hobby, emotional support therapist, or personal cheerleader while he does the bare minimum."

Ginny crosses her arms. "Honey, you're twenty-five years old. You're gorgeous, smart, and driven. There's no reason why you can't have a great romance!"

"I've dated plenty of reasons why." I fight the urge to self-consciously smooth the unruly strands of my wavy chestnut hair and instead focus on working a knot out of Betsy's. "What would I even put on a dating profile? 'Loves overthinking, flashcards, and avoiding gluten so my intestines don't explode'?"

"That's your problem right there." Ginny gives a knowing nod. "You don't appreciate yourself."

Helen perks up. "Gluten?"

Ginny groans. "Gluten, Helen! We've been over this a hundred times. It's the thing in wheat that might kill Emma. What's it called again, Emma?"

"Celi—"

"Celiac disease," Ginny plows over me, turning a triumphant gaze toward Helen. "Do try to keep up with the times."

Betsy scoffs. "Gluten wasn't a problem in my day. We ate Wonder Bread, drank from the garden hose, and turned out just fine."

"Yes, dear. And we walked to school uphill both ways in a snowstorm. I know. I've shared the same story." Ginny rolls her eyes, taking out her lipstick tube and reapplying her flawless lips.

Helen glances around before sitting on her phone, dropping her voice low. "I think the whole gluten thing is a conspiracy theory."

I hold up a hand before this conversation spirals into full-fledged paranoia. "Helen, are you sitting on your phone?"

Helen shifts uncomfortably in her seat. "Well, they could be listening!"

Betsy reaches for Helen's chair, making a move like she's about to pull the phone out from under her. "Oh, for heaven's sake—"

"No!" Helen yelps. "They might hear us!"

I pinch the bridge of my nose, exhaling. Salon night is going *great*.

Before Betsy can start on a tangent about a coupon she found for some infomercial's high powered ear plugs, I blurt out, "You're up, Ginny!"

Ginny gets up to swap seats with Betsy, clearly taking in my features while she's at it.

"I think you'd do well on any dating platform. You've got an hourglass figure that reminds me of that blonde bombshell in the '60s. Oh, why can't I remember her name? Betsy?"

Now it is Betsy's turn to look smug. She puts a reassuring hand on her best friend's arm. "Marilyn, honey. And damn, she was sex on a stick."

"Betsy!" I give her a look before glancing around, hoping Mr. Rhodes or his tattle-tale assistant, Karen, isn't within earshot.

"What?" Her brows raise in mock innocence. "That's what the kids are saying these days." She turns to Ginny. "Isn't it?"

Ginny nods. "That's what I hear. Point being, you're a chestnut-haired Marilyn, with those huge emerald-green eyes and gigantic, well, you know." Ginny gives a pointed look at my breasts, leaving little room for me to misconstrue her obvious meaning. "You're clearly hiding an incredible figure under poorly-fitting clothes. But I can help with that."

I suppress a sigh before gesturing for Ginny to lean back. "Speaking of beauty, let's get those locks shining." Ginny scoffs, peering into the smudged mirror for a moment, her hand absently running through her hair.

"I used to have thick hair like yours once. Oh, it feels like it was yesterday. Betsy, do you remember those Velcro rollers I would torture myself with? All in the name of having curls like yours, Emma. I have no doubt I would've hated you a little in high school."

Betsy gives an adamant nod.

I raise my hands in protest. "I'm sure Betsy can agree, curls are not all they're cracked up to be. I have frizz like you wouldn't believe."

Ginny positions her hand to look like a mouth and mocks me while I talk. "Sounds like pretty girl problems to me."

"She should know." Betsy glances up from her magazine. "She was the prettiest."

The sound of the running tap water fills our silence, and I watch the laughter fade from Ginny's watery blue eyes as she stares at her reflection. I wonder if she recognizes herself there, the deep wrinkles, papery skin, blue veins, or if she's wondering where that youthful beauty in her prime has run off to and how she can bring her back.

"I think you're stunning," I whisper, before starting to massage her scalp.

She reaches up and pats my arm, but doesn't stop staring into the mirror.

If you want to see what mischief these three get into, *This Is Not A Romance* **is available on Amazon now!**

Acknowledgments

To my incredible beta gals, thank you for believing in me when this book was a chaotic Google Doc and some half-baked ideas. You read, encouraged, rolled your eyes in the best way, and told me to keep going. I wouldn't have made it to *The End* without you.

To my family, who kept me hydrated, fed, and emotionally intact as I became obsessive with this project: I adore you.

To my husband. No. This book wasn't a warning sign.

Yes. I couldn't have done it without you.

About The Author

Adeline Aimes writes romantic comedies that are funny, heartfelt, and a little messy—kind of like real life. When she's not writing, she's baking gluten-free sourdough, hiking in the Pacific Northwest, trying to keep her house plants alive, and reading spicy romance novels under a blanket she swore she didn't need. She also feels funny writing about herself in the third person... So this took way longer to write than she'd like to admit.

You can follow along for monthly author updates by subscribing to my Substack here (Adeline Aimes Substack) or email newsletters here.

Find her on Instagram @adeline_aimes_author, TikTok @adelineaimes_author or her website at adelineaimeswrites.com!